### *Someone stood in the doorway.*

Brie spun on her chair and faced the tall, half-lit form of her husband. "Don't do that!"

Steve said nothing.

Slowly she lowered the hand she had raised to calm her racing heartbeat. Steve looked . . . off, his brown eyes bland and unfocused. His normal expression had faded from his face, and all her foolish ideas of possession returned in force.

"Steve, this had better not be some kind of joke," she said, standing to better defend herself. *Defend herself? This was Steve, her husband!* Ignoring the inner protest, she kicked her chair out of the way.

Steve didn't flinch at the clatter of wood, merely awkwardly extended one hand toward her face and stepped sluggishly closer.

Then he began to smile, a cold, victorious, *alien* smile.

Dear Reader,

It's spooky, the way our Shadows novels just keep getting eerier, more romantic—and *better*—all the time. Take this month's offerings, for example.

First up, new star Evelyn Vaughn returns to "The Circle" in *Burning Times*. This sequel to her immensely popular first book, *Waiting for the Wolf Moon,* features Brie and Steven Peabody. But Steven is not quite himself these days, and if Brie can't figure out what's wrong and then return him to himself... Passion and possession make a heady mix in this story that, once begun, will prove impossible to put down.

Our second book this month is also *this* author's second book. Allie Harrison made her debut as part of our "New for November" promotion. Now she's back, and in *Dead Reckoning* she's outdone herself in the sexy scare department. Once you're dead, you're dead, right? Maybe not—as Lauren Baker learns when a series of "accidents" begins to threaten her life. Only one man could be behind them, and only one man— Colt Norbrook—could save her. But would even Colt be a match for an evil from beyond the grave?

But the not-for-the-faint-of-heart fun doesn't stop there, because we'll be bringing you two new Shadows novels every month. Don't miss them!

Yours,

Leslie J. Wainger
Senior Editor and Editorial Coordinator

Please address questions and book requests to:
Silhouette Reader Service
U.S.: 3010 Walden Ave., P.O. Box 1325, Buffalo, NY 14269
Canadian: P.O. Box 609, Fort Erie, Ont. L2A 5X3

# EVELYN VAUGHN

# BURNING TIMES

Published by Silhouette Books
**America's Publisher of Contemporary Romance**

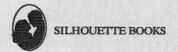 SILHOUETTE BOOKS

ISBN 0-373-27039-9

BURNING TIMES

Copyright © 1994 by Yvonne Jocks

Printed in U.S.A.

**Books by Evelyn Vaughn**

Silhouette Shadows

*Waiting for the Wolf Moon #8
*Burning Times #39

*The Circle

## EVELYN VAUGHN

has been a secret agent, a ghost buster, a starship captain, an elf, a prince and a princess. When not involved in role-playing games, she teaches junior college English and is an unapologetic television addict. She has lived in five states before settling in central Texas, and has traveled most of the United States and Europe. She has been writing stories since the first grade. Although she has not yet found Mr. Right, she is enjoying Mr. Write with every book!

With thanks to my critique group, editors,
network pals, family and speedreading friends,
this book is dedicated to
my favorite married couples:

Carolyn and Dan
Erin and Paul
Kayli and Matt
and
Mom and Dad

# PROLOGUE

The pumpkin-colored cat normally spent quiet evenings sprawled across the forbidden kitchen table. But tonight he remained alert, a ball of fur, ears pointing toward... it.

It didn't belong here. It was old and incorporeal, nothing but flickers of memory and tastes of identity. And hatred. Its stale scent and slow, pulsing sound did not even register in the physical realm. And it was seeking outward, bits of it crossing the Veil. Rediscovering its existence.

The cat laid his ears back and rose defensively, a growl low in his throat. As tendrils of invisible darkness neared him, the growl escalated into a challenging wail.

It hesitated, retreated back into itself—but the cat knew neither he nor his mistress, busy in the backyard, had caused the retreat. The being was not strong enough to exist outside its own realm, outside its portal.

Yet.

Settling back into a watchful crouch, the cat hissed.

The entity wasn't after cats.

But it was after something.

# CHAPTER ONE

*Tis said the devil plagues us with witches.*
> —The Journals of Josiah Blakelee

Something felt very wrong—for no reason at all.

The Lake Pontchartrain Causeway stretched more than twenty lonely miles across black, choppy water. Overhead, the full moon lurked behind clouds...except full moon was last night. Alone in his '82 Volvo, Steve Peabody shook his head to kick-start his brain. "Blue moon," his wife Brie had said; the second full moon this month.

Thoughts of Brie fueled his irrational unease.

He noticed his knuckles, pale against the steering wheel in the orange glow of the dashboard lights, and deliberately relaxed his grip. Then he realized his car's speed, and let up on the gas, too. The need to get home pressed in his chest, an unnameable weight that had settled there after he tried calling home from the Halloween party and the answering machine clicked on. He'd left the number, asked Brie to call him back.

She hadn't.

Only this afternoon she'd repeated her insistence that she didn't "do" Halloween parties—a fact three years' acquaintance had borne out. "Go on without me, honey," she'd insisted. Since one of his newspaper's largest sponsors had invited him, he did.

The digital clock on his silent car stereo now read 12:08. The witching hour, some would say.

She'd probably gone to bed early.

The moan of the Volvo's wheels deepened as he left the bridge for solid land. The dark expanse over the lake shrank to a looming tunnel of tall pines lurking outside the beam of his headlights on either side of the ditch-lined road. *Home. Get home. Something...*

"What?" he asked out loud, annoyed at this unrelenting, inexplicable tension. He considered paranoia a weakness. Who, what, where, when, why—*those* provided evidence, showed reality. "Intuition" wasn't worth the air it was plucked out of.

Red taillights, like glowing eyes, flickered in the midnight darkness; he had to stop-and-start through a minor traffic snarl in front of the local haunted-house attraction. Maybe he just didn't like parties, he mused, frustrated. Maybe he just wished he'd stayed home with his wife, passing out treats to neighborhood children. *That* might plausibly explain this burning need to get home.

How would *he* know if something were wrong?

When the road cleared, Steve had to struggle to keep from speeding through the small Louisiana town of Stagwater. Not soon enough, he pulled up in front of his and Brie's duplex. The two-story building huddled between tangled vacant lots on either side, with a huge oak and thick wood behind it. A faint glow seeped through the drapes of both living rooms. Brie's Blazer sat at the curb, between the old Pinto that belonged to his next-door-neighbor, who was also his sister, and one of her friends' cars.

*So why didn't Brie answer the phone? Why didn't she call back?*

*Why don't you go in and find out?* As he left his car and strode across the squishy lawn, his unease got worse, becoming a heaviness in his chest, a dread. Fear solidified, hard, in his throat—maybe she *couldn't* call back?—and he leaned into the front door as he pushed it open, bracing himself against . . .

Something.

A cluster of candles drew a red glow from the Chippendale furniture that crouched on ball-and-claw feet, candles on the coffee table, candles mounting the narrow stairway, candles hovering in a hanging iron holder.

Beyond the den, the hallway to the dining room lay in darkness.

Steve drew breath to call her—to hell with logic, this was his *wife* he was worried about—but at that moment, from that darkness, she emerged.

He forgot to exhale.

She'd always been bewitching. Tonight, the smoky blue eyes that caught the light first seemed almost feline. Her red hair fell in a fiery tangle about the folds of a black hood nestled on her shoulders. Strangely, she wore a robe, like a monk's, but Steve's gaze followed the open neckline down a completely unmonkish plunge that hinted at cleavage he knew and loved. The material—silk?—flowed around her and absorbed the subtle candlelight that flushed across her cheeks, but her wild hair caught and reflected the flames in russet sparks.

Brigit.

Something shivery hovered in the room, past the rich scent of melting beeswax, past the ethereal harmony of a Celtic ballad about swan maidens on the stereo. Steve ignored it to gaze at his wife.

Those smoldering eyes brightened as she smiled. "No trouble getting home?" Brie asked. "I tried calling the party, but they said you'd already left." When she swept toward him, her absurd black hem hissed across the bare wooden floor.

"What are you wearing?" he demanded, more sharply than he'd meant to, and shut the door. When he looked up, she'd stayed her approach and planted two sleeve-hidden hands on her hips. Uh-oh.

She opened her mouth, considered her words. "Gee . . . what night is it, hon?"

He felt a little silly, especially after the ridiculous sense of doom that had driven him here, and he folded his arms. So it was Halloween.

Another smile tugged at Brie's full lips, and she dramatically lifted one arm and pointed toward the plant stand beside the door, like the grim reaper choosing a soul.

He noted the nearly empty bowl of candy bars. "You couldn't answer the phone because you were entertaining trick-or-treaters dressed as a . . . a . . ." A monk, or Death? Did either wear raw silk?

She hesitated, her eyes searching him. "I only entertained trick-or-treaters till about nine. Then Sylvie invited me next door. Cy and Mary were over."

Suspicion, and that same knot of unease, whispered unintelligible warnings; he fought to stick to facts. "I thought you didn't do Halloween parties."

"It wasn't a party." She shrugged and wrinkled her nose. "Would you rather I wore my corset and garter belt?" she asked teasingly, coming to him, sliding her arms around him in a belated welcome-home hug.

A different shivery sensation sapped his skepticism. His hands drifted up; his fingers brushed the rough silk over her shoulders. Then he held her, too, clutched her tightly to him in a wordless dare to anybody else, anything else. She leaned into his strength. He felt her softness mold against his stress-weary body, seductive through the loose folds of her costume.

"The corset and garter belt? That *would* be a treat," he murmured into her fiery hair. He could relax now. He was home, with his wife. But something still felt...dark. A new threat in the house, almost... "Nothing's wrong, then?"

"Were you worried?" Brie nuzzled into his neck, her breath steamy under his jaw. He inhaled deeply, as if she were his drug. Smoke. "I should have left a message on the machine for you when I went next door."

When she trailed her nose off his jaw and up his cheek and tipped her beguiling face up to him, those dusky eyes expectant, those full lips parting eagerly, he took her mouth with his. At the seductive taste of her, desire rushed through him, hot and inevitable. Burying a hand in her tangled curls, he grasped her hair almost too tightly while he kissed her, while he lost himself in her.

She sighed in approval, melted into him and their hunger.

His inexplicable dread didn't go away; it just became suddenly expendable. For her. Hell, for her, at this moment, Steve would sell his soul.

Maybe he already had.

*'Twas much like emerging from a heavy sleep, only so much as to recognize that sleep and resubmerge. Something called to lost memories, beckoned forgotten intents, and yet...*

*For what should it risk the pain of awareness? Better to drown in the void of death, keep the pain at bay, as by a philter...*

*A witch's philter?*

*Consciousness snapped at that image with a hunger that o'erwhelmed its confusion. A hunger for redemption. A hunger for revenge.*

*Disoriented, it struggled to remember.*

Brie Peabody reared up in her empty bed with a sob. Half-real memories of a mutilated Egyptian king and a sacrificed forest lord—both wearing her husband's face—smothered her. A nightmare? Her panicked eyes began to focus: home, morning, the bed she and Steve shared, right here in the twentieth century. She was no widow, was neither dusky-skinned queen nor woodland lady. She was no kidnapped daughter.

Red flannel sheets were tangled about her legs as if she'd struggled with them; she tried to kick them off, and when they clung she grasped them and tore them away, threw them off her as she would have liked to throw off the lingering sense of tragedy. Muggy November air licked at her nakedness, barely cooling the sheen of sweat that coated her body. She pulled her knees up against her chest, buried her face in them until her heart slowed its cadence.

November air. Of course. Last night had been Halloween.

Now fully awake, she recognized images from her dream as the pagan legend of the sacrificed Holly King. She'd recounted the story to her friends last night. Beneath the sheltering oak tree, Cypress Bernard had related the similar Egyptian myth of Isis and her murdered Osiris.

Slowly Brie uncurled, adjusted herself to being safe at home. She'd personally restored the oversize mahogany bureau and wardrobe that crowded the paneled bedroom, heavy with age. She'd refinished the floors herself. Predawn gray struggled in through the heavy red drapes she'd sewn—night lingered longer and longer this time of year.

Her subconscious had merely blurred the similar stories, that was all. Nothing to dust off her dream journal for. Her panic at imagining Steve in dual roles as doomed husband required little introspection to decipher.

Registering the soothing background hiss of the shower, Brie shuddered away the last vestiges of the nightmare. Steve. She rolled out of bed, yanking on a short scarlet robe as she crossed the wooden floor to the bathroom. This was one of the many benefits of being married: on-site comforting.

When she pushed the door open, tendrils of steam reached out to her like living things. For a moment she paused, one foot on steam-slick tile, caught in a flashback of dark underworld shadows from the deepest recesses of her nightmare. *Kidnapped into darkness...*

Then the shower stopped, the curtain rattled back with a wet sweep, and her husband stepped out of the claw-footed antique bathtub, knotting an oversize towel around his slim waist.

A different, more appreciative paralysis stole over Brie. Her gaze lingered on the water droplets marbling Steve's flat stomach, his chest, his shoulders—tanned from months of jogging shirtless—before climbing high enough to meet his sharp-eyed curiosity. Dripping hair, darker and straighter than its usual light-brown sweep, clung to his temples and cheekbones, partially hiding his raised eyebrows. Steve had the clean-cut face of a scholar, a poet, a...well, a newspaper editor.

An incredibly sexy newspaper editor. If Brie had met him in high school he'd have been the class president and track star and she'd have merely been the artsy misfit, Crazy Gwen's daughter, adoring him from afar. Luckily, she'd met him when she was in college, where nobody knew Crazy Gwen.

She tried to swallow back the sudden knot of anxiety that rose in her throat. She was still her mother's daughter.... Last night she had come disastrously close to revealing just how much.

"You okay?" Steve asked now, brown eyes concerned. The dampness of his hand caught on the silk of her robe as he paused to caress her back. She arched into his strength like a cat, some of her tension draining away. "Nightmares?"

She knew better than to accuse him of being psychic, whatever her long-held suspicions. "How'd you guess?"

"It was an equal-opportunity nightmare," he admitted. After drawing his palm up over her shoulder, skimming her cheek with the back of his fingers as he broke the seductive contact, he leaned past her to snag a hand towel. She watched his planed muscles flex as he scrubbed his hair dry. When he finished, he caught her gaze in the mirror—in the moment before he palmed the hair back, he looked far wilder than Steven Christopher Peabody had ever been meant to look.

*Holly and ivy woven into his hair, brown eyes reflecting the flame of a bonfire, cheekbones highlighted and jaw lost in wavering shadows... She* recoiled from images of her own nightmare. "You, too? What did you dream about?"

He bent to kiss her. The kiss tasted of toothpaste and smelled of woodsy shampoo and resurrected a chaos of memories from last night. "Can't remember. Tell me about yours while I dress." Then he swept past her, with the barest graze of hard shoulder and nubbly towel, into the reddish half-light of the bedroom.

"Just...nightmares." She leaned against the doorjamb to watch him dress, apprehension about the night before settling in her stomach like nausea. Not that she hadn't enjoyed their lovemaking! In fact, there had been an intensity to Steve's passion, an exciting, primal edge of desperation.

*He knew. Somehow, he knew she wasn't what she seemed.*

No, how could he know? She made herself stand up straight, casual. She should be used to keeping secrets; it was part of her heritage.

But she'd never meant to keep them from him.

Steve shed the towel and, too quickly, covered his cute butt with a pair of teal briefs she'd gotten him for his last birthday. Then he disguised the rest of his athletic body with the usual business shirt—slouchy and silk, casually classy, like him—slim green tie, and khaki trousers, occasionally glancing at her. She knew him well enough to see the contemplation behind his attention. *He knew she wasn't—*

No! His own nightmare had probably upset him, that was all. Steve didn't like to admit being upset by anything.

She asked, "Do you think you could take a long lunch and help me pick up the tallboy I bought at the estate sale?"

He glanced up from his socks. "Sorry. Town council's having a meeting on the new stoplight—the one past the railroad tracks. Some genius spent *beaucoup* bucks on a light with a special left-turn arrow, and heads are gonna roll. Could be the biggest scandal Stagwater sees all year."

His enthusiasm surprised her; Steve loved his job, but he normally kept it in perspective. "Over a traffic light?"

"Mmm-hmm...." He slid on shoes and went to the mahogany bureau to comb his hair. "It's a real mess, because there's only the two lanes. Picture this: Someone behind a go-straighter wants to make a left turn, watches his arrow come and go. When the light changes and the guy in front goes straight, the left-turner's stuck waiting out the oncoming traffic, blocking any go-straighters behind *him*. Blood pressures soar. Violence erupts." He dropped the comb back onto the bureau and turned to wink at her, once more his neat workday self.

"Can you get out of it?"

"Nope. Can't use the shoulder because of the ditch. And the right-turners."

"I mean, can't Kent do it?" Kent, the *Sentinel*'s ad salesman, was also the paper's only other full-time reporter. But...maybe Steve didn't want to get out of it? The water residue on the tile floor cooled beneath her bare feet; standing on one foot and then the other, to shake the moisture off, she stepped into the bedroom.

"Sorry." Steve rolled his shoulders. "Since Kent and Louise cut their honeymoon short to make deadline last Thursday, I gave them today off. And my free-lancers have day jobs. If someone else can help you load the stuff, I'll unload it after work." Passing her, he paused in his cuff-buttoning to level a finger at her. "*If* someone can help you load. Don't do anything crazy."

The twinkle in his dark eyes eased her anxiety. When she moved to bat the finger away, he caught her hand, and a playful arm wrestle ended with her tucked securely against the silk and hard muscle of his chest, her head beneath his freshly shaved chin, in a hug. When he planted a goodbye kiss on her hair and murmured, "I love you," she melted into his strength.

"I love you, too," she returned, then added, as ever, "Always have. Always will."

Too soon he backed away. She felt suddenly cold.

"I met *you* doing something crazy," she thought to remind him even as he made for the door.

Steve paused in the doorway, considering. "No, Red, you did something crazy *when* you met me." Then he grinned. It was his special grin, for her. He didn't suspect her secrets. Yet. "Quit while you're ahead." He ducked out of sight.

She heard his receding footsteps drum the stairs, then the bang of the front door. A moment later, she heard the purr of the Volvo's engine. She'd read too much into his fascination with traffic lights. He wasn't trying to cover up distress. Steve was very thorough, that was all. Dedicated.

Her mother's warning came back at her, a taunting I-told-you-so: *Be careful what you wish for, Brigit. You just might get it.*

When Brie and Steve met, Brie had known the gods were smiling down on her. Here stood all the normalcy, stability, dependability she'd ever dreamed of, in a surprisingly attractive package. It was almost three years ago that she'd been working a Dallas soup kitchen on Christmas day, her own rebellion against years of never celebrating the holidays on the twenty-fifth. He'd arrived to do a story on the charity and stayed to dish out stuffing beside her. In the course of the conversation—a stream of small talk to disguise how momentous their meeting felt—she'd learned that car problems had kept him from his family's traditional Christmas in Chicago, so she'd offered to drive him. Not knowing how little sentimental value Christmas held for her, or how well she could protect herself, Steve had called her crazy. But he'd accepted the offered road trip and, arriving in Illinois mere hours into December 26, she'd discovered the most wonderfully normal family in the world.

The Peabodys had made her feel not only welcome, but as if she belonged, too. They'd put her in Steve's old room—he'd good-naturedly volunteered to take the couch downstairs—and she could still remember how it had felt to lie in his bed, staring at his track trophies, his old typewriter, the pictures still arranged on his bureau. Steve as a gap-toothed little leaguer; with his sister at camp; at his high school prom—that picture had a small wedding photo of his prom date, maybe three years older, with another man, tucked affectionately into the corner of the frame. She'd lain awake for hours, savoring the love and stability that permeated this place—and thinking about the man downstairs.

The next year's Christmas had been even more wonderful, sharing the room—and the bed—with her husband.

*Be careful what you wish for.* Brie knew her fairy tales. Every boon has a catch, every blessing a curse. The irony of getting Steve was that she didn't deserve either his love or his trust. She'd thought to leave her secrets behind when they married, but she hadn't.

She'd lied to them both.

Brie ducked into the clammy bathroom and started the shower with a violent twist of faucets, shedding her robe, hoping to lose her guilt under the age-old cure of running water. She closed her eyes against the hot water; if a few uncharacteristic tears squeezed out, even she needn't know.

She wasn't truly the woman Steve had fallen in love with. She wasn't the person he'd married. Worse, circumstances forbade her even having the decency to tell him why.

Steam whispered at her bare skin, awakening vestiges of her nightmare. *Kidnapped into darkness...* No, she knew *that* autumnal legend, too; her friend and circlemate, Mary, had told it during last night's Samhain ritual. The lord of the underworld kidnaps the Greek goddess Demeter's daughter, and the earth mother's mourning sends the world into a season of cold, and darkness, and death.

That one, at least, Brie couldn't cast with herself or Steve. She had in no way been abducted into marriage, and Steve was no lord of darkness—despite her mother's dislike of him.

"Everyone is a balance of good and evil," Gwen Conway had warned. "Your Eagle Scout makes me wonder just how deeply he's buried his dark side...and what it's been doing while he wasn't looking."

But then, Mom had never liked Steve, because Mom was prejudiced.

Steve wasn't a witch.

With a moan, Brie turned her face up into the spray and twisted the hot-water faucet.

# CHAPTER TWO

*As quickly as I saw her, I must marry her. She hath bewitched me.*

—The Journals of Josiah Blakelee

"Council Meets on Traffic Light."

Steve stared at his yellow pad and groaned through a mouthful of sandwich. As if those Stagwater elders, several of them fairly portly, would fit on a traffic light! He wasn't sure what was worse; the stupid headline, or the fact that after more than five years as a professional journalist he'd become too distracted to do a piece he could have whipped out in high school. Images of candlelight reflecting on red hair and bewitching blue eyes drew his thoughts from work to a woman who ought not, after three years, to seem quite so mysterious.

He ripped the entire page out, crumpled it and hooked it across his tiny office into the wastebasket. Two points.

"Traffic light discussed." He considered that, then crossed out "discussed" and wrote "disgust," just for the heck of it. *The silk of a black robe slipping off pale shoulders, caressing feminine curves in its fall to the floor.*

He scribbled out the words and got up to get more coffee.

Except for his own office, the *Sentinel* headquarters—a converted old one-bedroom house that nobody would have bought for a residence—stood eerily empty. The typewriter and computer remained off; no fluorescent desk lamps glared against the interior gloom. With two of the three-person staff out, the place felt...dead. He'd even received fewer calls than usual this morning; none of his thousand-plus flock of subscribers seemed to have any complaints or compliments about Saturday's issue, or even any subscription questions.

The opportunity to publish and edit a weekly newspaper, coming as it had so soon after their marriage, had been a minor miracle—but then, such lucky breaks had filled Steve's life, since and including meeting Brie. He'd surprised himself, accepting her offer of a Christmas road trip, and he'd spent half the drive north wondering what could have possessed him...he'd thought himself immunized against beautiful women. But Brigit wasn't the usual beauty. She dressed casually, wore little makeup. Her hair hung free and unstyled. Yet her feline eyes glowed with life and energy, her pointed chin never dropped, her smiles were direct and...seductive?

In the passenger seat of her old Delta, Steve had thought about *that* quite a bit. Bunked on his parents' couch, knowing this beautiful stranger lay upstairs in his old bed, he could hardly sleep—hardly get comfortable—for thinking about it. But no amount of mere thinking would salve the elemental need she awoke deep within him.

It had been like that from the start, a *need*. He wanted to be with her—to play Parcheesi with her, to have a snowball fight with her, to sit up by the fire and listen to her talk about her art classes. Their first kiss, which had started as an innocent peck beneath the mistletoe, had flared into a make-out session so heavy that they'd both jumped guiltily when his mother called out that supper was ready. Their "first time" had been on the way home, in the Delta's roomy back seat, parked at a remote rest stop outside Amarillo. Another foolish, impulsive act that his usually dominant reason had protested as too soon, too public, *illegal,* even as he fed himself into the flame that was Brie Conway. Gasping for breath between fiery kisses, exploring her curves over her jeans and beneath her sweatshirt, ready to explode, he'd tried to regain control. "I feel like I'm taking advantage of you," he'd gasped, his words muffled by her mouth, her neck.

"Give me some credit." She'd pulled away long enough to take his face in her hands, meet the searching of his eyes with the excitement of hers. Her smile lit his soul. "I'm not that easy to take advantage of."

He'd trusted her, lost himself in her. In *them.* It had been liberating, transcendent—terrifying. Even now, some part of him feared the forfeiture of himself every time he took her in his arms. Heck, every time he *looked* at her. He'd just learned to ignore the discomfort and savor the excitement.

He refilled his mug for the fourth time that morning and took a swallow of chickory-laced coffee. At today's rate of productivity, he'd forfeit more than himself—he'd lose his livelihood! Maybe it was just as well that, after two years of marriage, his and Brie's family still numbered two: him and her. They wouldn't have to dress the children in rags while he collected unemployment and went to the county hospital's psychiatrist!

Groaning, he scooped a handful of letters from the floor beneath the mail slot and headed back toward his own little room—secretary cum office manager Louise, his adman's new bride, also had the day off. And he would think about *business* now. *Not* those crazy nightmares about pilgrims. *Not* how Brie had looked beneath him last night while they made love, her head tossing on the pillow, her damp lips parted . . .

"Hey, Stevie."

He spun so fast that hot coffee sloshed onto his wrist; he put his mug down and shook brown drops off his fingers. His kid sister hovered in the now-open doorway, head cocked uncertainly. Okay, so the family numbered *three* people, since a brokenhearted Sylvie had moved here last year. Sylvie was as close to Brie as to Steve; the two women had hit it off ever since that first Christmas. That made some sense, considering how crazy *he* had been about his redheaded chauffeur. Steve and Sylvie were truly birds of a feather. Sylvie had good taste, like him. She was also slim, brown-haired, and maybe too serious, like him. But she'd perked up over the past few months. Sylvie had found love. *Like him.*

"Hey, Sylly, how are you?" He belatedly caught her in a one-armed hug. "Why aren't you at the bookstore?"

"Because it's lunchtime?" she suggested. "I thought I'd swing by, see how you're doing."

*Signpost up ahead: The Twilight Zone.* Sylvie had always shown up whenever he was upset about something, ever since childhood. Except, he told himself, he wasn't currently upset about anything.

"I'm doing fine, thanks," he assured her, reclaiming his coffee and ducking back into his office. "I'm short two people, and I still don't have anything immediate for you to help with—unless you can read and summarize these notes."

She followed him and perched on his desk as he dropped back into his chair. "Not if *you* wrote 'em. You sure you're okay?"

"Why wouldn't I be?" Well, color him defensive.... He flashed her an apologetic look. "A bit tired. I can't believe Potter had a party on a Sunday night, Halloween or not." *And speaking of Halloween...* "Brie was at your

place, right?'' The moment the words left his mouth, he
regretted them, and he glanced out the window to avoid his
sister's searching gaze. It sounded as if he were checking
up on his own wife!

"She was," returned Sylvie easily. "Is *that* what's
bothering you?"

"Never mind." He leaned his elbows on the desk,
scrubbed one hand down his face and tried to drag his
mind away from Brie. "So how about you? The car holding out? No more problems with that leak? Your haunted-
house guy treating you right?"

She zoomed right in on the question about which he really wanted reassurance. "Wonderfully. Rand and I are
getting handfasted in about a month, after he rests up from
October."

Steve stared, waiting for the punchline. *Handfasted?*

"Humor us," she said. "It's an ancient marriage cere-
mony, lasts a year and a day. The theory is, if it's a good
marriage, you renew your vows every year."

"Sounds kind of uncertain." Leaning back in his chair,
he took a bite of his partially eaten sandwich. He couldn't
imagine having those kinds of loose ends dangling off his
life. He liked things tied up neat and permanent, thank
you.

"That's the point. If you're uncertain, maybe it's not
such a good marriage," she pointed out.

He stopped chewing. *What makes you think Brie and I
are uncertain?* Then he realized that she was speaking in
the abstract, and he swallowed.

"And if it isn't good, you don't have to suffer through
the guilt of broken vows, or the complications of a divorce. I think a lot of personal worth hinges on keeping
vows."

He continued to stare at her; she ducked her gaze and asked, "What?"

"Couldn't you just get engaged and then married, like normal people?"

"It is a marriage," she said defensively. "I told you."

"Right. Handfasting. Where do you get this stuff?"

Sylvie just shrugged and looked away. What, was it a secret? He frowned at his own assumption. *Get a grip, Peabody.* "Okay, fine, it's your life—excuse me, your *space,*" he conceded. She might be getting goofy, but he loved her and didn't want to hurt her feelings. As for her boyfriend... "Let me know the date, and I'll see if I can't find some bell-bottoms and love-beads."

"Are you sure you're okay?" she repeated, and an edge of uncertainty prickled at the back of his neck. He'd felt the same sensation last night, right after he got home: the stillness in the air before a storm, the awareness of an unseen threat. "For real, Steve. I had a feeling I ought to check."

Like she had some kind of ESP radar—not that he believed in junk like that. Especially if it insinuated that he wasn't on top of things! His and Brie's bills were paid, their health records current, their cars recently inspected... Catching himself ticking off a list of possible problem areas, as if he believed her hunches, he drew an annoyed breath. Then he tried a grin, to show just how fine he was. "I've *been* fine. I *am* fine. I will *continue* to be fine, especially if I can get this article written and this mail read today." *And if I can keep from fixating on Brie for a few hours.* It was one thing to keep a loved one in your thoughts, but geez! "And if you'd stop hovering. It makes me nervous."

Sylvie stood up, so he assumed the interrogation was over. "Well..." She hesitated—he detected a familiar sparkle in her eyes, and braced himself for a sibling scuffle. "As long as you're *really sure* you're fine—" And she fled.

He knocked his chair over, bolting up to chase "Sylly" out of his office. After she'd stopped in the doorway to hug him goodbye, the *Sentinel* seemed more eerily quiet than ever. He went back to his desk, took another dutiful bite of his now-dry sandwich. When he found himself staring at Brie's picture on his desk for God knew how long, he turned it to face the doorway. There was *nothing wrong.* He wasn't about to call home and check up on Brie as if there were. He wasn't going to rush out of here in the middle of a workday, with nobody to cover the phones for him. Brie was . . .

He felt a tired smile pull at his lips. She was *fine.*

He opened the first letter.

Dere Editer: I am discused that Stagwater made a big dele about Haloween this year. It is a plot by the whiches. They are everywear. . . .

He squinted down at the scrawled handwriting, finally distracted from thoughts of Brie. A plot by the *whoms,* maybe, but the *whiches?*

Ah . . . *Witches.* Right. Surprised at the depth to which some readers' credulity would sink, Steve crumpled the letter and hooked it toward the wastebasket.

Two points.

Brie glanced in her rearview mirror at the white van trailing her Blazer along the two-lane highway and marveled at her "luck." The walnut tallboy didn't fit in her vehicle, but the estate solicitor's nephew, whom she'd met before, at Sylvie's bookstore, had just happened to be there to offer delivery. No "nudges" on her part required. She often got her way, unasked, like that. Her mom thought the advantage hereditary—just like their secrets.

When she left home for college, Brie had also tried to leave the Craft. Though she'd easily stopped casting "spells," she'd had more difficulty quitting the "little magic" of sending willpower nudges at iffy situations. Still, she had learned magical restrictions from the cradle: no manipulative magic, no harmful goals, no negative energy. It wasn't that huge of a step to "no magic." And, like any unused skill, her magical abilities had atrophied.

Except stuff like the red traffic light ahead of her turning green at her approach. As usual. She couldn't just shut off this unconscious "luck" of hers, she'd decided—any more than she could escape her true self and her untold secrets.

Both vehicles breezed through Steve's "scandalous" light.

Steve. Her soul sank at the thought of his confusion last night, his reticence this morning. She shouldn't have worn her robe for her circle's backyard Samhain rites—or celebrated Samhain at all! But even alone in her dorm room at college, desperate to be normal, she'd surreptitiously lit candles to observe major sabbats. She couldn't *not* celebrate Samhain, any more than a child could give up Christmas.

She checked on the van via rearview again, and noticed a frown line between her drawn brows. Rebellious and confused or not, she shouldn't have married Steve when she was already under oath. But the first time she'd met his clear brown eyes with her own, her heart hadn't given a damn about *shouldn't*s.

Many Old Families, clans that could name every ancestor executed since the Middle Ages, took oaths of secrecy-to-unbelievers. Brie had taken hers at fourteen—one of the two most important vows in her life. The other had been to love, honor and cherish Steven Peabody "until death do us part."

Maybe she could have kept both oaths, had the Craft not drawn her back. But when she'd met Steve's sister, a natural empathy besieged by negativity but open to the idea of magic, she *had* to teach her the basics. Then Sylvie had moved to Stagwater last year, depressed and withdrawn, and to help her make friends Brie had coordinated their current four-woman circle. She'd meant to quit as soon as Sylvie was settled.

Really.

She suddenly realized that she'd driven through town now, and hardly noticed it. Not that Stagwater, Louisiana, was so difficult to miss, especially with green lights all the way. With a disgusted sigh, she palmed her turn signal long before the street to her duplex.

*Sure* she'd meant to quit. She'd enjoyed having the excuse to stay, to flex her innate powers again. *She was a witch,* albeit not by her mom's standards, and couldn't stop being one.

A witch madly and passionately in love with her unbeliever husband, and sworn to secrecy against him.

Hopelessness tightened in her chest; she forced it away. She'd think of some way they could work it out. She had to.

Outside her window, lots thick with saplings, briars and overgrown scrub isolated the houses from one another. This afternoon the duplex seemed to cower from the encroaching wild. November had subdued the woods behind the house to a tired green of baked pine and towering live oak; anything deciduous had already withered to brown, skipping the autumn colors completely. The

cloudless blue sky was already deepening toward dusk....
Darkness would fall too soon tonight, and earlier yet tomorrow. The Year Wheel was turning.

She parked alongside the curb beside the double mail-
boxes and plastic *Stagwater Sentinel* boxes—the area's
constant dampness required waterproof receptacles for the
newspapers, no thrown-on-the-lawn stuff. After she cut the
engine and sat back, her shoulders dropped; only then did
she place her disappointment.

No Volvo. Steve wasn't home yet.

She wished she didn't sense a touch of relief, as well.

While she climbed to the curb, the white van pulled to a
stop and its driver hopped out. Andy Beaudry wore holey
jeans, a tie-dyed shirt and raggedy high-tops. His dark-
blond hair sported a tiny braided tail in back, and a quartz
crystal dangled from his ear. Brie bit back a smile, imagining what her mother would say.

Mom, with the "insider's" condescension of some hereditary witches, would find Andy's stereotypically New
Age trappings amusing, as she might a child playing dress-
up. Gwen Conway reserved the same attitude for Califor-
nia channelers, psychic fairs, and fortune tellers. The
worst, she'd say, were charlatans, and the best poked their
noses into other people's business. Brie had always known
her mother was a snob. It was one of the elements she'd
mistakenly associated with the Craft and wanted to escape. Her family's tradition had all the seriousness of a
longtime religion, which it was—even the raising and directing of energy, the magic, was secondary. She knew
Mom felt equal disdain for Brie's own Circle. "Wicca
Lite," she'd say, except Gwen Conway didn't even use the
word *Wicca*. Too trendy.

And yet, Mom would probably prefer Andy as son-in-law to Brie's straitlaced and stable husband. At least children playing dress-up had their hearts in the right place.

Unlike Steve?

"Where do you want the cabinet, Ms. Peabody?" Andy asked, now, sliding the van's cargo door open with a *growl-thunk.*

"My workshop's around back." Carports outnumbered garages around here—again, because of the damp—but the converted duplex, a Depression-era home in the boxy style she fondly called French Perversion, had neither. She and Steve had worked together to wall in their half of the spacious back porch to make an extra room.

*Steve, stripped to the waist, sawdust clinging to his sweat-slicked skin as he held a board in place against the vertical four-by-four strut...* Smiling at the memory, she started at a question from Andy. "What?"

"What do you do?" Once Andy had eased the bulky walnut bureau from the van, they carried it across the mushy lawn.

"Woodwork and restoration," she explained around their load—her favorite piece from the sale. Most local antiques were, because of Louisiana's history, of French or Spanish design. This sale had boasted several battered Colonial pieces. "It's a home business—Craft Queen."

"Cool double entendre" came the youth's muffled reply as they navigated the brick corner of the duplex.

"Excuse me?"

"Goes with your pent."

Breath catching, she looked down at her sweatshirt. How'd he know? Grammy's gold medallion carefully concealed the five-pointed pentagram, a symbol of witchcraft, within Celtic knotwork. Even Steve hadn't recognized it, and Steve could be damned observant.

They reached the workshop door, and she nudged the knob with her knee, then pushed into the coolness of her workroom, her mind racing. After lowering her side of the tallboy to the cement floor, she leaned against it to catch her breath. Andy must have *looked* for the hidden design! With the neopagan movement so strong, witches and witch-wannabes were everywhere...few of them aware of the strict silence many old traditions kept.

"Cool place," her young helper commented now, looking around the room. Her hulking machines—jig-saw, band saw, and drill press—waited against the inside wall, near the electrical outlet. Her workbench stood under a waist-high window overlooking the huge, moss-draped oak tree shadowing the backyard and the tangled woods behind. All the remaining wall space hosted Peg-Board and floor-to-ceiling shelves, cluttered with tools and boxes of acquisitions, including what she'd been able to carry from the estate sale on Saturday. An ugly still life painting in a beautiful oak frame leaned against a slant-topped Bible box, its walnut spotted black by moisture damage. A chest with handmade hinges and crude dove-tailing, pine planks suffering from shrinkage, sat beneath her workbench.

"Listen, Andy, about the pentagram..."

"I like it," he said.

"I keep a low profile, so I'd appreciate it if you don't mention my, um...leanings."

"No prob."

She relaxed, her reluctant responsibility to oath and blood fulfilled yet again. Belatedly she remembered her manners. "Thanks for coming out of your way. Would you like a cold drink?" When he nodded, still examining the room, she ducked into the kitchen. Grabbing two colas from the fridge, pausing to add cola to the shopping list, she stepped back into the shadows of the workshop.

"Are you pagan, too, or—" An oddness in the air, an unnatural thickness, silenced her. She paused, looked around. Did the light seem different than moments ago?

"Andy?" Nothing. Unless . . .

Something seemed to move at the edge of her vision. She spun to face it. The jagged edges of two handsaws, hung on pegboard, glowed with a faint redness. So did the tips of her neat row of screwdrivers; they dripped with it. But movement?

Nothing.

Then . . . a noise behind her. Again she spun, stared at the power tools lining the wall like instruments of torture. Their metallic scent corrupted the soothing smell of sawdust. Cold from the sodas crept into her hands, up her wrists, as she stared into the shadows, trying to see, to hear over the sound of her own strained breath.

Was it nothing? Or a . . . whispering?

A coldness in her soul began to surpass the cold in her hands. She shuddered, despite her sweatshirt and jeans. Her gaze darted from the painting to the tallboy to the chest. *Something was wrong. . . .*

Then someone grabbed her from behind.

"No!" More defense than protest, the shout forced air from her frozen lungs, made her draw a fresh breath, helped her strike out with a flare of protective energy.

"Ow!" Andy Beaudry recoiled, pale— Uh-oh, he must be a sensitive. He cringed like a kicked puppy, trying to reorient his scattered energy. "Heck-heck-heck!"

Her fear had focused on the depths of the workroom, but he'd been behind her, probably outside. He couldn't have caused the spookiness. "Did I hurt you? Geez, of course I did." Light-headed herself from the sudden drain on her power, she crouched beside him, relieved to see some color returning to his face. "I thought I heard something.... Come on, ground yourself."

Not a bad idea, actually. She took a few deep breaths, imagined roots sinking deep into the earth. She also drew her own energy close to her—shielded herself—to avoid sensory overload from Andy. Her pulse slowed; her internal balance returned. She spared a moment to visually scan the room again, but nothing seemed amiss.

"Yeah, yeah, I've got it," Andy panted, following her lead with uneven gasps, shuddering off her attack. "You pack some kinda power, lady!"

"Are you okay?"

"I'm okay, you're okay." Andy breathed deeply, straightening, and then his eyes focused on something over her shoulder. More astral alarms—even rusty, she recognized the warning of her sudden chill. "Hello," he said warily.

She followed his gaze to the kitchen door. But the figure that leaned with feigned nonchalance against the doorjamb was no specter.

It was Steve.

Steve often looked tired when he got home—the curse of the self-employed. Tonight, the part in his light-brown hair had disappeared, likely from his habit of dragging a hand through it when frustrated. Tension tightened his jaw and shadowed his eyes. His tie dangled from his trouser pocket; he'd unbuttoned his shirt collar enough to show a hint of chest hair on his tanned neck; he'd rolled his sleeves above his corded forearms. But his posture was surprisingly stiff, alert.

"Hello." He repeated Andy's greeting in a dangerous tone.

*Manners, Brigit.* Straightening, she gave one of the colas to her helper—her fingers could barely move, her hand felt so cold—and stepped to Steve's side. The animosity that roiled off him surprised and worried her. "Steve, this is Andrew Beaudry, from the estate solicitors. He brought the tallboy home. Andy, this is my husband, Steve Peabody."

"Bright blessings," said Andy. *Lords above!* She flared her eyes at him in warning, and he blinked his apparent surprise that her "low profile" extended to her husband.

Steve squinted at him. *"What?"*

"It's just a greeting," Andy said defensively. "Don't let your aura go scarlet." Steve did look a little reddish, she thought—and she didn't read auras. Then she realized the setting sun cast a slant of pink light through the doorway and into the workshop. That might explain . . .

Steve expelled a long breath. "Yes, well, it's my aura, I'll make it any color I want. Do you need to be paid or something?"

If the red sunlight had come through the door, that could explain the bloody color of her tools! Belatedly Brie registered Steve's brush-off of her helper.

Andy shrugged before she could comment. "Nah, the drink's all I need." Then he smiled shyly at her. "See you around, Ms. Peabody. Go carefully."

And he trudged around the brick wall of the house, disappearing from sight.

Steve stood as if rooted, his stare enforcing Andy's departure, and she had a moment to study him. He held his shoulders and back tightly, as if braced against something. A headache? His eyes narrowed, sharp, he almost looked like a stranger—but no, she'd bet he'd Steve-ishly furrowed his brow under that sexy fall of mussed hair. "Bad day at work?"

"What makes you think that?"

"You being a rude jerk was my first clue." She'd known that her observation, even said softly, would get his attention. "What was that all about, hon?"

"You're asking me? *I'm* the one who came home to find you fawning all over Moonbeam, there."

She stared at him. What? Fawning all over... Abruptly he strode back through the kitchen doorway.

Stunned, she vaguely became aware of the shadowy stretch of room around her. Maybe the sunset *had* caused the eerie light—and maybe not. Even if last night hadn't been Samhain, famed for free-roaming spooks, the universe was full of otherworldly things. Best to mind one's own business if they minded theirs. As long as whatever it was, if it was anything at all, was just passing through—as long as the circle's ritual hadn't drawn uninvited spiritual guests—she probably needn't worry.

"I welcome that which comes in peace, and bid all else be gone," she murmured. It was more declaration than spell. She didn't have the energy...but it never hurt to clarify things.

"Where the hell's the beer?"

She frowned. Who was this, Steve's evil twin? Ducking inside, she shut the door behind her. Imagination or no, she also bolted it and leaned back against it. *There.*

Steve stood beside the refrigerator, staring at her. Well, she sure wasn't going to explain that she'd been distracted by a "spooky" feeling. Anger hovered close enough already. Steve's manic realism, which she usually found comforting, would only antagonize her right now.

"The beer's in the vegetable drawer. And Andy was doing me a favor," she told him. Steve was always good at listening to explanations—not that she had anything to explain. "You really shouldn't have dismissed him like he was some peon."

To her surprise, Steve planted his hands on the red-tiled countertop and gave her a look that, were he a trained magician, could have knocked her back far worse than she'd zapped Andy. "Then perhaps you should go after him?"

She hadn't been *close* to being angry, she realized.

*This* was angry.

# CHAPTER THREE

*Suspect the willful woman.*
> —The Journals of Josiah Blakelee

If Steve had struck her, he couldn't have shocked Brie more. Steve didn't get angry. He was too *nice,* too damnably objective—wasn't he? *She* got angry—at rude drivers, outrageous prices, slow waiters—and *he* talked her out of it. That was how things worked in the Peabody household.

She didn't temper her sharp surprise. *"What?"*

To his credit, Steve seemed equally taken aback—briefly. Then he turned away and yanked the refrigerator open, burrowed into its depths. "You heard me," he insisted, sullen.

Definite bad day. "What's happened?"

Abruptly he slammed the fridge, beer in hand. Several magnets clattered to the linoleum, followed by the fluttering notes they had held. For a moment he stood there, eyes closed, jaw tense. When he opened his eyes, anger flared out. "What *did* happen, Brie?" He held the beer so tightly that veins showed on his arm. "What exactly did I just interrupt?"

She would have taken a step back, if she hadn't already been pressed against the door. "What's gotten into you?"

"Some sense? Some reality? Maybe the realization that I have no idea who you are. Or try all of the above." He strode around the counter to stand before her; she jumped when he popped open the beer can. "You've been going for God knows how long, with God knows who—why not go now?"

"Don't be stupid!" she snapped back, battered by the force of his anger, and her sudden, irrational fear of it.

"Tell me what I don't know then," he dared her. "I know you looked pretty cozy with the space cadet. I know you've been sneaking around behind my back. But I'm so damned ignorant, how about filling me in on the details?" He leaned over her; she felt suddenly vulnerable. Hostility billowed off him. "Tell me what you've been hiding, *Ms*. Peabody. 'Cause I can only think of one thing you'd have to keep from your husband, and it makes your little tête-à-tête with Moonbeam a minute ago look pretty damned suspicious."

*Sneaking around. Hiding.* Her stomach knotted. *He knew!* But no, he suspected—he suspected the wrong thing! *An affair?* She'd hardly looked at, much less wanted, another man since the moment she *saw* Steve. Forces stronger than them had drawn them into one another's orbits. Didn't he feel that?

Coldness gripped her stomach when she realized that, staring up at his anger, she could hardly feel the bond, either. Their anger interfered, throwing everything off kilter.

"Come on, tell me," he prodded, brown eyes searching hers. For innocence, or guilt? "You've got something to tell me, right?" The break in his voice clinched it. After over three years, he really thought she'd screw around on him.

The sonofabitch.

"You're right," she snapped. "You don't know me very well." Maybe she should have expected that, since she'd kept the secrets. But she could never have expected this. "And I sure as hell don't know you."

His dilated eyes stopped their searching. He shrugged, leaned back on the counter, took a long draw of beer. "Guess that makes us even, huh?" Had he been watching her, wondering? Why hadn't he ever mentioned it? *How much did he know?*

"If you've had questions, why haven't you asked them?"

"Would you have told me the truth?"

*Space Cadet.* How many disparaging names did he have for people who followed paths like hers? She couldn't admit her Wicca to somebody who didn't believe in magic— or in her. "I've never been unfaithful to you! You should know that!"

"Would you have told me the *truth?*" he repeated, as if she didn't understand. Maybe it showed—she *didn't* understand. She trusted Steve *not* to taunt her, not to mock her.

*Moonbeam.* "Stop interrogating me like—"

He hurled his beer can into the sink so hard it ricocheted out and bounced to the linoleum, with the litter and the magnets. *"Would you have told me the damned truth?"*

In the echoing silence, they stared at each other. Fight or flight. She turned to get away while she could still control her temper. His hand closed on her shoulder, spun her around. She grabbed his wrist, but he caught her hand with his free one, tight.

"Why?" he demanded, pleaded. "Why are you the one with the answers?" He breathed hard, high color in his face, wildness in his eyes, hair spiked down over his forehead. His chest rose and fell with each breath, clinging to the silk of his shirt. She could almost hear his heart rac-

ing...or was that hers? And was it only fear pulsing
through her, as she waited for his next move, drowning in
his anger, or something equally instinctive, and far less
appropriate?

This was, after all, Steve. *Her* Steve. That knowledge
tempered her alarm with fascination.

The hand imprisoning her shoulder loosened to caress
slowly to her neck, to brush her cheek. Out of habit, she
leaned her face into his delicate touch—such a contrast
with the hand that still manacled her wrist. Her head fell
back as his long fingers stroked beneath her chin, explored the contours of her face. Her tug to free herself was
embarrassingly weak.

Steve leaned into her and nuzzled her neck, his breath
hot, his lips dry. Her eyes drifted shut as his cheek scraped
gently across hers. Now she was glad to be propped against
the door; it gave her support while she melted from the inside out. Angry...wasn't she angry? But he breathed in the
smell of her, nibbled at her ear, and she knew that any
minute now, he'd apologize, explain what had *really* upset him. They'd kiss—maybe it would be more than kiss—
and make everything okay.

"Tell me," Steve murmured into her ear, his voice husky
and ticklish. "Tell me what it is you've been doing."

Dismay chilled her. Eyes flaring open, she tugged again
on her hand. That he wouldn't release it, but instead
tightened his painful grip, fully broke the spell. She ducked
from his seductive tracing across her throat. "Let go."

Instead, Steve tried to take her mouth with his. She
twisted her face away, and realized just how thoroughly he
had her trapped. His athletic body pinned her back, and
his hands held her own over her head. He'd braced one
knee firmly against the door, to block her exit. *That* scared

her—truly scared her. And that she could be frightened of her husband's strength scared her more.

Fight or flight—with all exits blocked.

"Let go, Steve," she warned hoarsely, ducking his second attempted kiss. Apprehension, and the dangerously volatile power of anger, unbalanced her. "Or I'll make you sorry."

Steve raised his head from her, blinked apparent surprise at her distress. Slowly his grip loosened, as if he had to fight himself to uncurl his fingers. His hand slid from her numb wrist. He stepped back awkwardly.

Expelling a relieved breath, she searched his eyes, hoping to see an explanation. She saw only accusation.

Steve said, "Too late."

She pushed past him and fled the kitchen, and went down the hall. She barely paused by the front door—*perhaps you should go after him*—then, breath shallow, bolted up the narrow stairs. *Moonbeam. Space cadet. Only think of one thing you'd have to keep from your husband.* Like Jekyll and Hyde.

She ducked into the bedroom.

Her pumpkin-colored cat, Romeow, blinked awake from his nap on the bed and stood, yawning wide while he stretched into an arch. He considered her with solemn, unblinking concern while she slammed the door behind her.

She stared back, trembling, echoes mocking her. She was behaving childishly, falling into a defensive mode she should have outgrown long ago. Yes, Steve had no right to suspect her of infidelity—but had she a right to keep the secrets that roused his suspicions? She gathered the cat into her arms while she sank onto the bed, buried her face in his fur.

How long had Steve let doubt ferment within him? Maybe he'd had a valid reason not to ask about it—that penchant for not "going with" any story with loose ends. Or maybe he'd been scared. What must he have gone through, to react this strongly when he finally *had* confronted her?

Her own guilt pressed down on her; she couldn't breathe around the weight in her chest. What had she done to him?

When Romeow squirmed his discomfort, she loosened her hold and stared, unfocused, out the window. Surprisingly, the murky red sky wasn't quite dark yet. At least not outside.

But it soon would be.

*It felt the husband instinctively fight its nebulous influence, felt their connection slipping, and struggled desperately to win command. No! 'Twas meant, their alliance; 'twas necessary! 'Twould not lose awareness again, not after—*

*But it knew not how long it had been . . . what? Confusion further weakened their connection. The draw of breath in living lungs, the pulse of blood through living veins, mocked its own half existence. The husband, alive, continued alone.*

*And it, not alive, but yet not done with life, remained trapped, alone in this stagnant void. Stolen vision darkened over like a falling curtain, like the Veil between their realms. The Veil that, yestereve, had thinned enough for it to awaken to evil—to salvation.*

*E'en now, exhausted from extended displacement, it could sense life beyond the Veil glowing into this timeless nowhere like a beacon.*

*'Twould find its way back, would return to reclaim the power of touch, of taste, of sight. The woman would do*

*her husband's bidding at last. If from its exile it could cast thoughts and emotions onto one so steadfast as "Steven Peabody"—even thoughts and emotions this Peabody found guiltily familiar—it could rend the Veil. Somehow.*

*As soon as it rested. And remembered.*

Steve extended a hand and gripped the edge of the sink—and only then staggered under a wave of dizziness, as if the anger itself, the sheer, pounding rage, had been keeping him on his feet. Now, as it drained and the red haze of fury faded from his vision, his strength drained, as well. He had to stand for a long moment, swaying, propped against tile and steel, before his breathing felt normal and his head relatively clear.

Where had *that* come from?

He took a step back and felt a ceramic magnet crunch beneath his shoe. Looking at the floor was a mistake, because beer was puddled around the mess he'd knocked off the fridge door—an upside-down photograph, a shopping list, and a second cat-shaped magnet, this one only broken in half. Automatically, still unsteady in the aftermath of the argument, he crouched and scooped up the magnet remains, the can, the list.

His eyes gravitated to the words on the list—he'd always sought solace in words. His hand shook, with cold or shock, so that he could hardly read it at first. *Tampons,* Brie had written in her impatient scrawl—she still wasn't pregnant. *Steve's cereal. Cola.*

They'd had the photo, which dripped beer when he lifted it, taken three months before in New Orleans when they were celebrating their second wedding anniversary. They both held champagne flutes, both smiled happily. He wore his tux, and Brie wore a strapless black number with her wild red hair swept back, tiny rubies dangling from her ears down the creamy column of her throat. That was before he'd given her the necklace. . . .

He straightened and tossed the photo into the sink with the rest of the mess. The mess he'd made with Brie was far worse than one ruined picture.

He felt unbalanced, as if he'd just run a marathon—with a migraine. What the hell had happened? No; he rejected the confusion. He *knew* what had happened. He'd gotten angry. Simple as that. He'd gotten home after a distracting day, felt a touch of last night's illogical apprehension—maybe he was coming down with something!—and when Brie hadn't greeted him he'd glanced into her workroom to find her bent over that retro-hippie. She'd looked so beautiful, almost unnaturally so, with her loose hair catching fire from a scrap of sunset, and her jeans molding the seductive curves of her bottom and legs—and she had been with...*that*. That scrawny, tie-dyed Maynard G. Krebs of the nineties.

And they'd seemed *right* together. They hadn't been dressed similarly, they didn't look alike, and their ages had to miss by a half decade, at least. But that mystery of Brie's, that wildness which he, Mr. Dull-and-Dutiful, wouldn't know without her, had met some kind of incongruous match in that overyoung, New Age beatnik. And he'd felt left out. Jealous.

He took a deeper breath, trying to regain himself with his slowing heartbeat. He'd been *envious,* he told himself, not jealous. As much as he'd obsessed about Brie all day, of *course* he'd been put out to find someone else enjoying her company, no matter how innocently. He spent too much time away from home, that was all.

As for the business about her keeping secrets—he hadn't even considered the idea until the words left his mouth.

Odd, that she'd denied nothing—answered nothing.

He dragged a hand over his sweaty face. *Get a grip, Peabody.* He'd behaved abominably, he was man enough to apologize, end of story. He was, after all, a completely rational person, and from now on he would stay that way.

If he lucked out, maybe Brie would be rational too.

After climbing the narrow stairway, he knocked on the bedroom door. There was the chance that if he marched right in he'd have to dodge assorted toiletries. They also, he noted with a weak attempt at a smile, kept the gun in the bedroom.

He got no answer.

"Brigit?"

More silence. Then she called, "Yes?"

"We've got to talk."

He had a moment to study his shoes before she said, "I'm not sure I'm ready to talk just now, okay?"

Exhausted, he leaned against the wall. "Well, heck, Brie, I haven't exactly prepared note cards, either. But if we wait till we're ready, we may never communicate again!"

"Okay," she called finally, reluctance in her voice.

Hardly an engraved invitation, but he'd take it.

Brie hadn't turned any lights on, and she didn't look up when he opened the door. Instead, she sat on the bed, stroking her fat old cat and staring out the window at the dregs of the sunset. Dying streaks of flame clawed at the duskier purple as they slipped away, throwing everything before them—treetops, electrical wires, Brie—into black silhouette. Even the crystal suncatchers hung before the window could manage no more than a random glint of crimson. Only the edges of Brie's hair caught the sky's color, her hair and the gold pendant she always wore.

Someone unfamiliar with his wife might not have recognized her vulnerability, or her desperation. He knew better, knew *her* better—or he thought he did. Guilt at her hurt magnified his own. He had to brace against the urge to lunge across the room and gather her into his arms, to pet her hair and kiss her face... and against an equally strong urge to lay his head in her lap in a silent plea for *her* to comfort *him*. Luckily, his self-control worked again. He'd temporarily abdicated physical-gesture privileges with that stunt downstairs.

He winced at the fresh memory. He'd scared her—maybe not as much as he'd scared himself, but scared her nonetheless. Best to deal with her fears first—because Brie always came first, of course, not to avoid soul-searching.

Really.

"I am very, very sorry," he said, carefully remaining in the doorway. "I acted like a jerk. You didn't deserve that."

She raised her eyes to meet his, her smoky gaze wary. He could see her weighing possible answers—*Brie,* the temperamental one of the pair. After the hair-trigger temper he'd exhibited, he doubly appreciated her effort, even as he missed her spontaneity.

Her cat jumped off her lap and slunk out of the room, giving Steve a wide berth and hissing at him as it left. Great.

"Why did you?" she finally asked.

*I don't know.* That was lame... except that he *didn't* know, which bothered him more than his lingering exhaustion.

She continued to wait, outwardly calm, but her fingers smoothed and resmoothed the comforter, tattling on her distress. She deserved an answer, so he'd better figure one out quick.

"I got angry. I've been in a mood—a bad mood, I guess—and when I came home and you were with... Andrew?"

"Andrew." The movement of her fingers on the quilting stilled when he used the kid's real name.

"I felt—" Surprised, curious…then threatened. Funny, how it had hit him like a blow to the chest before spiraling into jealousy, and then an anger the likes of which he hadn't felt for a long, long time.

This was *not* the moment for an unrelated walk down memory lane. "I felt belligerent, and acted on it. I shouldn't have." He held her gaze, feeling the knot in his stomach lessen with the diminishing guardedness he saw there. "Not with you."

Unfortunately, even though her caution faded, the questions stayed. She lowered her eyes before the weight of his and said, "Did you notice anything odd when you came in? Some negativity that could have set you off—" That she stopped when she peeked up to judge his reaction told him that he must not have masked his skepticism fast enough. "But you said you were already in a bad mood," she remembered, disappointed.

"Yeah." He shrugged. "Stress."

She said, "Because of me."

"Partly."

The word hung in the air between them, and Brie glanced back out the window. At least he thought she did. Darkness had triumphed; he could hardly see her now. Still in the doorway, he palmed the switch to the overhead light. The Tiffany-style lamp revealed the room, *their* room— and all the space between them. The window became a mirror, and Brie's hauntingly beautiful reflection caught his gaze, even as she presented her sweatshirted back.

"I'm sorry," she whispered.

Oh, God. He covered the distance to her in three strides, saw her flinch, and managed to stop himself at the high-posted footboard. "Don't be sorry—it's not your fault."

"But you said . . ."

"I was in a mood partly because of you. I meant you were on my mind—I was worried. I think too much, that's all." *That's why I need you.* "It's not your fault I worry."

He couldn't read the nuances of her mirrored expression. Maybe she couldn't read his, either, because she turned on the bed to face him. "Were you worried about me cheating on you?"

Well, one of them had had to bring it up. "No. Absolutely not. Consider that temporary insanity. I had no call to accuse you of keeping *any* secrets." He braced his hands on the bedpost, leaned his chin on his hands, and tried to grin. It was a poor grin. "I mean, that's a pretty dumb thought, huh?"

*Way to sound convinced there, Peabody.* Oh, well, he'd screwed up so badly in the past half hour, how much worse could it get with a touch of unattractive vulnerability?

Brie stared back at him, eyes clouded and miserable.

She wasn't reassuring him yet.

He shrugged away that portent of doubt. What did he expect? They'd been through this downstairs. "Of course it's a dumb thought—forget I even asked. I don't know what's gotten into me. I might be coming down with something . . ."

She shook her head. "It's not . . . entirely you, Steve. I won't let you think it is."

*No.* He wanted to shut his eyes against the confession in her stubborn, worried expression, but he couldn't move. A violent protest of disbelief wrenched at his gut. *No.* She *wasn't* seeing anyone; she'd *said* so. He wouldn't believe it, not even if she did confess. It didn't make sense.

But the secrets, on the other hand . . .

He recovered the ability to blink as pieces fit together. The way she'd run from his ridiculous accusations, instead of tearing him to shreds. His own obsession with her activities, recently—*Brie was over at your place, right?*

"Your nights out with Sylvie and the others?" he guessed. She never changed those planned outings, ever. But what could Brie possibly do wrong with *his sister?*

"It's not anything bad," she said quickly. "I'm not involved in drugs, or illegal activities, or underground political movements." Her eyes flashed. "And I am *not* cheating on you. Don't you ever accuse me of that again, Steven Peabody, or you're asking for trouble."

Maybe because of his relief—wary relief, since he wanted to trust her more than he did—he felt one corner of his mouth quirk in dry amusement. "Tell me something I don't know."

She widened her eyes at his choice of words, even as he caught his own double entendre. Wouldn't Freud have a field day with that? "I can't," she said.

She was confessing to keeping secrets—but wouldn't confess the secrets? He moved to the other side of the bedpost and sank onto the foot of the bed, a good four feet from her. "You don't trust me."

"Remember when we got engaged, and went to see my Mom?"

Clearly. Mother Conway was a real character, with her mobile home, and her cats, and that piercing gaze of hers. She hadn't liked him, which he—a fairly likeable guy—had found disturbing. And she'd seemed so knowing, he'd almost wondered if maybe *she* was right and *he* was mistaken about himself.

"That night I said that there was some stuff from my past I didn't think I could ever tell you about. Remember?" He noticed a likeness between her eyes and her mom's now. "Remember?"

*My life isn't exactly an open book.... I love you, Steve, and I trust you, but there are things I can't let you ever know. Can you handle that?* At the time he'd suspected some past incident she was unreasonably ashamed of, or simply couldn't confront. His imagination had glanced across the possibility of everything from incest to a juvenile criminal record to an abortion. She'd piqued his journalistic curiosity—but she'd looked so desperate as she awaited his response, as if her life hung on his answer. He remembered thinking that, for her, he could handle anything.

"I said, 'What matters is our present and our future, not your past,'" he told her. "I was willing to leave it at that, too. But this is *now,* Brie. This isn't just you, it's us. What is it you aren't letting me know about *us?*"

She opened her mouth, closed it, swallowed. She looked trapped, threatened by him. With a sinking feeling, he remembered the scene in the kitchen.

"Nothing I can tell you," Brie managed.

In three years, he'd never once moved to hurt her, never once threatened to leave her. They'd survived monetary difficulties without fights. They'd calmly decided to wait another year before considering infertility counseling. Together they'd made it through the deaths of his parents, and the conviction of the driver who had killed them— what was there she couldn't trust him to handle? So he'd lost his temper downstairs. So what? If having a bad temper were a crime, Brie would have been behind bars years ago.

Immediately he wished he hadn't pictured his wife in jail, even facetiously. His imagination had fed on news for too long; he could consider everything from the absurdity of sex-change operations to the horror of fatal diseases, instantly. All of which he could handle, if only she'd let him!

At least if he knew, he'd have only one thing to worry about instead of a million.

"I thought we could talk anything out," he said, with remarkable outward calm. If they couldn't, there was a lot more wrong with them than her damned secrets.

She winced as if he'd shouted, but she held her ground. "Not this, Steve. I promised never to tell."

"Promised who?"

When she wouldn't answer, he stood and moved to the bedside table, so close to Brie he could smell her spicy perfume.

She watched him pick up the phone and start punching in numbers. "Who are you calling?"

"Sylvie." The only person around here who'd known Brie before their marriage.

Brie depressed the disconnect button. "Don't."

"She's involved, isn't she? If this is her secret, *she* can refuse to tell me. You don't have to cover for her."

"I'm not covering for anybody!" She removed her hand from the telephone cradle and huddled on the bed again. She didn't relax when he hung up. "I wish I were."

He shoved his fists into his pants pockets. "Could you tell a therapist, or a marriage counselor?"

Her blue eyes widened. "A what?"

"A marriage counselor. Because I can't go on this way. Something's wrong."

"But it doesn't have anything to do with you! Can't you trust me that much?"

"Why should I? You don't trust me." When she only set her mouth in that stubborn line he knew so well—*thought* he knew—he said, "Maybe whatever it is doesn't have anything to do with me. The fact that you won't tell me does. It's manipulative to say you're hiding something and try to leave it at that." Anger sent a pain between his eyes, stiffened his neck and back muscles. That he kept control, instead of losing it, as he had downstairs, didn't relieve the pressure.

Maybe it made it worse.

"I only told you because on some level you obviously already knew. I didn't want you to think you were crazy."

He didn't thank her. He didn't say anything. When Brie reached up and touched his arm, he almost flinched.

"I'm sorry," she said, again. "I couldn't talk to a marriage counselor about this."

Then the room got really quiet. Deadlock. He fished his tie from his pocket, pretending not to notice her hand falling away as he belatedly moved to the closet. He could still accomplish simple tasks like hanging up his ties, even as the most important part of his life crumbled around him.

"How about a compromise?" she whispered, stilling him. He didn't turn to face her, but he strained to hear her words. "Give me some time.... I'll work on it. I'll try to think of something. I'll call my mom. Maybe she can help me...."

Somehow, the interjection of Mother Conway in the conversation lent it a comforting normalcy. The woman might not like him much, but he could hardly imagine her condoning anything truly immoral or illegal in her daughter.

"This has to do with your family?" He came to sit beside her on the bed, taking her hands. Maybe he'd misread this. Her hands felt so right in his; their gold rings matched.

"Sort of," she hedged.

"Your dad?"

She frowned, tugged at her hands. He didn't release them. "I don't have a father, remember?"

"Then what—"

Her smoky gaze silenced him. "A month," she said solemnly, pleadingly. "If I can't come up with a solution of some sort . . . well, we'll see."

*We'll see.* An odd way to refer to something that could destroy their marriage. But he'd give her the time. Did he have any choice? One month to figure out who she was . . . and maybe, considering the scene downstairs, who he was, too.

One final month.

"I'll go fix something to eat," he said, bending. Out of habit, he brushed his lips across her temple, let the spiciness of her fill his lungs for a brief, bittersweet moment. "Maybe nuke a frozen dinner." And he moved away from the beautiful stranger on his bed.

"Steve!" Her voice was sharp, almost panicked.

He stopped, but didn't look back.

"I really do love you. I always . . ." But it was an easy phrase, overused and hollow.

When he left the bedroom, he didn't feel loved.

# CHAPTER FOUR

*She maintains her innocence, yet women deceive—
and witches moreso.*
                              —The Journals of Josiah Blakelee

Somewhere along the line, she'd let herself believe in forever. That, Brie decided with a strangled breath, staring at the black, blank window, was why she hurt so badly.

She and Steve had been inseparable since that first Christmas, and yet, despite the totality of her happiness, she'd always wondered when it would end. Even after they'd moved in together, she would lie awake, surrounded by the black of night and by his warm, secure arms, and she'd fight off fear of their eventual parting.

But they hadn't parted, they'd married. Time, happiness and Steve himself had lulled her into a false sense of security.

Now the threat returned. Because of her, because of her secrets and her witchcraft. And she couldn't do anything...

Or could she?

She drew a steadier breath to collect her scattered energies. She wasn't the average afternoon-talk-show victim of fate—she was a witch! Even out of shape, she had certain abilities! She could cast a little glamour spell on herself to increase her attractiveness, could draw some extra cover

over any future Craft activities. She could project "Love me without question" easily to someone as open as Steve.

Rejecting the very idea, she grabbed up the phone and punched in familiar numbers. The ethics of her magic forbade such manipulation—and what kind of perverse love would that be? She took numb comfort in the ringing on the end of the line.

Besides, she did not want to ever, ever know whether she could bend his will to hers.

"Hello?"

She'd meant to ask about the vow. And yet when she heard the voice of her mother, her teacher, her high priestess, Brie's restraint cracked, and she surprised even herself. "Mom, do you know anything about possession?"

A hint of a Texas twang now softened Gwen Conway's Connecticut accent. "It's nine-tenths of the law, dear."

Now that she'd admitted her crazy suspicion, Brie wanted to spontaneously combust—poof—and be gone. Of course Steve wasn't possessed! And yet there had been that moment of eeriness in the workshop, before he got home.

And possession could be cured.

She swallowed, made her voice casual. "Mom, I'm serious. How could I tell if someone were possessed?"

"You'd probably know, dear. I've only once seen a case of demonic possession. Foaming at the mouth, groaning, shrieking—the possessed person, of course, not me. Filthy language in strange voices . . . You get the idea."

*Buzz! Wrong answer, but thank you for playing.* "Like in *The Exorcist*." Steve might not have seemed himself in the kitchen, but he *had* been human. He was, in fact, as mundane as they came—Brie could imagine him being voted "Least Likely to have a Paranormal Experience." *Or*

*"Least Likely to Marry a Witch."* But to imagine that the problem was not their marriage, but some mysterious, external force, comforted her. Falsely.

"Who do you think might be possessed?"

Uh-oh. Brie said, "Never mind," and her mother laughed out loud.

Brie braced herself.

"I'm sorry, dear—but the idea of your Eagle Scout levitating..." Gwen snuffled to a stop. "Who would you get to exorcise him? A justice of the peace?"

"Never *mind*, Mom. I didn't call about possession, anyway." No guts, no glory. "I called about the vow."

"Mmm-hmm." So much for shocking Mom. "I've been expecting this. 'Silence'—"

"'Is the secret of secrets.' I know." Brie had learned those basics—to know, to dare, to will, and to keep silent—in childhood. She'd learned all kinds of things. Little comfort such esoteric teachings brought, when the man she loved, the man she needed, thought she'd betrayed him.

Especially when he might well be right.

"I don't think you want to hear my opinion, Brigit."

*I don't.* But it was her only hope, at the moment. "Hasn't anyone ever broken the vow successfully?"

"Other than the few who confessed under torture? My second cousin Arthur told his wife about the Craft." Brie's hope hardly had time to flare before Mom added, "Three years later, he'd divorced anyway. Even lost custody of his kids."

Mom didn't lie. Lies weakened a witch's ability to create reality with words.

Brie heard Romeow, downstairs, yowling to go out. She felt like yowling, too. "Because he betrayed the Old Ones?"

"Because he betrayed himself."

Oh. So much for her only hope. Downstairs, Romeow yowled again, more impatiently.

Brie's mom said, "I'm sorry if you're unhappy. Maybe..."

Suddenly Romeow's mournful cries erupted into cat-fight screeching. Steve's voice cursed back in very un-Steve-like language. Something crashed to the floor downstairs.

"Gotta go, Mom!" Brie was already hanging up the phone and bolting from the room and down the hallway. At the landing, she stopped to absorb the situation.

By the door, at the foot of the narrow stairs, Steve was bracing something against the wall. Something orange, something writhing, something that growled. Romeow!

She lunged down the stairs. "Stop!"

"Open the door." The cat matched Steve's command with a low-throated wail of warning.

"Romeow..." She reached for her pet, but Steve side-stepped between them, blocked her with a shoulder. She caught a glimpse of his hand, clutching the squirming cat by its scruff so tightly that Romeow's eyes squinted.

Steve sucked in a sharp breath. "*Now*, Brie!" Maybe he wouldn't hurt Romeow further if she obeyed. With a snarl of her own, she undid the chain lock and opened the front door, crying out when Steve literally threw her cat into the front yard. She darted out onto the lit porch in time to see the orange streak vanish into the shadows across the yard. He wasn't limping. He couldn't be hurt too badly.

As fear for her cat lessened, anger rose. It was bad enough that Steve had to act like a jerk with her, but to pick on helpless animals! She spun on him—but his own direct, disillusioned gaze stayed her anger.

Instead of loosing a string of epithets, she swallowed a mouthful of air.

"You thought I'd hurt him." Steve didn't shout, didn't hit anything or throw anything, didn't accuse. But the pain that laced the question made it more potent than any of those he'd hurled at her in the kitchen.

"You were—"

He turned away, stalked down the hall and back to the kitchen.

For a moment she stared after him. She *had* believed he'd hurt Romeow. The cat had been screeching, Steve was so much bigger... and he was the same man who had hurled beer cans and pinned her to doors not an hour ago.

The same man who'd been kind and dependable for three years, otherwise.

She found him washing his hands at the kitchen sink, sudsing past the elbow, uncaring if his rolled sleeves got soaked. Negativity—the residual remains of anger and upset—hovered in the room like a stench. Then, as Steve rinsed, she saw the long red gashes that were the marks of his battle with the cat, deep, bleeding wounds, not the playful scratches she sometimes got in a too-exciting game of catch-the-string.

Suspicion that she was an idiot settled like nausea in her stomach. While Steve turned off the faucets, she snatched a dish towel from under the sink and handed it to him. The gashes on his arms left red smears on the towel as he dried.

Maybe Romeow was defending himself, but... "I'll get the first-aid kit."

"I can do it." Steve winced as he patted his other arm with the towel.

"I want to, okay?"

He looked as if he might disagree, but he leaned sulkily against the counter. Rather than waste time searching out the stepladder, Brie hitched herself onto the sink to reach the overhead cabinet where they kept the kit. Kneeling on the narrow drainboard, she felt her balance waver. Then Steve's hand settled against the small of her back to steady her. She closed her eyes for a long moment, glad he couldn't see her face. So comforting, his touch. Strong. Familiar.

Though maybe not as familiar as she'd once thought.

Surely he hadn't tried to hurt her cat! If she couldn't trust him that far, she had more problems than a vow of secrecy. She handed him the kit and hopped to the lino-leum.

"We should find a better place for this," he noted. It was better than "nice weather." She took the towel and dabbed at his still-bleeding arms.

The kitchen smelled like microwaved Italian food. Steve smelled like warmth, faintly lingering after-shave—and blood.

"I moved it away from that leak under the sink." She noticed red splotches soaking through the shoulder of his shirt, too. "Romeow really did a number on you, huh?" She began to undo his shirt at the collar, catching the first button with her fingernail to slip it from its starched prison.

Steve parted his lips, as if to protest, but didn't move to stop her. Three buttons later, he said, "I thought you were worried about the number *I* did on *him*."

"I sometimes leap before I look."

"Really?"

She relaxed at the note of humor behind his sarcastic inquiry, and met his very close gaze. It was intense and wary. He did smell like blood, but he also smelled like Steve. "Really." Some of the wariness faded from his expression. Not all of it, but a little tenderness coexisted with it now. "I'm sorry I assumed—I'm a bit tense this evening, after...."

*What exactly did I just interrupt here?* She willed away the too-fresh memory. Bad topic of conversation.

"Yeah," Steve agreed, instead of making her finish. When she undid the last button, he shrugged the shirt off, wincing as silk came free from the scratches on his shoulder. He eased each arm from the soggy sleeves, then let the shirt sag from his waistband.

Face-to-chest—bared, golden chest with just enough muscle to affirm his fitness and just enough soft brown hair to complement his maleness—she swallowed back an inappropriate purr of appreciation. The depth of his brown gaze, when she raised her eyes to his, cinched it. Steve *was* the best thing ever to happen to her. Only a fool would risk such good fortune, even for something as deeply ingrained as her heritage.

"We ought to let the bleeding slow down," she advised when he reached for the kit. "Tell me what happened."

Dispassionately he examined wounds on himself that would have had her in furious tears. "Your cat attacked me."

"Really?" She held the gaze he lifted to her, pleased by the twinkle of warmth that touched it. He was trying.

Then even that meager warmth cooled into confusion. "He was yowling to go out, so I started to open the door, but I forgot to undo the chain. And he—" Steve moved to shove a hand through his hair, then noted his torn palm and stopped himself. "He just freaked, tried to squeeze out. I couldn't undo the chain until I closed the door again, and his head was in the way, so I tried to move him and—pow. Psycho kitty. Trust me, when you came down, I was holding him off."

"But why would Romeow—"

"I'm supposed to know?" He closed his eyes, as if to belie his sharp tone, but she knew he still hated that she'd believed, even briefly, that he would hurt her cat. "Maybe there was another cat outside."

She studied the linoleum. They'd had Romeow neutered half a year ago; he shouldn't have freaked over another cat. Maybe he hadn't tried to get *to* anything, but to get away.

From the something in the workroom? Or—?

Steve touched the underside of her chin, and she met his concerned gaze. "I didn't lose control, Red. And the fuzzball used to be a stray; he can take care of himself."

In answer to that, she tugged the blood-smeared towel from him and gently touched it to the scratches on his bare shoulder. So much for his smooth tan—not that he'd care. Steve had no awareness of his good looks. "*You* aren't okay."

"These?" He caught her hand, held it loosely as he leaned close to her neck to whisper, "These aren't anything."

His fingers, on the underside of her wrist, both drained and recharged her, as if his touch completed a circuit of which they were both part. She tipped her head to look past his wounded shoulder, into his eyes. He bent, took her lips with his, kissed her gently. Cautiously.

A pure, healing energy filled her, from her curling toes to her tingling scalp. And then it left. She wanted to cry out when their lips parted. *Nothing has changed. I'm the same person I've always been.*

"Geez, Brie," he muttered, his voice thick. "I—" But whatever he'd been going to say, he swallowed instead. Maybe he knew that kisses—even delicious, magical kisses—wouldn't break through the wall between them.

She wished she could blame that wall on his earlier anger, but it went deeper. And she didn't know how to fix it. "I think you've stopped bleeding." But when he nodded and reached for the kit, she touched the back of his hand to stay him—and maybe just to touch him, too, invisible wall or no.

"Aloe vera would be really good on these," she suggested, to justify the movement. "Cat scratches infect easily."

"I'll use this stuff." Steve selected a yellow tube from the kit. He just wasn't a home-remedy kind of guy, she reminded herself to quell a disproportionate sense of rejection as she took the tube. He wanted things proven and approved.

The exact opposite of the Craft.

She carefully applied the drugstore cream to each angry scratch, then wrapped his arms with clean gauze. She considered telling him to soak the wounds in an Epsom-salt solution before bed, but decided not to burden him with any more such cures and put away the cream without comment. Wasn't his sheer normalcy one of the things she loved about him?

If only it didn't contradict so many of her own beliefs.

"I look like I tried to commit suicide," Steve joked as she turned to find a better place for the first-aid kit. It slipped from her suddenly numb fingers, burst open as it hit the linoleum and scattered tubes and bottles past their feet. "Don't say that!"

The sudden silence, sharp after the plastic crash, thickened the wall between them. Steve stared at her. When she didn't offer an excuse for her sharp words—how could she, when *she* didn't understand the shudder that had gripped her?—he crouched to collect the strewn first-aid supplies.

"I'll get that," she murmured, embarrassed, and knelt to take a jar of aspirin from his bandaged hand.

"Fine," he snapped, standing. "Take care of everything."

From the floor, she watched him rescue his dinner from the microwave and stalk out of the kitchen. She listened to him ascend the stairs, probably to the temporary office they'd set up in the baby's—in the spare bedroom.

He could be made to forget. The receding energies of the waning moon could be tapped to banish his concerns about her secrecy. A little chamomile in his coffee, with the right charge . . . a black candle for negation . . .

No! She would not work magic on anybody without his permission. That, too, was a vow.

Besides, she thought ruefully, still on her knees amid this latest mess, even if she could make him forget his suspicions, they would return, sooner or later.

Things that you ran from always caught up with you— three times as powerful.

*A shade. In the silent nothingness of its exile, it—no, he—recoiled from the force of harsh memories, even as they explained what he had become.*

*Screaming girls had fallen to the floor of the Ordinary House, clearly in the grasp of great evil. "Her shade torments me!" young Ann had cried. "Make her stop!" And he had turned in horror and fury to confront—*

*No! But, his physicality long lost, he had no eyes to close, no arms to raise in protection. Now that the memories had found him, he could repel them not. He knew it all again—the frustration, the fear, the anger.*

*The betrayal.*

*And through renewed pain and repeated suffering, he remembered that which was of most importance: his name. Blakelee.*

*He was the shade of Goodman Josiah Blakelee.*

*Pitted against a devil's whore, once again.*

Brie reared up in bed, unable to cry out through a panic-strangled throat. Images of her nightmare, of accusing faces and pointing fingers, pushed in at her from the darkness.

She mouthed a quick childhood banishing spell, to help push her terror back to whatever realm had spawned it. Her subconscious had carried her marital problems into her dreams, that was all. That had to be all.

Huddling back against the mahogany headboard, she realized from the slope of the mattress that Steve must have finally quit working—or avoiding her—and come to bed. She could hear his steady breathing, close in the night. It set a rhythm for her own to match as she slowly calmed. If she reached out, she could touch him, wake him. Surely, despite their fight, he would hold her and comfort her if she woke him.

But to tell him she'd dreamed of being accused of witchcraft came far too close to revealing her own secrets.

And he would comfort her in the voice from her nightmare.

*His voice.*

Silently she crept from the bed, from the room, and down the stairs. She stopped only at the linen closet, for another blanket and pillow, before taking refuge on her camelback sofa. She hoped that, away from his scent and breathing and warmth, she wouldn't dream again of Steve rejecting her because of her witchcraft. She hoped she wouldn't dream again of herself denying that heritage before a crowd, negating her very being.

She didn't.

Instead she dreamed, again, of Steve as a pagan forest lord. The holly king. Not he who sacrificed—but he who was the sacrifice.

She didn't even trust him enough to sleep in the same bed with him?

Steve had awoken with a start and, finding the bed empty, fought off a panic as foolish and intense as the one from Halloween. He'd barely paused to snatch up his bathrobe as he bolted from the room, slowing only as he descended the narrow steps and saw Brie, safe and asleep, in the living room below.

She must have woken up after he went to bed, and relocated to the more preferred couch.

Feeling as if he'd been punched, he'd retraced his steps up the stairs to take his shower and get ready for work. Since he didn't go into the kitchen—he had no appetite—he managed not to wake her until he lifted his keys from their hook, opened the front door into an almost cool, rainy predawn. Then he glanced back, searching for some security in the sight of his wife's huddled form beneath the old blanket, her red hair wild across her pillow.

Those smoky blue feline eyes stared back at him.

They held a hint of fear.

He wanted to grab her, to insist that she had nothing to fear from him. Yes, he'd lost control yesterday. Once!

But maybe once was all it took.

So when Brie said nothing, neither did he. He just stepped out onto the porch, into the gray mugginess, and shut and locked the door behind him.

Between them.

# CHAPTER FIVE

*What blasphemous iniquities hast she committed in the night?*

—The Journals of Josiah Blakelee

"If this vow of yours causes that much trouble," said Mary Deveraux, sitting lotus-style on one of Brie's sabre-legged kitchen chairs, "maybe we can find some loophole."

"That's not how it works," Brie told her friend and circlemate. Not that Mary could truly understand vows of secrecy. The petite blonde even wore a T-shirt reading Blessed Be! and a bright silver pentagram, point up, for anyone to see. When Mary cocked her head in thought, pentagram earrings peeked out from beneath her short, honey-colored hair.

*Why not just wear a black cape and a pointy black hat?* But Brie recognized jealousy in herself, and when she remembered her own robe from Samhain she felt doubly guilty.

Again. Still.

She looked to her sister-in-law for support. Sylvie shrugged. "I already screwed up back when I told Rand about it—I'm keeping my mouth shut from now on."

Brie had invited all three of her circlemates to lunch, but the third, Cypress Bernard, had canceled because of a staff meeting. Brie had hopes that... Okay, she didn't know *what* she hoped they could do. On the upside, they'd made it through soup and sandwiches with neither empathic Sylvie nor psychic Mary screaming, "There's evil in this house!"

On the downside, relating her recent nightmares about Steve learning her secret in some kind of courtroom setting had turned into an unwelcome discussion about that vow.

As if it were subject to debate.

"Like, if you swore not to speak about the Craft, maybe you could write about it instead," Mary suggested. "Or I could tell Steve for you, and—"

"Don't you dare!" It wasn't as if she hadn't already considered and dismissed each of the younger woman's ideas—hundreds of times. "You talk as if this were some mere legality to be gotten around. It's a *vow!* A lot of things are legal but break vows—divorce, bankruptcy..."

Mary had leaned forward, her intense expression belying her meditative posture. "And sometimes those things are a person's only hope. What, exactly, did you vow?"

Brie recalled the covenstead in West Texas. A strong wind that night had sent torchlight dancing across the rocks, tugging at her hair, wrapping her robe around her legs. A full moon had bathed her with a sense of belonging and purpose. "I, Brigit Conway, willingly stake all that I am, was, and ever shall be on this vow," she now recited. "May my powers desert me and my allies turn against me should I ever reveal my association with the Craft, or any of its secrets, to an unbeliever. In this and all lifetimes—so mote it be."

Her friends stared. "Some vow," said Sylvie, finally.

"And they made you take this witch vow when you were *fourteen?*" Mary always sided with the assumed underdog. But Brie had known exactly what she was doing.

"And at what age were you confirmed, Mary Margaret?"

The blonde grinned. "You'll notice it didn't take."

"When your mom is high priestess, it takes." And none of this helped her current situation. She and Steve had fought on Monday; by today, Thursday, little had improved—Romeow had even moved in with Sylvie. Fanned by Steve's resentment, and her wariness, the wall between them grew. She phoned other relatives in the Craft, but none could tell her more than her mother had. She'd even tried to find a Wiccan marriage counsellor. So far, the closest one she'd located worked in Arkansas.

She doubted she could sell Steve on driving to Arkansas for counseling. Just the idea that they had *considered* counseling hurt like hell, way too much for her to discuss it with her friends—and particularly Steve's sister. Instead, she said, "So, y'all have been here an hour. Have you felt anything unusual?"

Sylvie looked like a slimmer, female Steve—especially when she folded her arms and raised one eyebrow. "Other than you being nervous and frustrated? The vibes feel sour, but—"

Mary said, "It's gone." *That* caught their attention.

The smaller woman's hazel eyes had clouded from trying to "see" into realms beyond the red-tiled dining room, with its refinished mahogany table and chairs. She frowned—then blinked and looked at them. "No. I thought maybe I saw something, but it's gone. If it was here at all. I'm a precog, remember? Not a postcog."

"There was something in my workshop, the day Steve lost his temper," admitted Brie quietly, her gaze moving toward the back door, past the kitchen counter.

"You jest." Mary unfolded her legs, stood, and padded to the offending doorway. "Saint Steven lost his temper?"

And not just on Monday. She hadn't even mentioned last night! As a peace offering, she'd brought a mug of coffee into the second bedroom, which they optimistically called the baby's room, where Steve was proofreading typeset copy for tonight's pasteup. She'd found him at his card-table desk, in front of his computer, staring. At nothing. His hand, resting on the tabletop, had clenched and unclenched in a mannerism she'd never noticed before, and the planes of his face seemed almost sharp, his brown eyes unfocused, depthless, like gates into someplace she never wanted to go. And he'd looked at her with those seemingly alien, angry eyes and said, "Confess."

One word—an unmeetable demand. She'd held his accusatory stare for as long as she could stand it, then whispered, "Go to hell!" and spun, and left the room.

She hadn't reached the stairs when she heard Steve's shout of "God*damn* it!" and the crash of books and packing boxes impacting the floor. She'd slept on the sofa again last night. When Steve had left on his run this morning, and then gone to work, he hadn't tried to be quiet. He'd slammed the door.

She realized that Sylvie was watching her, concern in her Stevelike eyes.

Mary splayed her hands on the workroom door. "I don't know. The energy here feels weird—not evil, just...disturbed. Maybe there *was* a beastie of some kind. It's not here now. You think maybe something's influencing Steve?" She smiled, and her pentagram earrings lapped against her throat. "He hasn't been foaming at the mouth or levitating, has he?"

"He's never lost his temper before," Brie answered defensively, embarrassed by her own crazy conclusions. "It was possible."

"The only way to be sure would be to hypnotize him."

"Ha!" said Brie and Sylvie in unison.

"So we do a cleansing." It was the obvious course of action. "Bet you're due for one, anyway. Coordinate times with Cy, and send every drop of negativity on its way. Andrew Dice Clay couldn't pick a fight here once we're done."

Brie hesitated—doing even a standard working here, with Steve already suspicious, seemed unwise no matter the goal. Then Sylvie said, "Mary, could you wait outside for a minute?"

The blonde looked from one Peabody to the other, then shrugged and slipped into her sandals, which she'd deserted at the entrance to the dining room. "Okay. See you in a few."

Sylvie waited until Mary had shut the door behind her to turn back. "Listen, Steve would freak to think I was talking behind his back. You know he hates to feel conspired against."

Brie almost laughed, but it wouldn't have been a pleasant laugh. "Yeah, I know."

"Well...him losing his temper—that's not necessarily a sign that something is influencing him. Steve once had an awful temper."

"What—you mean throwing tantrums about bedtime?"

"When he was fourteen, he almost killed another boy."

Brie stared.

Sylvie leaned across the table. "When I was in the sixth grade, and Steve was in the eighth, Mom and Dad sent us to day camp—you know, where kids do crafts, learn trampoline..."

"I get the picture." Actually, Brie had never been to day camp, but it was more important to know about Steve.

"Well, Steve got into this rivalry thing with another boy, Joey something. I thought it was friendly, since Steve never seemed upset, but then, you know Steve."

As if Sylvie wore her heart on *her* sleeve—but yes, Brie knew. She only nodded, so as not to interrupt.

"One day we were playing baseball. Steve and Joey were each made captain, and Joey picked me before Steve could. And since I wasn't much of a player, he started making fun of me—you know, stuff like 'Oh, God, *Sylvie's* up next? We're dead.'"

Only several years' intimacy with the Peabody clan made it possible for Brie to detect a remnant of hurt in her friend's tone. Even now, with a happy engagement and successful career, Sylvie regretted her childhood awkwardness. Her surge of hostility toward this Joey brat made her wonder—fear—how furious Steve must have felt.

"At one point Steve and Joey had words," Sylvie remembered. "Nothing major. Then Joey threw a fastball at me, unexpected like, and hit me in the face." The frail brunette grimaced. "Next thing I know, I'm on the ground—well, partly in Steve's lap—and everyone's standing around me looking scared. And you-know-who says, 'Look at the crybaby.' Steve got this *look*. He didn't say anything—just got up, walked over to Joey, and lit into him. I was so stunned I forgot I was hurt, and ran over with the rest of the kids to watch."

It didn't sound like Steve, of course, but he'd sure had incentive—heck, if she'd known that Joey kid, Brie would have been figuring out a good toad spell, karma or no karma.

Sylvie must have read her expression, because she quickly added, "He grabbed a bat, Brie. Joey was on the ground, all bloody and whining, and Steve grabbed a bat, and I *knew* he'd swing. When I caught it, he almost yanked me over. Then his eyes started to clear, and he dropped the bat, and he looked..."

Brie waited.

"Scared," Sylvie finished. "I think he scared himself. That's why he got so controlled, Brie. Because the couple of times he's lost his temper, he's *really* lost it."

Brie shook her head, trying to reconcile the Steve she knew—the man she'd married!—with what his sister described.

"Anyway," finished Sylvie as she stood, trying to sound more cheerful. "I didn't want you thinking Steve's turned into some kind of pod person if he's shown a bit of temper. You've been together awhile. He was bound to slip sooner or later. But a cleansing sure can't hurt."

"I've got to find time when Steve's not here," said Brie softly. "Tonight's his late night, but it's too soon."

And Sylvie grinned, her smile as warm as Steve's could be. When he smiled. "I have a plan."

"So," said Steve, after taking a deep gulp of draft beer. "You're handfasting my sister." He and Rand Garner sat on stools at the bar, in Stagwater's local dive. The place smelled of smoke and sawdust. Country-and-western music twanged from the jukebox, and the clacking of pool balls intimated a Friday-night game in the back corner.

Garner put his own mug of root beer down on the faded Formica bar and grinned wolfishly. "Why do I get the feeling I'm about to be shot at again?"

Steve said, "Excuse me?"

The grin faded.

This slim special-effects artist wasn't someone Steve would've picked for Sylvie. In contrast to Steve's crisp work shirt and trousers, Garner wore a T-shirt depicting a skull, faded jeans, and shoes with no socks. And he wore his black hair pulled back in a perky ponytail.

But he'd taken the initiative and asked Steve out for a let's-get-to-know-each-other after-work drink. And he apparently made Sylvie happy. So Steve took another draw of beer and tried to lighten up on his pit-bull imitation.

"Handfasting has nothing to do with fast hands," Sylvie's fiancé promised, holding up three fingers. "Scouts' honor."

Okay. "So tell me something."

"The capital of New York State is, in fact, Albany."

Steve stared, thrown by the non sequitur, until Garner widened his eyes innocently. "*Oh* ... something *specific!*"

Steve continued to stare. Garner looked away to find a bowl of peanuts. So much for male bonding.

Steve fought off the thought that he should be home with Brie—though, to be honest, he hadn't been having a terrific time at home recently. Who would, with a wife who alternately avoided questions and treated you like something out of a horror flick? Yes, she was still the most beautiful and fascinating woman he'd ever met. She haunted his every thought. But his worry about her—about them—was giving him monstrous headaches.

"Look," said Garner. "I know where you're coming from. I respect it. But whether your sister and I marry by priest, rabbi, reverend, shaman, or high lama—as far as I'm concerned, we're married. And not just for a year and a day."

Couldn't argue with that. "So who *is* officiating?"

"Sylvie's pal Mary."

Steve choked on his beer, and accepted a handful of napkins to mop up the spill with. "Is that *legal?*"

Garner took another long draw of root beer. "Is Louisiana a common-law state?"

Steve sat back on the stool and folded his arms, eyes narrowed. "It has pretty lax firearms laws."

His future brother-in-law cleared his throat nervously at the dour warning . . . until Steve grinned.

Garner scowled in admiration as he stood to dig in his jeans pocket. "Good one. The deal is, Syl's not real comfortable with engagements, after her last one. But we'd be a bit crazy to marry this soon. *But* we can't stand being apart—I know, I know, sloppy romanticism alert. So we handfast next month, and in half a year, assuming, pray God, she still wants me, we do the justice-of-the-peace thing as a technicality." Having retrieved a quarter, he rolled it through his fingers. "Me, I wouldn't mind having the J.P. the first time, but I'm not rushing Syl. Besides, you know your sister." He raised his voice a little. "'I don't worship the legal system, and I won't have one of its priests at our handfasting.'"

A pool player, walking by, paused and cast them both suspicious looks. Garner batted his eyelashes, and the local gave them both a wide berth.

Yeah, that weird statement sounded painfully like Sylvie. She'd gotten truly weird lately. "What about you?"

Garner grinned. "I just worship your sister—and my lucky stars." And he headed toward the jukebox.

Steve noticed the tables against the wall, where Friday-night dates played footsie or held hands, and wished he didn't suddenly feel so overwhelmingly jealous.

Between the waning moon, the setting sun, the closing week and the darkening season, all the aspects were right for a cleansing. Natural energies on several levels receded, like an outgoing tide of ageless strength, easily harnessed to carry lingering traces of upset from Brie's and Steve's home and disperse it harmlessly into the universe.

Brie and Mary had spent the afternoon thoroughly cleaning the duplex. When Sylvie and Cypress arrived, straight from work, the circle immediately started their earth magic.

As they moved from room to room for the first step, sprinkling salt, Brie half expected some hidden evil, once threatened, to leap out at them. When Cy went into the workroom and gave a small shriek, she dived to her defense—only to find her black-haired, black-eyed friend stepping back from the still life.

"That is the dog-ugliest painting I have ever seen!" And Cy chucked some salt at it from a safe distance. While Sylvie and Mary joined her laughter, Brie mentally pried her fingernails from the ceiling and made herself relax. The whole *purpose* of the cleansing was to replace banished negativity with positive vibes, like laughter.

By the time they'd exposed the duplex to incense, candlelight and sprinklings of water, it practically pulsed with positive energy. Then they set about creating protective wards, to keep future ghoulies, ghosties and long-legged beasties out. Cy, the closest their small group had to an expert on crystals, provided the stones to magnify the invisible walls—protective onyx to go over each doorway, and rose quartz for either side of the front door.

"To add a little enforced cheerfulness to anybody who passes through," the exotic-skinned witch explained from where she knelt by the door. Cy still wore her green suitdress from work, but she'd removed her heels and hose for comfort. "We'll put the main crystal—" she gestured toward the large, cool hunk of clear quartz in Brie's hands "—in the center of the house. It keeps the others on track."

Even Mom might find this useful, Brie mused. Though respectful of stones in general, Mom had become increasingly disenchanted with crystals as their New Age popularity rose.

It had been a long time since Brie felt comfortable talking Craft talk with her mother.

"And they keep negativity out," she put in.

Her heart sank as Cy stood awkwardly in her fitted skirt, brushing her hands together. "Lady, don't I wish... Anything that wants in bad enough can do it—but if you're up against that kind of evil, you need to be expending daily energy for heavy-duty shields. Also, anything you've invited in can come back. Like vampires. But no random negativity will approach the place. And if anything bad does cross the wards, you'll know. So should Steve—but he might not know he knows."

Which reminded Brie. "I made some dried flower arrangements for over the doors, to hide the onyx. I had some leftovers, so if y'all want some, we... What?"

Cypress and Mary were exchanging significant looks. "You're right, girlfriend," drawled Cy, her voice lapsing into a hint of Creole. "She's bad off."

Brie put her hands on her blue-jeaned hips, and directed her annoyance at Mary.

"I'm worried about you," insisted the blonde. "How much have you gone out of your way already to keep this vow? Would Steve give up that much of himself for you? It's medieval."

Sylvie perched on the edge of the easy chair. Cy made a sipping motion with her hand and disappeared into the kitchen for refreshments. Both knew Mary and Brie.

One. Two. Three. Mary was a late blooming witch, and had found the Craft during these fairly liberal times—she couldn't know. Four. Five. Six. Brie took a deep breath herself, and sat on the sofa. "You ever hear of witch blood?"

Sylvie nodded, but Mary shook her head.

"It's the theory that witchcraft is hereditary. Sometimes whole families were killed when one member was accused of witchcraft. I have witch blood. I have ancestors who were strangled or hanged or burned as witches, some named Brigit. When my family says 'Never again the Burning,' we're talking about something real, horrible, and very possible. Just because it's not too dangerous to be a witch now, here, doesn't mean in another century things'll be the same. *That's* why my family tradition demands secrecy. Because once a secret is revealed, it can't be taken back. Not ever."

"But this is your *husband*."

"My mother's line has seen enough persecution to err on the side of silence." She could see that Mary was unconvinced. "Oh, never mind. I come from a long line of Celtic witches and you come from a long line of French Catholics."

"And Catholics were never persecuted?" Mary asked her challengingly.

"You ever hear how the Inquisition burned heretics?"

"You ever hear how the British exiled the Acadians?"

Sylvie rose from her perch and stepped between the two. "C'mon, you guys—it's not fair to debate whose ancestors were more oppressed without Cypress here," she teased.

Mary flopped onto the sofa at Brie's side. "'You guys' again," she echoed—any negativity they might have built had vanished at the teasing. The cleansing was working.

Brie couldn't stay angry at someone who meant as well as Mary. "Remember, she's a Yankee."

Cy returned with her water. "Leave you folks for a minute, and a wizard's duel breaks out." She gave them all a stern look. "And I vote for Sylvie's ancestors."

"Sylvie's?" Brie looked at her sister-in-law, trying to remember what Steve had said about their wholesome American-dream family background.

"Oppressed?" echoed Mary. Even Sylvie looked bemused.

"Oh!" Cy grinned. "I thought you said *re*pressed!"

"Now stop that!" commanded Brie, trying not to smile. Even Sylvie had joined in the affectionate laughter. But Brie would not use the word *repressed* to describe Steve. Particularly not her private Steve.

Then, suddenly, Sylvie quieted. Brie went on guard. Did she sense something?

"You know," her sister-in-law mused, "beliefs that are repressed do exist. They're just momentarily inaccessible."

She was talking about Steve—and belief in magic.

Brie stared. She had to be kidding.

Steve reached for another crawfish. He and Rand had partaken of local tradition, "pinchin' tails and suckin' heads." "So Sylvie's weirdness doesn't bother you?"

"How's she weird?" asked Garner.

"She's into all that New Age, Shirley MacLaine stuff." He couldn't think of another way to describe it.

"Well, I'm not exactly Mr. Sanity myself," Garner pointed out.

"What I mean is," Steve tried again, "what if her weirdness were just the tip of an iceberg? What if she turned out to be someone you didn't recognize? You haven't known each other that long—how strong a bond can you have developed?"

"Animal attraction?" suggested Garner.

"Not enough." He meant that emphatically, remembering the first kiss he and Brie had devoured under the mistletoe, that first time in the back of her car, those mornings and lunch breaks in his old apartment—heck, even Halloween night!

Geez, was it hot in here? He took another swallow of beer. "Not if you learn you never really knew her. She could be a drug addict, or a multiple personality, or a cult member, or something, and you wouldn't find out until it's too late."

"Too late for what? To stop the wedding?"

"No!" That wasn't it at all. He wanted to be married to Brie—couldn't imagine *not* being married to her. He just...he just wanted to know the Brie he'd married. Otherwise, he loved some figment of his imagination, some image he'd constructed around a sexy redheaded whoever-she-was.

"I guess," said Garner slowly, "that I'd have to trust her. I mean, if I trusted her enough to marry her..."

"You could be wrong." Steve pointed a crawfish at him. "*She* obviously doesn't trust *you,* if she's hiding it."

"Might not be so easy." Garner raised his voice over the zydeco music that was bouncing from the jukebox now. "I bet she'd tell you if she could. I mean me." He took a quick swig of root beer.

Steve studied him, suddenly suspicious. "Whose life are we talking about here?" He didn't want to suddenly doubt this guy. He'd had fun for the past hour.

Garner folded his arms. "Some idiot in love. You want another beer?"

"No. Thanks." It was a ridiculous, baseless suspicion. And yet— "I think we ought to be getting home."

"Something wrong?"

Steve frowned. "How would I know if it were?"

"Okay, bro, just a friendly question." Garner was the very picture of trustworthiness, despite the ponytail.

So why did the way he checked his watch seem significant?

"Speak of the devil." Cy, nearest the living room, lowered the brown ribbon she'd woven through branches of eucalyptus and ivy. "I heard a car door shut."

Brie's pulse quickened as she scanned the table for anything suspicious. Even seen through guilty eyes, the dried and silk flowers, ribbon and pipe cleaners could hardly be construed as occultic. The others started to put their stuff away, having decided long ago that the easiest way to keep from slipping around Steve was to limit exposure to him. *How much have you gone out of your way already to keep this vow?* Mary had asked. *Would Steve give up that much of himself for you?*

She'd narrowly missed Brie's real worry: How much of her didn't Steve know, and how much of her might he dislike if he did?

The voice that called "Hi, honey, we're home!" from the front door unbalanced her—it wasn't Steve's! Then she saw how Sylvie's face lit as she flew to greet her fiancé.

*Get a grip!* She followed more slowly, half listening to Mary's and Cy's chatter. Steve's mood could indicate if their cleansing had worked and, lords above, she did hope it had.

The sight of Romeow, perched on the stairs as if he'd never left, encouraged her—but Sylvie and Rand, in mid-embrace, caught her off guard. So did the sense of loss that tore at her. *Where was Steve?* She suddenly wanted, needed—

"Hi, honey." His voice, easy and amused from where he stood by the coffee table, soothed her. Again he'd rolled up his sleeves and undone his collar. He looked more relaxed than he had in a week. He held her gaze as he hefted the new ward crystal, his own more curious than wary. More like the Steve she'd fallen in love with.

She crossed the room to him, to the warmth of his energy.

"Sorry we have to run," excused Cypress from somewhere nearby. Brie vaguely heard the exchanged goodbyes.

"Hi," she murmured to Steve, grateful for the faint twinkle deep in his brown eyes. She wanted to reach out and push a lock of hair off his forehead, to touch him. She felt more awkward about that desire than when they'd first met.

"Nice rock." To her relief, he put it down.

"Cy brought it." She heard the front door shut, and glanced in that direction. Rand whispered something into Sylvie's hair, making the brunette smile. Rand accepted Sylvie completely, her seriousness, her Craft.

As opposed to Steve? But Brie had never given him the chance.

His arm, warm and secure, draped casually around her. She turned to him, fearful, hopeful—and melted into the support of his embrace, smelling after-shave and soap and the faint muskiness of him, savoring it. *Don't let go.* She didn't say the words, but his arms tightened around her anyway.

*Empath.* She wanted to voice the accusation, but didn't dare.

"We're outa here," she heard Rand say. "Take care, Steve-o. Brie."

"See you." Steve sighed. Maybe it was rude for her not to add her goodbyes, but she'd gone almost a week without a good hug. She wouldn't lose this one so quickly.

The cleansing, she decided, had *definitely* worked.

*Something further blocked his escape through the Veil.*

*Josiah could sense the couple, hear muffled bits of conversation, detect flickerings of movement. 'Twas all. He tried to extend his awareness toward the husband, and brushed traces of foolish concern, but 'twas o'ertaxing.*

*Sorcery. The very air about the mortals had changed.*

*Yet he would gain the husband again, would claim sight, voice to question, hands to touch, to fondle... to kill. Patience was a virtue, after all. The pleasurable air with which the sorceresses had wrapped themselves must fade— and he would not. Then the witch's own deviltry would deceive her.*

*She thought to sense her foe, when he again entered her home.*

*But Josiah—Josiah's portal—was already inside.*

# CHAPTER SIX

*Her imprisonment costs me dearly: two shillings and sixpence a week.*

—The Journals of Josiah Blakelee

Brie squinted at the light that struggled through the bedroom's red drapes and realized she was awake. She stretched cautiously beneath the covers, trying not to disturb the cat asleep on her legs. No nightmares. No fights. The cleansing *must* have worked.

Pipes in the bathroom squeaked, and the sound of water faded, revealing the softer patter of rain outside. No wonder the light seemed so gray. Not yet ready to leave bed, she snuggled into the woodsy scent of Steve's pillow and listened to the shower curtain rattle back, the whoosh of a towel being yanked from its rod. Too bad she slept so heavily. Maybe if she'd caught him before his run or, his shower, they could have gotten in some long-overdue conjugal bliss. She and Steve had never been ones for abstinence.

Maybe he wouldn't mind showering again? Last night's chaste cuddling, spooned against the security of him, wasn't enough. She wanted physical affirmation of their marriage.

Did he?

The bathroom door opened, emitting ghostly tendrils of steam, and Steve emerged in a pair of ancient jeans, pulling a faded green T-shirt over his head. She caught a glimpse of tanned ribs before the shirt fell into place—it hung a bit loose on him. Was he losing weight? Even so, he looked good, golden and lean. His damp hair, mussed by the shirt, gave him a slightly wild look . . . he was overdue for a haircut.

"Morning," he said as she sat up, and he detoured to the bed to kiss her hello. His warm lips fit perfectly against hers; she savored the taste of his toothpaste, the combined scent of his piny shampoo and sandalwood soap and his after-shave—like a forest. How easy it would be to pull him down on top of her, to strip off the teddy she wore, to roll onto him in lusty invitation—

And how easy for him to climb awkwardly from beneath her, embarrassed that she'd read more into last night's comforting embrace than he'd perhaps meant. The moment passed; he straightened to go comb his hair. *Coward,* she told herself—and maybe him. But this was the weekend. They had time to let things happen naturally. Everything would be okay.

"So what do we do today?" she asked, withholding her own risqué suggestions—and avoiding the risk of his rejection—for now.

"Timmy didn't call for delivery help, and there's no local events to cover," he noted, turning with his quiet half smile. "Not much to clean, either. The place looks great. Those new thingamajigs over the door—what are they?"

The ward stones. Her optimism flickered against cold dread. The weight of her secret still haunted them. She should have known he'd question—

"They smell good, anyway," Steve added, palming his change and wallet off the bureau and filling his pockets.

Oh. The dried-flower arrangements. "Eucalyptus." She managed to keep her voice from trembling as she feigned nonchalance, but the warm security of the bed and the morning now seemed tainted by her deception. Romeow flattened his tufted ears as she swung her feet to the floor; Brie noticed that Steve's attention focused, briefly, on her legs. He *was* interested.

Everything *was* going to be okay. The walls between them wouldn't vanish instantly, but the cleansing had bought them time. A rumble of thunder preceded a flickering of the bathroom light, reminding her of how they'd once had their electricity disconnected, during their first year. They'd grilled meals on their apartment balcony—and made love by candlelight.

"We could have a cookout," she suggested.

Steve raised his eyebrows to the watery window.

*Damn.* "Doesn't it do anything but rain around here?"

"You'd rather we stayed in Dallas," he said challengingly. "With a low-paying job. At a now-defunct paper."

"That wasn't what I meant!" Their eyes locked, too defensive too quickly. On unspoken agreement, they looked away.

Okay, so everything wasn't okay yet. At least she could stop jumping at shadows, find a solution Steve could handle.

They had all weekend.

The cat tested a Chippendale chair with his front paws, then hopped onto it en route to the tabletop. Once properly established, he settled into a happy sprawl, a faint purr. If that trespassing being remained, it could reach him no more than could the hound down the street—the one that was kept behind hurricane fencing. Cozy in the positive vibrations that filled his home, Romeow yawned—only to be caught and rudely deposited on the floor by his mistress's mate.

* * *

Steve put down both cat and toolbox, and leaned on the
kitchen counter, watching Brie without her knowing it. In
her workroom, framed by the open door, she scraped pasty
varnish remover off the top of an antique bureau. With
each stroke, her bottom, beneath frayed cutoffs, swayed a
bit. Since she wore an old burgundy shirt of his with the
sleeves butched off, he could see the smooth muscles of her
arms, above protective rubber gloves, flex as she worked—
and could catch glimpses of the pale sides of her breasts
through the oversize armholes. She'd caught her hair up in
a baseball cap, and he detected a sheen of perspiration on
her flushed neck. Hard work, stripping furniture. She'd
thrown herself into it as if demons were snapping at her
sexy tail.

He swallowed, hard, and knelt beside the toolbox to
open the cabinet doors under the sink. He still got the
manly jobs, lawnwork, and auto repair—and plumbing.
Turning on the trouble lamp and extending it into the
cabinet space, he located the familiar leak. Rusty elbow
pipe. He'd bought new pipe three weeks ago, while at the
hardware store to get a new washer for Sylvie's shower.
He'd fixed his sister's plumbing that night, then gotten
distracted writing an editorial, without doing their own
sink. Brie hadn't complained at all.

She didn't nag.

He hooked the lamp on a separate pipe, rolled onto his
back and wriggled his way under the sink. Okay, so he
liked his wife; no news flash there. He still wanted to dis-
cover what the hell kind of trouble she'd found. Maybe he
could help. He wanted to get everything out in the open,
so that they could be themselves again.

And, most of all, he wanted to lift that silly baseball cap
and let the wildfire of her hair tumble free, to lick the

saltiness from her throat, to have her, right there on the concrete floor in the sawdust—

He squirmed to get more comfortable in the suddenly too-cramped confines beneath the sink. *Control yourself, boy.* He couldn't pretend nothing was wrong, just to satisfy his baser yearnings. He had to stay honest about his expectations.

And now, more than ever, he couldn't afford to lose himself in her. There was more to their marriage than sex.

So why, instead of seeing the elbow pipe, did he see Brie's cutoff-clad bottom? He closed his eyes—which didn't dispel the image—and a horrible, crazy thought struck him.

What if there *wasn't* more to their marriage?

Regaining the tabletop, Romeow yawned deliberately in the direction of his mistress's mate, this time without interruption. The mate missed this insult, of course, having found a too-small lair of his own. Just as well for the cat.

Stretching out fully, front paws reaching in one direction and hind paws the other, Romeow hesitated—and sniffed. His humans felt skittish; their nerves contrasted with the magical brightness that surrounded them.

Concerned, he rolled over to regain his feet, and pointed his ears toward . . . it. His fur bristled.

It wanted out even worse than the hound down the street.

Brie finished swabbing grime from the still life that had "frightened" Cypress—a nothing picture by a nothing artist, in a beautiful oak frame that was three centuries old if it was a week. Unfortunately, the amateur artist had smeared not only streaks of oil paint, but varnish as well, so thick it blurred the painting's corners, onto that frame.

She'd have to remove that before separating the canvas, or she'd risk wood damage.

At least it made a break from the exhausting work of stripping the Colonial tallboy. Wringing out the dirty rag, she carried the bowl of dirtier water back into the kitchen and set it beside the sink. Then, tipping up her cap to wipe her forehead, she allowed herself a moment to enjoy the sight of Steve's T-shirted waist and jeaned legs where they emerged from under the cabinet. The old jeans were erotically faded; she bit her lip to hold back an appreciative purr.

The hollow clunking sound of Steve's plumbing slowed; she realized he must be watching her own bare legs. "Hi," she said, crouching closer to the linoleum. "How goes it?"

"I've been at this, what—half an hour? The thing's practically welded on." He gave the joint of the pipe another whack with his wrench, then propped himself on his elbows to grin at her. "More like plumbing you'd expect to see at Garner's haunted house—it's sure scary enough."

She smiled back. "So how'd it go between you and your future brother-in-law?" If the conversation sounded forced, so be it. Better than wary silence.

Steve leaned back, and tapped the pipe again. "He's a good enough guy. But I got the weirdest feeling that he was running interference." And he lowered the hand with the wrench, a flick of his gaze showing he awaited her response.

She fought the too-familiar sick feeling—Rand *had* been running interference. *Steve knows.* She wished she could tell him everything and deal with the situation from there. Like a crude remedy for a wound: burn it, and treat it for burns.

But her oath forbade even that invited catharsis. No wards could keep that truth away; no cleansings could solve it. Not as long as Steve didn't believe.

Sylvie thought he could handle the idea of the Craft— certainly better than he handled Brie's secrecy. Could she ignore even the faintest possibility of being able to combat his cynicism? His own latent empathy provided the opening she needed.

"You had a feeling?" she asked teasingly.

She heard his disgusted sigh as he drew up one faded denim knee, then resumed pounding on the pipe. "Never mind."

So much for his "repressed" paranormal beliefs. She escaped to the living room. Scanning CDs, she grabbed one by a Celtic harper, as a stressed smoker might snatch at a cigarette. Then she paused, put it back. Steve didn't like the Celtic stuff. Instead, she put on the soundtrack from *The Little Mermaid,* their favorite dating movie. She could relate to the mermaid's willingness to lose part of herself and escape her watery life for her prince's sunny world.

*Sacrifice.* She touched the Celtic CD, remembering the Gaelic ballads that had filled her childhood. "It was worth it to marry him," she whispered in answer to the doubts that gnawed at her. No matter whether he'd sacrifice so much or not; this was no contest. And as long as his feelings for her had not yet disintegrated beyond repair, it was *still* worth it.

She stalked back into the kitchen. "Steve..."

Just then the bowl of dirty water, responding to the vibrations of his hammering, tipped over the edge of the sink.

Steve let out a muffled howl, followed by a thunk of his head against wood, a curse. He wriggled from his cramped workspace and glared up at her, face framed by dripping hair and a water-blackened T-shirt. When he noted her distance from the sink, his accusation faded to a more indirect annoyance. Maybe she could spill the bowl from the doorway—she could have once, had she truly wanted to. But he'd never consider that possibility.

He caught the dish towel she tossed. "What did you want?"

Now or never. "Do you love me?"

Steve lowered the towel from his face, unblinking. "What?"

*She* glared—he'd heard her just fine.

He finished wiping his face and tossed the towel back to her. Then he leaned against the cabinet door, folding his arms and resting them on one knee. "Of *course* I love you." His tone was almost sullen—but very honest. "What the hell would make you think I don't love you?"

She hadn't realized just how much she needed those words until he spoke them. She could hug him for them, kiss him, thank him for what she'd taken for granted only weeks ago—but when she stepped forward, a flicker of wariness in his eyes stopped her. He didn't seem alien or frightening. He just looked like a handsome, wet, *reluctant* Steve.

Which made her next question more difficult. "Why?"

He continued to study her in that appraising way of his, reminding her that he was, above all, a journalist. She shifted from one bare foot to the other, praying for a serious answer. She couldn't take much more distancing repartee.

"Because you're so sure of yourself," he said finally, and she let herself slide down the wall until she sat on the floor herself, listening. His weren't loving words—she could tell from his tone that he thought she wasn't acting sure of herself at all, at this moment, but apparently considered that a momentary lapse. "I keep hearing about empowerment, women trying to find themselves. . . . You already seemed empowered."

*In more ways than one.* Matriarchal roots and a sense of female divinity went a long way toward empowerment. How ironic that her very confidence, and the quality he liked best in her, came from the Craft that caused their troubles.

"And I love you because you're strong," Steve continued, tilting his head in careful consideration. This time, when she scooted to his side, no hesitance touched his thoughtful eyes. In fact, he lifted her cap from her head, throwing it aside as her hair fell free, then lowered his index finger to stroke her lips. "And very, very feminine. . . ."

She kissed his finger, and when she saw no further reluctance shadow his expression, she caught the finger between her teeth and licked it. Steve leaned nearer, distracted her by kissing the corner of her mouth with tickling persistence until she turned into the sultriness of that kiss. She shivered with the power of the moment; his warm hands rubbed the gooseflesh smooth over her bare arms, her shoulders.

"And," he murmured, lifting his mouth from hers, but not protesting when she leaned into his damp chest, "there's depth to you. Something I'm not sure I'll ever fully reach, something..." The wordsmith hesitated at the obvious word.

"Mysterious?" she suggested, searching his planed face, caressing him with her eyes. *You love me for the very things that are driving you nuts, Steven Peabody. Admit it.*

*"Different,"* he said, obviously aware of the implications of her suggestion, and not about to get caught in them. He skimmed his palm over her jeaned hip and fingered the fringed edge of her cutoffs, smiling with teasing wickedness when she squirmed against him.

The phone rang. They met each other's gaze with a mixture of frustration and amusement—and a silent agreement to let the answering machine get it. Luckily, she'd recently recorded a short message. "You know the routine," recited her taped voice. "Name, rank, and phone number." *Beep.*

"Oops, don't bother picking up," said Sylvie Peabody's voice. "I have the sudden feeling that this is a bad time, so I'll call back later. Bye." *Beep.*

Steve let his head fall back against the cabinet with a slight thud. "Speaking of different."

She could either draw him back into their foreplay—or make another attempt to bridge the real differences between them. Oh, hell. "You sound like you really do disapprove of her," she noted carefully, plucking the material of his T-shirt, now dampened to forest green, away from his chest. "Just because she can sense things other people can't." *Not unlike someone else I know, who's too thick-headed to recognize it.*

"Because she *thinks* she can sense things other people can't." Steve raised his head again to look at her. "We didn't answer—*that's* how she knew we were busy."

Okay, she decided, leaning back and adjusting herself more comfortably against the prop of his bent knee. She'd handle this from another angle. "Suppose you're right, and she doesn't have special abilities." She congratulated herself on saying that without making a face. "What's the harm in her thinking she does?" *Or that I do?*

Steve opened his mouth—then closed it and frowned. Ha! He had to think about that one. But he was a fast thinker. "Because she could make a fool out of herself, for one thing."

"That's not your problem. She's a big girl." *So am I.*

*"And,"* he continued, leaning into the debate. Losing the support of his knee, she had to sit up alone, her bare legs cold on the linoleum. *"And,* thinking she's got one kind of special power might make her think she's got others. Next thing you know, she's channeling Martians, peering into crystal balls, and refusing to go outside if her horoscope says boo. She'll get as doofy as your friend Mary."

"Mary's not 'doofy.'"

"She's your friend, I wasn't going to mention it, but her truck's got a My Other Car Is a Broom bumper sticker!"

Again Brie reigned in her temper. *This was her marriage!* "Fine. Let's just say Sylvie gets as 'doofy' as Mary Deveraux," she admitted. *Or me.* This time she made a face. Steve smirked. "For the sake of argument," she reminded him.

"Mmm-hmm..." His mouth straightened; his eyes still smirked.

"Would you love her any less?"

Steve seemed to sense the importance of her question, and he weighed it carefully. If ever he wanted a list of reasons *she* loved *him,* forthrightness would top it. She held her breath.

"No," he decided; relief fed her strength. "She's my sister—how could I not love her?"

Everything might truly be okay, after all.

Then Steve palmed his damp hair from his forehead and added, "I doubt I could respect her, though."

From the living room, the mermaid mourned her and her prince's separate worlds. Brie could feel her own hopes disintegrating, even as Steve tried to explain. "She's never thought any less of me for being so... well, dull. A control nut. Predictable." He winced at his own description.

"Dependable," she said, defending him. "Forthright."

"Insensitive," he translated—as if he regretted the very things *she* loved about *him*.

"Honest."

He grinned his embarrassed gratitude. "Pushy."

"Determined. When you care about something, when you believe..." Her voice trailed off as the depth of their rift sank in for perhaps the first time.

"Because I believe in the believable," Steve insisted, waving a hand toward the phone to indicate that his sister did not. "That's what adults do—see reality. *Children* create imaginary friends to take the blame for their mistakes, justify biases by claiming to sense evil in next-door neighbors; avoid responsibility by wishing on stars." He searched the room for the right example. "*Children* compensate for poor self-images by pretending they're magic...."

His deep, steadying breath couldn't hide the extent of his distress. When he met Brie's questioning gaze, concern clouded his eyes. "I just thought... I'd hoped Sylvie'd outgrown that stuff. I thought she'd taken responsibility for her life." And he shook his head.

*Trapped in some twisted O. Henry story.* Brie turned away to hide the tears burning behind her eyes. The very things she loved in him would never let him accept the Craft. Never.

She stood up, ignoring the questions in Steve's eyes. Their physical frustration was the least of their problems, and she had to be alone for a bit, had something with which she must come to terms. Everything was *not* okay. Because of her.

Unless she took drastic measures, things might not be okay ever again.


"You're *what?*"

Over a week after the announcement, Brie could remember the horror in Sylvie's tone. She paused in her careful removal of varnish from her antique frame, alcohol swab in one hand and turpentine rag in the other, distracted by the too-fresh memory. "You're going underground?"

"It's an old family tradition," Brie had tried to joke. "I'm sorry if this messes up any of the circle's plans...."

"Never mind the circle. I'm worried about you!" Her normally placid sister-in-law's tone had supported that statement. "I never pictured you as a kitchen witch. Are you sure—?"

"No. But it's for Steve. For Steve and me."

Now she wet cotton with more alcohol and resumed her battle against varnish, arresting the solvent's effect with turpentine before the wood's surface suffered. Quitting the circle made sense, damn it. Going out for every new moon, full moon and sabbat would feed Steve's suspicions. But if she restricted herself to private household observances using mundane tools—hence the term *kitchen witch*— perhaps they could resolve this secrecy issue and move on with their lives.

Romeow yowled by her workroom door. *I promised you a solution within the month, Peabody,* she thought almost sulkily in the direction of the living room as she stood and let the cat out into the dark yard. *You'd damn well better appreciate the sacrifice.* But she doubted he would.

Because nothing got better. Her nightmares had returned, too consistent to ignore: Steve accusing her of witchcraft. Steve watching her tortured. Steve insisting she confess—and, always, her denials. She'd have suspected psychic attack, but for her faith in the wards. Though the cleansing faded, the longer her and Steve's problems festered unresolved, the wards remained unbreached. If the dreams didn't express her resentment at leaving the circle, they had to be either garbled premonitions or snatches of a past life—and her already rusty abilities, further weakened by her denial of them, didn't say.

And each darker, longer night stole more of the sun's comforting energy from her.

Tonight's dark moon particularly drained her, especially since her circle—her *former* circle—was meeting without her.

Tonight, sitting beside the black window, she felt at the mercy of the universe, and of Steve's increasingly mercurial moods. He *was* losing weight. His usual clean-cut looks had taken on an intense, brooding quality. His lengthening hair seemed to be darkening with winter's approach, though the temperature had yet to drop below sixty. His eyes, always quick, seemed unusually sharp. *Not without some measure of dark appeal,* she admitted to herself. But it wasn't normal. And despite his increasingly frequent headaches, he refused to see any problems in himself.

Well, she decided as she applied more alcohol, he *did* have a problem. He had a wife who was tiring of making all the sacrifices for their marriage, and if—

Someone stood in the room's interior doorway. She spun on her chair and faced the tall, half-lit form of her husband. "Don't do that!"

Steve said nothing.

Slowly she lowered the hand that had tried to calm her racing heartbeat. He looked ... off, his brown eyes blank and unfocused. Innate intelligence had faded from his slightly parted lips, and all her foolish suppositions of possession returned in force. "Steve?"

He blinked, as if disoriented—but, though his eyes focused on her, their strangeness remained. He moved forward.

His step faltered.

"Steve, this had better not be some kind of a joke," she hissed, standing for better defense. *Defense? This is Steve!* Ignoring the inner protest, she kicked her chair out of her way, caught a deep breath to combat cold apprehension.

Steve didn't flinch at the clatter of wood against concrete, merely blinked again. He awkwardly extended one hand toward her face and stepped sluggishly nearer.

He began to smile—a cold, victorious, alien smile.

How much of her fear was instinct, and how much shock at seeing her touchstone of stability acting so unstable? Brie directed tonight's limited arcane energy into defensive shields and closed the space between them. "Steve!" She batted his hand away easily. It was as if he weren't certain of his reach. Then she grasped his arm, her fingers closing around hard, tense muscle. She shook him, yelled. *"Steve!"*

And suddenly he was okay. He wrenched himself away from her the second time she cried his name, as if startled. Breath tore from his lungs, as from a diver surfacing. *"What!"*

While she stared, relief easing the thrum of near panic, he swayed and steadied himself against the recently stained tallboy. "Geez, Brie ... you nearly scared the life out of me!"

She'd scared *him?* "What the hell was that all about?"

"What?" How could he not know? His face looked unnaturally pale beneath his tan, even now that life—no, awareness!—had returned to his planed features. Spears of his normally soft hair clung to his damp forehead and temples. The tension between his eyes beckoned to her to soothe it. But—

"You! What the hell were you doing?" Okay, so this wasn't soothing. She was, in fact, doing her banshee imitation. But how could he deny the abnormality of this?

Steve squinted—or was he wincing? "That's odd," he admitted finally, grudgingly. "I don't remember what I came in here for. Is this thing wet?" He raised his arm, rolled his eyes at the wood stain on his beige sleeve. "Great."

Like he could change the subject. "You were sleep-walking or something." *Emphasis on the "or something."*

He gave her his dry aren't-we-overreacting-a-bit look. It did not help her temper. "I'd have to be asleep for that, now wouldn't I?" Then, as his gaze grew more intimate, his expression softened. "I really scared you?"

Her hands fisted in frustration; something was going on. How could he not know it? "Like something out of *Night of the Living Dead*."

He smiled with strained assurance. "I've been working hard, Red. Maybe I'm a bit overtired," he said as an excuse, extending his hand, with his usual natural grace this time, and brushing her cheek with his warm knuckles. She closed her eyes, savoring the solace of his touch. She wanted to believe his mundane explanation. "You've been watching the late show too much."

But she didn't watch the late show. And when she opened her eyes, she caught him in a full-fledged wince. "You have another headache."

Steve claimed one of her clean rags to wipe at the wood stain on his shirt. "I've taken aspirin, okay? And no, I don't want to drink peppermint tea or sniff lavender. I can take care of it."

Yet more home remedies sacrificed on the altar of Steve's rationalism. "You should see a doctor. Something's wrong...."

"With me?" She'd touched a nerve. "I know you're the one with all the information in this marriage. Now you know best for me, too? It's *my* head. I'll handle it my way."

"But you aren't handling it!"

"*I'm—*" He stopped, wincing in pain as they both realized how rarely he shouted. And yet this time his anger seemed neither alien nor otherworldly. This, she could clearly see in every tall, straining inch of him, *was* Steve. His anger didn't frighten her this time.

But he fought it. "I am fine," he said, carefully quiet. "Kindly stop accusing me of being unable to care for myself."

"But—"

"It's none of your business!" He raised a sarcastic eyebrow. "You understand that argument, right?" And he spun and stalked unsteadily from the workroom.

She stared after him, then looked around, disoriented in the aftermath of the argument. Had the trust between them eroded so far that he wouldn't even let her help him? Whatever was going on, surely she could help...as a mundane, if no longer a practicing witch. Less restrictions, this way.

The room suddenly felt stifling. Realizing that she'd finish no more work tonight, she began to pick up her jars, capping them and putting them onto their shelf—

Turpentine! Snatching at her soaked rag, she swabbed desperately at the still life, where she'd last applied alcohol. Varnish and paint came away in a sticky smear where the solvent had eaten right into the painting. "Damn it!"

Count to ten. It was too late to do anything about it tonight. Reining in her dangerously undirected anger, she made herself put down the rag, kill the light and head upstairs. She tried not to look at Steve, who, despite the fact that the *Sentinel* had just gone out yesterday, was sprawled on the sofa, intently scribbling notes for the next issue on a yellow pad, to the background sounds of CNN. She looked anyway.

His profile enhanced the angle of his cheekbones, the clean line of his nose. Untamed brown locks licked at the beige of his collar, where, despite his weight loss, his shoulders strained beneath the shirt. His hand moved in quick, decisive strokes—very much Steve. He did not look at her.

Maybe she'd imagined this possession idea, after all.

Rather than lurk there, hands itching to touch Steve's tense shoulders, fingers longing to play with his lengthening hair, Brie turned and headed up the narrow stairs. Perhaps she'd phone her mother again.

Maybe she'd imagined nothing.

*Had the husband wished to avoid his woman, Josiah might yet have failed, but Peabody's desires conveniently aligned with his own. After long days of reaching, Josiah had finally found Peabody's awareness again—and through those eyes beheld the red sin of the witch's hair, the fire of her eyes, the glow of her flesh—*

*And as he gazed, and knew lust, he broke through the last tattered threads of the Veil and found himself not in Steven Peabody's mind—but in Steven Peabody.*

*He stepped with Peabody's foot, reached with Peabody's hand, awkward after so many centuries, but blessedly corporeal—and inexplicably gaining strength with each passing moment. He'd tried to speak—not merely to color Peabody's thoughts, but to use his own words. But the husband's disbelief fought the control with more willpower than Josiah wouldst have suspected. The witch, with each cry of her husband's name, had wrenched more of his control from the shade. Peabody defiantly shuddered him off. And then Josiah—incorporeal, yet still blessedly free—watched the fools dismiss him as a head pain.*

*With practice and effort, he wouldst yet turn the husband's strength to his will . . . and yet now, free from his spirit's stagnant tomb, perhaps Josiah needed him no more.*

*He could trail the witch to her bedchambers without assistance, now. If he tried, perhaps Josiah could also command her—and defeat her—alone.*

# CHAPTER SEVEN

*For I have dwelt wherein evil dwells, through no fault of mine own.*

                              —The Journals of Josiah Blakelee

Just inside the bedroom, in the wedge of light from the hallway, Brie paused. She felt the sudden urge to run to her mother. But Gwen would think like a witch—which would *not* help, if Steve was right and she *was* overreacting.

She'd not felt the wards broken, after all. She couldn't imagine why ghoulies, ghosties or beasties of any leg length would be interested in someone as mundane as her husband. Sure, she'd grown up believing in paranormal dangers, as well as abilities—but why was she so certain, *this* time? Of all the people she should trust to know their own minds, Steve headed the list.

Maybe the Fates had bad news about switching worlds. *How long...*

At the hissing words—were they even spoken?—her upset drained before a far stronger chill.

*...hast thou...*

Not the bedroom! She had to feel safe somewhere!

*...been a witch?*

The duplex seemed suddenly silent, empty. Could Steve have left? She turned slowly, wishing she hadn't counted on only a swath of hallway light and her night vision to see by.

*Why...*

Hulking pieces of mahogany cast long shadows.

*...didst thou...*

Three reflections of her own pale face stared back at her from the triple-mirrored vanity, floating, disembodied, as her black jersey blended into the darkness behind her.

*...become...*

The faint glow of the light on Sylvie's back porch cast a bloody glow through the half-drawn red drapes. Dangling suncatchers caught the hall light like glowing eyes.

*...a witch?*

As plodding as any inquisitor's, the voice slid from everywhere and nowhere. A brief image of a courtroom, of screaming girls writhing on the floor, touched her mind like a memory of something she'd never known. Her nightmares.

*What demon...*

"Shut up." Her own faint voice surprised her. She extended a hand, tried to trace a pitifully thin circle of protective energy around her. Dark of the moon—and she'd already drained herself.

*...didst thou choose...*

She took a deep breath, finishing the circle, and again searched the bedroom. Nothing. "Shut up!"

*...to be...*

"Shut the hell up!" She stepped toward the doorway.

And the door began to swing shut.

*...thy lover?*

A mere draft might have caught it, so slowly did the door move. She reached out—then snatched her hand back. What if *it* was closing the door? What if she touched *it*? What if *it* touched her?

*Where...*

The wedge of light in the bedroom thinned, becoming slimmer and slimmer as the darkness grew.

*. . . didst thou consummate . . .*

Idiot—grab the damned door!

*. . . thy union . . .*

She lunged, and her grasping hand hit the door instead of catching it. It clicked shut under her blow.

*. . . with thy incubus?*

She murmured a banishing spell, but had no strength left for it. She couldn't handle this alone, not tonight.

*What was the name . . .*

"Steve?" Disoriented, she groped for the doorknob, but knocked the lamp to the floor instead. Its crash echoed.

*. . . of thy master . . .*

Where was the doorknob? She pressed herself against the door, scrabbling at the wooden surface. "Steve!"

*. . . among the evil demons?*

There—the knob! But it turned beneath her hand!

She screamed and, in lunging back, fell into the darkness. The opening door caught her foot as she landed on the hard wooden floor, and a tall form, silhouetted against the bright hall light, loomed over her.

It called her name—"Brie?"—and her heart's hesitation to trust the safety of Steve's voice scared her most of all.

He knelt over her in the shadows, definitely Steve—stained sleeve, mussed hair. In the stillness of slow relief, she glanced around. She didn't expect to see anything.

But now she didn't hear anything, either. Steve had shown up, and it had stopped. These things didn't happen in Steve's world; he didn't believe in them. At the moment, she didn't want to believe in them either.

And she'd thought *he* was getting weird?

"Brie, what's going—?" He couldn't finish his question; she rolled instinctively into the safety of her husband's arms, and they closed around her.

First Steve had gotten dizzy in the workroom—obvious stress, considering how exhausted he then felt—and Brie had tried to blow it out of proportion. But none of that mattered. His resentment had vanished when he heard Brie's scream, and what mattered now was that his spitfire wife was shivering in his arms as if she'd seen a ghost.

"Hey, Red, it's okay. I'm here." So maybe that shouldn't comfort her, considering their recent altercation... but she burrowed her face into his neck, accepting his protection. From what? Belatedly he looked around them. The bright overhead in the hallway lit the room pretty well, and he couldn't see anything wrong, except for the broken lamp beside the doorway... Better unplug that. When he moved to reach for the socket, though, Brie's arms around him tightened. Okay, he could unplug the lamp later.

He settled onto the floor beside her, gathered her closer, almost into his lap. "Um, Brie?" Her hair smelled spicy, like incense... like her. How long had he subconsciously connected her to such enticing, smoky smells? "What's wrong?"

"You didn't hear it," she whispered, after gulping another breath of air. The dullness of her tone scared him, and he pulled away enough to see her face. No, she didn't look as if she were in shock. Her blue eyes still sizzled under arched brows; she still had color in her cheeks, her lips.

"Hear what?"

She opened her mouth—then shut it, her hand rising nervously to the Celtic medallion she always wore. "Sort of a voice," she admitted finally, biting her lip in indecision. She turned to look fully at him, tipped her face up entreatingly, her fingers clutching at his back. "First you go sleepwalking, and now I'm hearing disembodied voices. Steve...either something really weird's going down, or I'm losing my mind."

*Then we'd have something else in common.* He pulled her to him again, buried his face in the curling softness of her fiery hair. He hadn't held her in so long. "Try none of the above. Rand and Sylvie were probably out back, talking," he told her soothingly. The concept of such a conversation was hardly frightening, but what else could she have heard? "You're okay now, right?"

The shivering had stopped, and her breathing had slowed. Instead of panting, she drew shallow breaths that tickled inside his collar. Slowly he became aware of her arms, still holding him tightly; the curve of her jeaned thighs, hot atop his own; her fleece-covered bosom rising and falling against his shirted chest.

They hadn't made love since Halloween.

"You *are* okay." He hadn't meant for his voice to sound quite so husky. "Aren't you?"

"It wasn't Rand and Sylvie," she whispered. Her steamy breath lit seductive sparks in his gut, and lower.

"What...um..." *C'mon, Peabody, vocabulary.* But with her turning in his arms, readjusting her knees so that one found purchase between his own, words seemed woefully unfamiliar. "Did you hear what they said?"

"It..." She looked quickly down, shook her head. "Never mind." When she again raised her face to his, her lost eyes focused on his lips, and it was *that look.* Expectant and nervous, innocent and sinful, all that lurking within the deepest, smokiest heavy-lidded eyes...

He didn't want to lose himself in those eyes, didn't want to pretend everything was okay when it wasn't. They hadn't solved anything... but he wasn't angry anymore, either. He'd traded anger for fear when he heard her scream. Trusting her had suddenly seemed far less important than keeping her safe.

And at the moment he didn't really give a damn what the "voices" had said. If there had been voices at all.

Brie tipped her heart-shaped face up to him, full lips parted, blue eyes veiled, and he wanted her beyond reason. As he always had... whoever she was.

His arms already encircled her; he hardly had to move to weave a hand up into her hair, against the base of her neck, to hold her still for his kiss. Her lips met his eagerly, parting, tasting, taking; in her clutching hands, the back of his shirt strained away from his waistband. Her knee, between his own, slid forward, and he groaned. His free hand retreated, beneath her arm, to cup her breast through the jersey. She groaned, too.

"The bed," he muttered, kissing and nuzzling. She was pulling his shirt loose in earnest now, running a hand beneath it, blazing a trail up his bare spine with her greedy palm. She knew what that did to him.

"Prude," she gasped throatily, even as he lifted the black hem of her jersey over her ribs, breasts and forearms, neck and elbows. Her hair tumbled back around her pale shoulders even as her wrists and hands came free, and the jersey fell to the floor behind her. His hands dropped to her waist, half on skin, half on denim.

"Broken glass," he grunted, but detoured around caution to bury his face in the swell of her breasts, harnessed by a lacy wisp of raspberry-colored bra. They jutted forward as she reached behind herself. The unclasped bra fell loosely from her, so that nothing but the medallion impeded his questing mouth from the curved velvet of her skin, her taut nipples. He ran his tongue up her in *just that way,* and was rewarded by a whimper of pleasure.

She fumbled awkwardly at his shirt buttons, muttering something wishful about Western shirts and snaps. He lowered her backward, straddling her back-bent body until her shoulders touched the floor. Then he grinned down at her and unbuttoned his own damn shirt.

She arched her hips upward, pressing herself against his arousal, dragging his attention to his pants instead. He yanked the shirt loose—thank God the cuffs weren't buttoned—and leaned over her, planted his arms on either side of her as she gazed expectantly up at him from a pillow of wild red hair.

Pain bit into his hand; with a curse, he reared back, snatching his injured palm to his mouth.

Brie sat up, too, so that her breasts tickled his chest, and eased the hand from his mouth. It wasn't a bad cut. "We really should do this on the bed," she murmured huskily, blue eyes dancing. "Glass, you know."

He narrowed his eyes at her, but when she raised his hand to her own lips, he couldn't even feign annoyance. The erotic heat of her mouth, her tongue, sapped his strength. This was one home remedy he fully accepted.

"Better?" she whispered, finishing her ministrations with a chaste kiss on the wound; still holding his hand, she leaned against the side of the bed and used its leverage to raise herself up, to slide onto the comforter.

He followed, stepping between her knees where her denim-clad legs still hung off the mattress, reclaiming his hand to deal with that little jeans problem of hers. Her panties matched the lost bra, pink and deliciously brief, angling over her flared hips like an invitation.

She kicked free of the denim and grasped his trousers, using her feet to drag them down his legs once she'd unzipped him. When he lowered himself onto her, savoring the friction of skin on skin, cotton on lace, she wove her legs possessively around his.

He stroked tendrils of her hair away from her face, trailed his fingers down her jaw, skimmed her collarbone, palmed the curve of her hip, taking the time to enjoy every inch of her. Her feet rode impatiently up and down his calves, sometimes tightening and sometimes falling loose in reaction to his touch. She lightly scored his bare back with her nails, occasionally gripped his shoulders to pull herself up and kiss him.

"Mmm...." she purred, rubbing herself against the hard heat of his arousal. "I've missed you."

"So much..." He shed his briefs as he echoed the sentiment; she raced him, shimmying out of her panties. Then they were pressed together again, sweat and heat, limbs twining, wriggling their way more securely to the middle of the bed.

Blessedly, deliciously, he lost control again. *Yes, yes, yes...* Sliding into her felt like coming home, like dying, like tasting heaven. Their groans harmonized, fell to quiet ecstasy. Then they both began to move, to match each other's rhythm, pacing one another. Time lost all reason.

The slice of light from the doorway seemed to brighten at the edge of his vision. It didn't matter. Brie knew just how to tighten around him; he knew just how to move against her. She arched her head back, exposing her neck, and he took it like a vampire, grazing her tender skin with his teeth, tasting her salty, smoky skin. Faster, oh, yes, faster, neither losing the other, building together forever, groaning together forever, peaking....

She convulsed beneath him, laughing sobs of delight; then her face blurred as he shuddered his own release into her. For a moment, he could have sworn they glowed ... another trick of the light. He choked out a groan, then a panting, gasping breath as he slowly sank onto her, managing to prop his chin against her sweaty shoulder on his way down. Her necklace chain bit at his cheek.

She chuckled into his ear, and nipped his earlobe.

Oh, my. Oh, God. What the hell had just happened?

Brie smiled at him. It was the satisfied smile of a woman well loved. If he could have erased the past week—the past *year*—of uncertainty from his memory, he'd have smiled back. But his lost control was returning, and he knew exactly what remained unresolved. *They* did. And even earth-shattering passion couldn't change everything that had come between them.

She extended a lazy hand and ran her nails through the hair over his temple, still smiling at him. Not quite against his will, he relaxed beneath the caress. Her whispered "I love you" soothed the rest of his reserve. "Always have, you know. Always will."

*She is bewitching you!* The thought came from nowhere; he rejected it. He was a rational adult. If he'd lost himself in her, it had been his decision to do so.

"You're very good," she murmured huskily, "at keeping the demons away." And she drew closer to him again, pressed her sweat-dampened curves against him.

*Charming. Luring. Tempting.* He should resist, should argue—their demons still existed.

*She's drawing you.* The strange thought brought with it a resurgence of desire; he did feel drawn to her scent, her softness, her heat. He pushed her back into the pillows, took her mouth with his. One of her hands left his back for a moment; the air around them brightened, almost as if they lay inside a bubble of light. He ignored the illusion. Right now, he just wanted to feel her, all of her; he wanted to be her husband in every way. She moved beneath him, lithe and hot and hungry, and he felt himself already responding. He really did want her—

*She is doing this to you. You are under her spell.*

Steve snorted at the idea. "Please!"

Brie blinked; heat paused in its buildup. "What?"

Oh, God—now he was talking to himself?

She lay there, waiting, confused. *Shut up,* he silently told the extraneous thoughts. He was in the middle of something here. *Just . . . leave me alone.*

And the edge-of-sight illusion of light expanded to fill the whole room. Steve actually glanced toward it, saw nothing but glittering suncatchers and dismissed it as fantasy. He scooped his hand behind Brie's neck, into her hair, threading silken fire and golden chain between his fingers, and drew her smiling lips toward his.

She met his mouth hungrily—seducing, bewitching, enchanting. Brie.

And after that he wasn't thinking at all.

*The bitch. She'd used the energy from their coupling to cast a protective sphere around them both. Even Josiah's screamed warnings could not penetrate the shield, once husband's will joined witch's spell.*

*He watched their ungodly revels, and felt frustration.*

*He had failed. He had finally managed to use his own words against her, but, like the witch long ago, she had answered not—and the experiment had sapped his power. The portal called him, drew him, offered sanctuary in the netherworld. He must accept failure. For now.*

*But next time, Josiah would use the husband who even now risked eternal damnation for the pleasures of the flesh—the husband's eyes, the husband's mouth, the husband's hands. And in time, together, they would make the witch confess her sins.*

*As he felt himself fading back across the Veil, Josiah only hoped he had the strength to resist tasting damnation himself. Before destroying her.*

Brie's eyes flew open as she came out of a deep sleep into dark nothingness. A scream pushed at her throat; then the familiarity of the steady breathing against her neck and the musky smell that surrounded her eased the panic. Barely.

Steve's arms encircled her; his cheek—she'd recognize those cheekbones anywhere—scratched lightly against hers. Their sweat and breath and heartbeats mingled. And yet the half-formed horror clung to her just as tightly. Struck by the comparison, she slid from the suddenly suspect security of her husband's arms and out of bed. Her chest felt heavy. Her throat burned. Darkness surrounded her; even Sylvie's porch light had gone off hours ago. The silence of the night pressed at her. *Get out.*

The security she'd found in Steve's arms tonight had been temporary; blissful, delicious, but temporary. Her nightmare had undercut it. And the voice that she'd heard—surely she hadn't imagined it!—had soiled the sanctuary of the bedroom. She needed to think clearly, needed to ground herself, and she couldn't do so with this inexplicable dread pushing in at her.

She'd channeled the energy raised by their lovemaking into a protective sphere...remnants hung about them still, silverine threads of light glittering from the astral realm. She'd not asked Steve's unlikely permission to so direct their shared power, but it had seemed a shame to waste this conflagration of energy—after her scare, she'd accept the karmic ramifications for this bit of security. Feeling across the floor, she found his shirt and pulled it on, then stepped outside the boundaries of the sphere and tested the night air. Nothing. No goose bumps. No raised hair on the back of her neck.

It was safe to get out.

She skirted the broken lamp and slipped into the hallway, down the stairs, through the kitchen and workshop and into the faint chill of a Southern mid-November night. *Get out.* Her nerves propelled her across the lush lawn, barefoot, buttoning Steve's shirt, until she reached the oak tree.

The oak was sacred, the king of trees. Even if her bedroom was no longer completely safe, even if Steve showed signs of instability, she could always take shelter among the broad, protective branches that swooped near the ground before lifting again toward the hope of sunlight. Sinking onto the rough bark of a low-hanging branch, Brie toed a few acorns through the dark grass and took several deep breaths. Her heartbeat calmed with each exhale. Romeow appeared from the shadows to sniff her ankle; then he launched himself gracefully onto the branch beside her and butted her hip with his head, purring. Her fears eased, just as she'd hoped they would.

Here, she could face her nightmare.

She still felt the bite of rope securing her wrists behind her back. She felt the weight and scratch of heavier hemp, loosely encircling her neck. People below her stared, some enthralled, some horrified. Beside her on the scaffold stood other good men and women, silent in the August morning. She'd been praying—not for her own life, but for her husband's understanding. And then her prayer seemed answered; from the crowd of soberly dressed witnesses emerged Steve. She longed to reach for him, knew she could not.

Neither did he reach for her. He held himself back, loath to touch one such as she. And even in the last seconds of her life, he'd commanded, yet again, "Confess."

She would find no understanding from him, no forgiveness. Sick with despair, she'd shaken her head.

And he'd turned toward the men who would kick out the scaffold—and he'd nodded. She'd felt a horrible lurch, a pressure behind her ear, a worse jolt—

Under the tree, Brie shuddered. Her subconscious merely blurred her two worst nightmares—Steve's rejection of her Craft ancestry, and the executions that ancestry had endured. But why? Everyone's dreams meant something....

Romeow scrambled up the tree. She knew Steve was there even before she raised her eyes, before her night vision spotted him in the doorway. He stood as if on guard, his dark terry bathrobe blending with the shadows around him. His intent gaze, beneath a fall of mussed hair, held her.

Was he protecting her... or hunting her?

She wouldn't find out by huddling under a tree. She rose and crossed the lawn to her waiting husband, torn between fear and an equally strong attraction.

"It's not safe out here at night," he said shortly, when she stopped before him. She could protest that he knew the low crime rates in Stagwater as well as anybody, that she could protect herself. But she *didn't* feel particularly safe... and she knew that, after Steve's strange behavior tonight, and then the voice she'd heard in the bedroom, she very much needed help protecting herself.

The sort of help that could ruin their marriage—what was left of their marriage. The scent of him still clung to her; she felt an intimate tenderness from their lovemaking, a faint whisker burn on her cheek. He'd come to her rescue. When she'd most needed him, he'd been completely hers. But passion wouldn't save their relationship, wouldn't heal the rift of distrust—and fear—that lurked between them.

It would only confuse the issues further. "I'm sleeping downstairs tonight," she said.

Steve shrugged, as if resigned; he'd probably sensed her decision even before she spoke. The shadow of worry didn't fade from his eyes. "Just come inside, okay?"

"Is something wrong?" But she stepped quickly inside.

He locked the door behind her. She escaped from the workroom, with its own spooky memories, into the kitchen. He followed, and threw the bolt on that door, too.

"What's *wrong?*" she repeated, imagining all kinds of threats advancing on the duplex. Romeow was out there!

Steve shrugged suspiciously. "I don't want you hurt."

"But what is there to hurt me?"

His stare lingered—she could sense the turmoil behind his level gaze. Finally he shook his head, shrugged again. "You'd be surprised." And he retreated into the living room. At the foot of the stairs he stopped, looked at the camelback sofa. "You want me to throw down a pillow?"

"I can get it." He was taking this awfully well, too well. She began to follow him up the narrow steps, then stopped on the second stair, staring helplessly at his strong, retreating back. Thinking of the bedroom reminded her of the nightmare, the explosive pain as her skull snapped from her neck, how her feet searched for purchase as she dangled...

The bedroom reminded her of the voice.

Perhaps sensing her hesitance, Steve paused, looked over his terry-clad shoulder. She caught a glimpse of pain

in his quietly handsome face before he hid it. The cruel
Steve of her dream was an illusion. She didn't want to hurt
the real one, to reject him again. No level of safety could
excuse that.

"Stay down here with me," she invited, wondering if
they could do so chastely, willing to try.

The ghost of a grin touched his lips. "On that sofa?"

"Or the floor." She forced another step—her pulse sped,
her breath thinned. Maybe she *could* climb the stairs if she
had to, or if he distracted her by sweeping her into his arms
and kissing her until she lost all awareness of everything
but him. But he could do that downstairs, too. And it
would only confuse things. "Or the backyard, or the
Blazer, just not in the bedroom. Not tonight. I don't feel
safe up there."

His concerned gaze probed hers. Would he lose respect
for her, because she'd heard voices? Was he insulted that
she didn't trust him to protect her from the bogeymen?

He shook his head. "No thanks." At the confusion she
didn't try to disguise, he attempted his weak smile again
and turned enough to brush his fingers across her white
knuckles where she grasped the banister. "Stay where
you're safe."

Brie drew a breath as if to argue, but Steve backed away
from her, up the stairs. Even if it showed lack of trust on
her part, her decision to stay downstairs relieved him. His
sick nightmare, in which he'd had Brie hanged, almost
made *him* question his trust in himself. His brief memory
lapse this evening, easily dismissed at 9:00 p.m., seemed
ominous at 3:00 a.m.

Not that he could ever hurt Brie.... What a ludicrous
idea!

But he left her to the safety of the sofa, all the same.

# CHAPTER EIGHT

*Wanton is every witch.*
—The Journals of Josiah Blakelee

As soon as Steve left the next morning, Brie called Sylvie. By lunch her entire circle—her *former* circle—had arrived at her home, with the surprising addition of young Andrew "Moonbeam" Beaudry, replete in black-and-white tie-dye.

"We're teaching him some basics of Wicca," Mary explained. "He was at work with me, learning some tarot, so I invited him on the condition that it doesn't bother you."

It did bother her—that the circle was moving on, adopting new members, hurt more than Brie had expected—but she wouldn't let destructive emotions like jealousy rule her, so she invited them in. Sylvie explained upon arrival that her fiancé was watching the bookstore, and a fashionably suited Cypress dryly declared herself to be on "a *real* power lunch."

Yet even with five witches, or four witches and a trainee, they could do little. Sitting in a circle, holding hands and seeking unusual vibrations, revealed nothing. Brie had already removed the remnants of magic left over from her and Steve's love-making, and Mary only once thought she saw something.

"Something *widdershins,* westward," the psychic directed. "Like a river running backward— Oh. It's gone now."

"Gone?" As in 'escaped'? Quickly Brie tried to access the powers she'd once had at her command, but she couldn't do it...and not just because high magic took long and dedicated practice, and she hadn't studied seriously for years. In quitting the circle, she'd somehow weakened herself even further. Certainly she could sense the energies flowing around her, the shortening days, lengthening nights, coming winter and new crescent moon. But nothing felt *widdershins.*

"I'm sorry," Mary said apologetically as, on unspoken cue, they released hands and opened their eyes to the overcast room. "I just didn't have time to be sure what I saw, before it was gone. If y'all didn't see it, it probably wasn't there."

"The wards hadn't been broken," admitted Cy. "And the only folks that should be able to cross them are Brie, Steve and the cat. Any chance this is some kind of poltergeist activity—you know, something of yours or Steve's creation, that went its own way, masked as your own energy?"

Brie tried not to think of the blank expression on Steve's face last night, tried not to remember his shuffling walk. "It could be anything," she admitted. "That's the problem! For all I know, I imagined the whole thing."

Sylvie draped a frail arm over her shoulders. "Nah. You haven't got that good an imagination."

At which Brie had to ask, "That's *good* news?"

Because if it wasn't imagination, what was it?

They reinforced the cleansing, circling the outside of the duplex not with mere salt, but with a sulphur mixture. They buried protective runes at each corner, to strengthen the wards. But Brie suspected that the lot of them—her an out-of-practice hereditary witch, Cypress an exotic mix of swamp magic and ancient arts, Mary and Sylvie both relative newbies, and poor Andy still unsure which elements corresponded with what powers—were in over their heads. Even her mother could hardly fight something until she could name it.

And Brie couldn't bear to consider that this elusive foe might be trying to go by the name *Steve.*

Though they couldn't accomplish much, she felt better for her friends' support. Too soon, Cy checked the gold Bulova on her dark wrist and left for a staff meeting. Then Sylvie left to relieve Rand—but she, the empath, hesitated.

"Will you be okay?" the slim brunette asked, and frowned Stevishly at Brie's attempted smile. "I'll close the shop for the afternoon. It'll only take me half an hour."

*"No."* This moodiness was embarrassing. "If the cat levitates, or demonic faces appear in my soapsuds, *then* I'll call you. Nightmares and silent voices are not worth you missing work." The momentary distracted look in Sylvie's eyes clinched it. "Besides, Rand's expecting you, right?"

Sylvie almost blushed—as near as a Peabody could—but nodded, and Brie sent her on her way. But she felt pathetically grateful that Mary and even Andy weren't working that afternoon, and remained seated.

Maybe she'd been hasty in quitting the circle.

Right, and maybe she should just phone Steve and ask for a divorce right now, to save them both the heartache of watching their marriage deteriorate from the inside because of her secrets and his . . . whatever was wrong with him.

If anything.

"Maybe you've got ghosts?" suggested Andy.

Brie and Mary both looked at him, surprised at the simplicity of his suggestion, and he shrugged his skinny shoulders. "It's just, y'all are so busy trying to find some outside force, and trying not to suggest that Mr. Peabody's possessed—which is a pretty funny idea, really...."

Brie glared.

Andy ducked his head nervously. "Anyhow, I was thinkin', what if the house is just plain haunted? I may not know much about witchcraft, but I do know about ghosts, and I don't think they'd set off a ward. The wards are in our realm, right? But ghosts usually stay on a separate plane, one that just sort of bleeds over into ours. Ya know?"

"The boy's got himself a point," admitted Mary, drawing her jeans-clad knees up to her chin with disgusting ease. She was, Brie realized, wearing red-and-white striped socks.

It couldn't hurt to consider the idea. "Sylvie probably has some books about dispelling ghosts." Brie sank onto the sofa. "I've never dealt with one myself, but..."

"I have," admitted Andy, his eager expression almost puppyish. "That's how I got interested in the supernatural."

Brie tried not to get her hopes up too quickly. "But if the duplex is haunted, why would we just notice recently?"

"Why don't I ask it?" The women exchanged glances. "My family," Andy reminded them, "is in the estate-sale business, remember? Selling off the belongings of the recently—or not so very—departed? I know about ghosts."

Mary grinned at Brie. "Who else ya gonna call?"

* * *

*Call.*

Steve glanced at his phone, then turned firmly back to the *Sentinel*'s accounts. He had no reason to call home.

Except for the niggling urge that wouldn't leave him alone. Like a thought of coffee during caffeine withdrawal, like a lingering responsibility on the rare occasion that he left work undone. He couldn't forget it. It hovered in the back of his mind, as clearly as the static from the police-band radio and the rhythm of the photocopier in the main office.

*Call.* It was like that damned gut-level fear that had sent him home on Halloween night. But there had been nothing wrong at home on Halloween, no cause for alarm.

Though the sex had been incredible.

From his chair, he flopped facefirst into a stack of invoices. God, but he was degenerating.

*Call.* The urge welled up in his chest and mind; with a disgusted sigh, he sat up and pushed his invoices back into a neater pile again as he claimed the telephone. He might not have cause to call, but neither did he have reason not to.

"E.T., phone home," he muttered, punching in the familiar sequence of numbers. If he started making mashed-potato sculptures, like Richard Dreyfuss in *Close Encounters of the Third Kind,* he hoped somebody would take pity on him and shoot him.

Brie picked up on the second ring. See, she hadn't been kidnapped by aliens after all. "Hello?"

"It's me." Well, that hardly earned him suave-and-debonair points. Still, he could hardly ask *her* why he'd called. He also nixed *Heard any more little voices today?* as a conversation starter. "I . . . just wanted to check in."

Or check up? He already regretted bowing to instinct.

"Nothing to report," Brie said, after too long a pause.

He narrowed his eyes at the phone. "What's going on?"

"Nothing you'd want to hear about," she said with a sigh, which only piqued his interest.

"Why don't you let me decide that?" He leaned his chair back to balance on two legs, using his shoulder to hold the phone to his ear. "You know, Brie, we'd probably make more headway if you'd trust me a bit."

"Okay," she said, her tone matching the stubborn expression he imagined. "I think we may have a ghost."

"Thanks for taking me seriously."

"We may have a ghost," she repeated. And she wasn't referring to the TV reception. Well, she'd thought she heard voices last night. And now that he thought about it, she'd had a few more nightmares than usual. When he scared her, with that little memory lapse, she'd likened it to *Night of the Living Dead.*

Worried now, he considered a radical connection. Could she think her family was cursed, or something? Was that her big secret? Surely not. That was more in Sylvie's line.

"You're serious? You think you saw something?" Even as the words left his mouth, he knew he should have deleted *think.*

"Never mind, okay? I'm probably a hysterical female, or whatever else you want to believe. Go back to work."

Right. "I didn't say you're imagining things—just that there's a logical explanation. Wind hitting loose shingles, or a radio left on. We can check it out tonight."

"Mary's over. We'll keep our ears open."

Now *there* was a comforting thought. "Did she bring her Ouija board?"

"Goodbye, Steve."

"Wait, wait . . ." The front legs of his chair hit the floor again. "Please?"

She didn't hang up.

"If you think there's someone there who shouldn't be, you get out, right?" His voice sharpened when she didn't immediately agree; a sense of threat from last night's dream still lingered. "Take the gun and go to Sylvie's."

"There aren't any serial killers casing the house," she insisted. "The town's clean out of them."

"Be careful anyway. Promise?"

Her voice fell soft. "I promise. See you tonight."

"Bye." Hanging up the phone, he considered that— imaginary hauntings aside—his suspicions had proven false. There hadn't been anything wrong at the house.

"Instinct zero," he announced, and took a sip of tepid coffee. "Logic gains a strong lead—" He shut up, mug still raised to his lips, when he noticed Louise, with a handful of mail, glancing curiously in his office door.

"They're way too much trouble, if you ask me," Mary said when Brie hung up the phone.

Hearing her memory replaying Steve's voice one more time, contrasting his concern against his cynicism, Brie only belatedly glanced toward her friend, who was spreading newspaper across the kitchen table. "What are?"

"Men. Is this thick enough?"

Brie nodded, and went into the workroom for supplies—rags and a bottle of wood reviver. Andy had wandered upstairs with his rucksack—he had to find the house's center of energy, he'd explained—and she hoped to get some work done while she and Mary waited for his report. But she didn't want to use the workroom, with its tools and antiques casting rainy-day shadows.

Mary came as far as the doorway. "When you're a kid, everything's fine. Boys and girls pretty much accept one another as equals, even if a game of doctor with the neighbor kid reveals some radical differences. Can I take those?''

Brie handed over the supplies and picked up the Bible box. Mary had long ago made it clear that she didn't like touching items from estate sales.

''And then you're a teenager,'' the blonde continued, doing her best to distract Brie from her troubles, ''and suddenly you can't just be friends. There's this sexual thing hanging between you—so to speak—and even if you aren't dating, people think you are, and if you are dating it gets even more complicated.'' She shook her head, and her crescent-moon earrings bounced against her neck. ''Ugh.''

Brie set the box, a slant-topped piece with butterfly hinges, on the newspapers. ''I didn't date much in high school,'' she admitted. *Crazy Gwen's daughter.* Had she truly thought she could escape that stigma?

''I haven't dated much *since* high-school,'' quipped Mary. ''What, you haven't noticed?'' She paused then, cocked her head. ''It's for me.''

The phone rang. Brie grinned as Mary picked it up; if Steve had seen that, he'd be thinking they'd set him up.

''I don't know,'' the blonde said after a moment. ''Teddy, this is a really bad time.'' Teddy owned the Wellness Club, where Mary worked as a massage therapist.

Though no precog, Brie suspected what was coming next. When Mary covered the mouthpiece, and looked at her apologetically, Brie asked, ''How long?''

''Less than an hour,'' admitted Mary. ''Normally I wouldn't take a last-minute appointment, but this is Miz Holcomb—she's eight months pregnant, with terrible backaches. Teddy says she was crying when she called.''

And, of course, Mary could no more ignore Miz Holcomb's need than she was able to ignore Brie's.

There were worse traits in a friend. "Go."

"But—" Still covering the mouthpiece, Mary rolled her eyes toward the ceiling and, presumably, Andy. "Not to manifest anything, but what if Steve comes home?"

"At three in the afternoon? Not likely." Brie had to restrain herself from knocking on wood. "If he does, I'll just ask him to wait out the ghost results—to humor me, if for no other reason. I don't need a chaperone."

Mary hesitated, one indecisive foot turning inward.

"Go help Miz Holcomb!"

With a shoulder roll that mixed defeat and relief, Mary told her boss she was on her way and hung up. "Under an hour," she insisted, stepping into her shoes. "I promise."

*Watch out for those vows, kid.* As Mary headed for the door, Brie called, "You're wrong about men, you know."

"How?" Mary turned to walk backward.

"Trouble, yes." Brie folded her left hand, on her lap, to thumb her wedding ring. Trouble... and sacrifice. "Too much trouble, never. Not with the right man."

Mary gave her a thumbs-up before pushing out the door. Brie, now alone, lifted her left hand to openly study her ring. The right man. Steve was so very right.

She just wondered if she was the wrong woman.

"Don't come home early," she whispered, barely pulling back her power before the wish could become a spell... even as mediocre a spell as she could manage, lately. She would *not* manipulate him. No matter what her crimes, she wouldn't add that sort of magic to them.

But, as she went back to work on the box, she felt very, very conscious of the clock.

Colonials had used Bible boxes to protect most of their books and papers, really—the slanted covers served nicely as makeshift writing desks—but since few pilgrims would own a book without first owning a Bible, the name stuck.

Mom, who'd first taught Brie an appreciation of antiques, wouldn't buy any piece saturated in Christianity, so her exposure to such book boxes—"shadow boxes," Gwen would slyly call the few that passed inspection—had been limited.

Brie narrowed her eyes at the dull, partially decomposed walnut piece in front of her. Wait a minute....

Taking a few deep breaths, she spread her hands over the box and sensed it. Lords above, but she'd fallen out of practice. Her focus wavered embarrassingly, and she received only vague impressions, all of them pleasantly tolerant. Opening her eyes with an exhausted sigh, she blinked wearily at the inoffensive antique, then thought to check the clock.

Mary had barely been gone ten minutes.

*Back to work.* This box had been restored at least once before; she could tell by the way the grain, in the bottom, ran crosswise to the grain of the sides. A modern touch. No wonder the bottom didn't need much work. She applied reviver to the rest of it, rubbing the homemade solution into all corners, one side at a time. By the time she finished the last panel, the first should be ready for drying.

She checked on the clock after two panels. Mary had been gone for seventeen minutes.

Steve, she remembered, hated the smell of turpentine in the dining room. And her wood reviver, which mixed turpentine with linseed oil and vinegar created quite a stench.

But Steve wouldn't come home for hours yet. And if he did, well, she could have people over, even those of whom her husband might not approve.

She tried not to remember Steve's accusations when he'd first met Andy. He'd overreacted then, admitted it, apologized. Nothing to worry about.

Nineteen minutes.

She wet her soft cloth with more reviver, and rubbed it slowly into the walnut. Over her shoulder, the clock ticked. Andy should be finishing, soon.

Outside, a car door shut.

Mary? She checked the clock, her heart heavy. It was too soon to be Mary. But it could be Sylvie, home early. Or Rand Garner, come to surprise his fiancé. Or Jehovah's Witnesses, come to proselytize—anything but . . .

The front door opened. "I left the paper early."

Thanks a lot, O evil god of bad timing. "I'm in the kitchen," she called to her husband.

At least her voice didn't waver.

Steve wrinkled his nose as he strode down the short hall from the living room to the dining room and kitchen. Yech—turpentine. Why Brie would ignore a perfectly good workshop to stink up the kitchen, he didn't know. Unless it had something to do with her ghosts.

She looked good; even in jeans and an old orange UTA sweatshirt, with her hair pulled back in an elastic, she had that sultry, mysterious look that had first drawn him. A few weeks ago, she would have come to him for a hug and a welcome kiss, warm after the cold rain outside.

He tried not to feel disappointed when she didn't. A lot had happened since a few weeks ago.

"So you left the paper early, huh?" she asked.

He blinked at that. "Yeah." She seemed nervous about something—still ghosts? "I wanted to make sure you were okay."

*She's been up to something. She's always up to something. You can't trust women.*

"I'm fine. I told you I would be."

The stench of turpentine distracted him. He winced away from it, a sudden pain shooting behind his eyes. Damn it, she knew he hated the stuff! "Last time I heard, you thought you saw a ghost."

"I didn't think I saw anything. I heard something."

*She's not telling the truth.* Steve shook off the thought, tried to focus on her. "Was the door locked?"

"It wasn't a real person," she insisted, her brows slanting down over those smoky, cat-like eyes of hers.

"So now you're communing with ghosts." Not real tactful, but damn, his head hurt. She'd soaked some cruddy hunk of wood—a Bible box, *'tis a Bible box*—in oily turpentine, and left the lid off the bottle. No wonder he felt ill.

"Not me," she hedged as he reached for the bottle. "In fact, I got someone else to— Oh!" And she jumped up to avoid the oily liquid spreading across the paper-strewn table, where his clumsy reach to cap it had knocked it over.

He could manage better curses than that, and did, snatching a dish towel from the oven. He threw it on the spreading stain while she righted the bottle.

"Steve, my mom made that!" Brie's screech did not help his headache—belatedly he realized that the towel he'd grabbed was one Mother Conway had sent on their last anniversary, hand-embroidered with more kitties. What was it with these women and cats? "The smell will never come out!"

He raised a hand to the bridge of his nose; the stench coming off it nearly gagged him. Maybe he should go out and try this again . . . but something she'd said finally registered. "What do you mean, you got someone else? To do what?"

Brie, gathering wet papers from the table and scrunching them into a two-handed wad, paused at his question.

*She's up to something. She's always up to something.* She carried the mess past the kitchen counter, tossed the abused kitty towel into the sink and dumped the papers in the trash. "I found someone who believes in ghosts to check us out."

"Who—?" Wait; the white van across the street. *Real observant, Peabody. Those reporter's instincts are still sharp as ever.* "This person wouldn't look like a Woodstock refugee, would he?"

"I was afraid you'd take this badly," she said, putting a lid on the trash can and stepping toward him. He stepped quickly back. Oh, no, she wasn't getting her manipulative little paws on him again. He needed his head clear!

Though that hardly seemed likely at the moment. "And you invited him over anyway?"

She planted her hands on her hips . . . did she plan it, so that her breasts jutted out? He wouldn't put it past her, wouldn't put anything past her, and his head was throbbing like a battering ram. "Did I need your permission?"

*Yes!* "And he's still here." *Pound. Pound. Pound.* Any minute now, the protective door around his mind would splinter under the assault. He stumbled toward the living room, hoping that escaping the smell would clear his head.

"He's upstairs. Are you all right?" Brie followed him, laid a hand on his cheek. "Maybe you'd better sit down."

*Pound. Pound.* Not only had she let that space case in, she'd sent him upstairs. He grasped the banister and started up the steps, dizzy with the surge of hostility that tried to drown him, his free hand clenching and unclenching. Brie dogged his heels. "You need rest—and *he* needs privacy."

"Bull!" They topped the stairs.

"I'm serious!" She grabbed his arm; he shook her off, stalked down the hall to the bedroom. *Liar!* The word screamed through his head. *Always a liar! What is he really doing here? What is she really up to? What—*

But when he slammed open the bedroom door, some small, sane part of his brain still managed to be surprised by the truth—just before sheer fury blinded him to all else.

"Sonofabitch!"

During Steve's long moment of shock, Brie peeked around him and took in the whole, horrid picture. The black candles around the bed. New Age synthesizer music on Andy's cassette player. The Ouija board—lords above, he'd brought a Ouija board into her house? And worse, much worse: Andy himself, kneeling on the bed, wearing a black robe, and obviously nothing else—practically sky-clad!

Steve sucked in a long breath, visibly tensing. His left hand curled into a fist, relaxed, flexed again.

She really wished she'd made the bed this morning.

Andy's eyelids fluttered, his eyes focusing, coming out of his trance. She couldn't see the expression on Steve's face, but Andy's eyes widened with more than surprise.

"This isn't what it looks like," she asserted, shoving past her husband to step between him and the idiot on the bed. Then *she* got a look at Steve's expression.

His coldness singed her. His jaw was set, but a muscle beneath his high cheekbone flexed angrily. His eyes bored accusingly into her, then flicked over her shoulder.

*He's going to kill Andy,* she thought with sudden clarity. Her nonviolent husband meant to kill somebody.

Instead, Steve remained rooted for another long moment. She could hear Andy behind her, scrabbling for his clothes. Then Steve spun and stalked out.

"Oh, my god, oh, my god, oh, my god," chanted Andy, voice trembling. "I thought we were dead. I really..."

She ignored him to bolt after Steve. She had to race down the stairs to catch him before he reached the front door, and only by throwing herself against it as he turned the knob did she keep him from walking out.

His still silence hurt more than names or cursing could have.

"I said it wasn't what you're thinking, and I meant it," she insisted, meeting his eyes. She wasn't sure she recognized the man behind them.

"I thought it was a nude man in our bed," said Steve, clipping his words.

"He wasn't—"

"It wasn't me."

"I never slept with him!"

Steve seemed to consider that. "Of course not."

She sagged, relieved, against the door. They *could* talk about it. It was all just a silly misunderstanding.

"It's the middle of the afternoon, and you didn't expect me home for hours," he added. "Who has time to sleep?"

She slapped him. The smack, the red stain on his cheek, scared her more than the painful way he caught her hand. He held it for only a moment, gripped it with almost enough strength to do damage. Then he used it to yank her away from the door, shoved past her and strode out into the rain.

She clutched at the doorjamb, fingernails digging into painted wood, stunned by their mutual violence. She couldn't just let him leave like this, thinking the things he did. "Wait!" The scream hurt her throat; she stumbled out the doorway, onto the damp porch. "You always said we could talk anything out, Steve. Please!"

He'd already yanked the door to his Volvo open, but he paused to look back at her. Maybe they'd work through this after all, somehow....

"I lied!" He hurled the words at her; she recoiled from the force of his hatred. "Surprised?" he yelled, climbing into his car. "I learned it from you!"

Then he slammed the door and peeled down the street, away from her, away from their marriage...and away from the apparent evidence that she'd betrayed it.

# CHAPTER NINE

*The wife who bends not to her husband's will invites
her husband's wrath!*
                              —The Journals of Josiah Blakelee

Brie stood on the porch, clutching a post, as the rain
misted unendingly down. He'd left. Oh, lords above, he'd
left her. And maybe not just because of Andy. *The candles. The robe. The magic.* He'd also left because of the
magic.

How had she let this happen?

"Um..." The hesitant voice came from behind her. She
spun to see a fully dressed Andy. "I hope I didn't cause too
much trouble," he mumbled, fidgeting with the ties on his
duffel bag. "You understand—I had to shed my physical
persona to get in tune with the energies, and—"

"Shut up!" she snarled, and advanced on him. He
cringed back into the house, nearly tripped over the orange flash of fur that beat him in. "I can understand the
candles, the music. I'm real wary about Ouija boards, but
maybe..." He started to nod, stopped at a glare from her.
"But, energies or not, you don't strip in a married woman's bedroom!"

Andy—Moonbeam—pouted. "What is he, your master?"

*"My husband!"* At least he was, until a few minutes
ago.

As soon as Andy left, she locked the door and curled into a ball on the sofa, too miserable even for tears. Romeow sniffed her face, then lay down against her stomach. She tried to tell herself that she could fix this—she'd been able to fix things all her life, hadn't she? But the memory of Steve's fury undercut every effort at hope.

"Calm down," she repeated, softly at first, but with increasing self-indictment. "Calm down." Mary would return soon. And she had to check on Steve. This angry, he could have an accident, be hurt, be killed! "Calm down!"

She'd thought herself stronger than this, more capable. It took more than heartache to reduce a Conway woman to despair. More than heartache and stress. Fatigue. PMS.

Except, she realized with a growing stillness deep in her soul, she should have had PMS last week. She pressed a fist to her mouth. She was late. Her cycle was late.

Now she cried.


Only once he'd made sure the others had also left early, locked the door behind him and checked that the shades were drawn against the damp street did Steve realize that he was at the *Sentinel* offices. He wasn't sure how he'd gotten there, but he assumed from the keys in his hand that he'd driven.

When the nausea hit him, it hit him hard. He grabbed for the edge of Louise's desk to support himself until the spell passed, then decided that was as good a place as any to crumple to the floor. He leaned his hot cheek against the cool metal side of the desk. Oh, God.

He could clearly remember worrying about Brie's ghost story, reluctantly heading home early. Brie had acted nervous, and he had spilled turpentine . . .

And there it got hazy—but not hazy enough.

The phone rang once before the answering machine in his office got it. His stomach cramped into a roiling knot, but he couldn't kneel on the linoleum indefinitely. Someone might come by.

"Come on, Peabody," he muttered, and, oddly enough, he felt a little better. "At least lose it in your own office." Using the desk for leverage, he hoisted himself unsteadily to his feet. One foot in front of the other got him through the doorway; once there, he could slap on the lights, lock *that* door, and collapse into the familiarity of his own chair.

Brie hadn't really slept with Moonbeam, had she? *The bitch, making him a cuckold. The deceitful, manipulative...* He recognized the red haze of fury as it spread across his thoughts, tendrils of anger trapping each memory. *Hold it, Peabody. Cease fire.* It faded.

Funny word, *cuckold*. Old-fashioned. Not one he'd normally use. And it might not even fit. He tried to replay the afternoon in his memory, tried to separate reality from the awful, malignant redness that blurred everything into seething hatred. Why had he been so insanely angry? Sure, the near-naked man in his bed—but he'd been angry before he went upstairs, hadn't he? He'd been angry in the kitchen.

Somewhere, he'd lost control. That wasn't like him.

*But she seduced him, seduced you, soiled all—*

No! He pushed back in his chair, stood, paced. He had to think about this objectively. Suppose it *was* true? He remembered something through the blur of hostility, something about *it's not what you think*. But suppose she was lying? *Women lie!* He fought back the anger. Damn it, think! Even if it was true, hadn't he ever had cause to be this angry before? As a child, he'd either run cool or hot, no in between, but he'd learned as he got older to *stay* cool.

He'd thought he'd succeeded. In court, facing down the drunk driver who'd killed his parents, he'd been furious, but he'd controlled it.

Why couldn't he control himself anymore?

He could have killed her today. Even through the scarlet haze that still blurred much of their fight, he knew he had wanted to hurt her, could easily have hurt her. His worst fear. That was why he'd left. If he'd stayed...

He took a deep, steadying breath.

Spilled turpentine... It was like piecing together the memories secondhand. When he learned Moonbeam was there, he'd lost it. He'd stalked upstairs like some macho movie hero, and there had sat that scrawny space case, circled by... black candles?

*Witches in Stagwater.* He'd gotten a letter to the editor along those lines, a while back. But...witches? Even doofy Mary, for all her pretenses, didn't really count.

The phone rang again, and he glanced, irritated, toward the answering machine as his own message came on. "You have reached the *Stagwater Sentinel.* Our offices—" With a jab, he silenced his own voice. Then he realized it was—might be—Brie, and raised the volume. "For calling." *Beep.*

"Steve, are you there?"

He fought back another, milder wave of anger at her voice, and stepped farther back from the desk where the machine sat. "Pick up, so I'll know you're okay."

Right. He was okay, and there were witches and warlocks running naked around Stagwater, to go with that stupid werewolf scare a few months back. *Why don't you tell me, Brigit? Don't you know?* He was getting as crazy as she was.

She did sound worried, and a tad annoyed. Another memory found its way home. Did she slap him? "You know that I didn't sleep with Andy! If you don't trust my morals, at least trust my taste. He's just a kid!''

He hadn't considered Moonbeam such a fine specimen, either, but what did he know? Suddenly he felt very, very tired.

Brie's voice persisted, hoarser now. "I didn't sleep with him. But I am sorry. For the rest. For..." And she sounded so lost that he reached for the phone. "Never mind," she whispered, and hung up first. The dial tone clicked to a stop; the tape reset itself.

He waited for his temper to flare again, like a stab of pain after a broken bone was bumped, but it didn't. His disorientation remained, complicated by exhaustion. But the anger had retreated as thoroughly as it had erupted.

The office's silence echoed around him. A single car drove by—rush hour in Stagwater—and even the always-blowing air-conditioning was silent for a November cool spell. He fell back onto the duct-taped vinyl couch where he sometimes crashed after 3:00-a.m. layout sessions.... He wasn't going home yet, that was definite. He couldn't go to Sylvie's, since she lived next door to him and Brie. And Rand Garner's gesture of friendship might not have been completely legit.

Like a dog with a bone, his memory worried the scene in the bedroom. Black candles. Ouija board. Witches?

Sitting up, he reached up to one of the metal book-shelves and hoisted the New Orleans yellow pages to his knees. Sylvie carried New Age-y books at UnderCov-er...but UnderCover was closing soon, and he wasn't about to encourage his sister's delusions by showing inter-est. Shops in the city, however, should be open at least until seven—and southbound traffic ran pretty light in the evening.

This was ridiculous. Had to be ridiculous. But it was a lead. If Brie had gotten sucked into some occult scam, it might explain why she'd been acting so strangely of late.

He hoped he wouldn't learn anything he didn't want to know.

Brie sank unsteadily onto the high edge of the old-fashioned tub, staring at the plastic stick in her hand. Pink. It had turned pink. It was positive.

*Or false positive,* she reminded herself. She'd been late maybe a year ago, and gotten a false positive by taking the test in the evening. Steve, avid reader of instructions, had warned her not to get her hopes up, despite an equally excited flush in his open face, a sparkle in his concerned eyes. And he'd been right; the next morning's test had shown negative, and she'd started her cycle a day later. The disappointment had suffocated her, but he'd been there to hold her, to comfort her, to assure her that the setback was minor and to pretend he wasn't hurting just as much.

Romeow propped his front paws on the tub's edge to sniff the plastic stick in her hand; she lifted it from his reach. Still pink.

She had refused to tell her friends her suspicions when first Mary, then Sylvie, came by, because Steve should know first. Only after they'd left had she driven to the drugstore for two pregnancy tests. She needed one for a more reliable reading in the morning—but she hadn't had the patience to wait till then. After the store, she'd driven by the *Sentinel,* but Steve's car wasn't there...which explained why he hadn't answered any of the five apologetic messages she'd left. He had to be safe. Lords above, let him be safe.

*And let him trust me, one more time.*

She threw the plastic stick into the trash, then tugged the rich terry of Steve's bathrobe more closely to her neck, breathing in the smell of him. This felt different from last time. She splayed her hand against her still-flat abdomen, and she could *tell*. She and Steve had made a baby. How could she simultaneously feel so happy, so anxious, so grateful?

And so frightened that Steve wouldn't be there to share the miracle, not just of childbirth, but of the baby's whole life. That he would reject them, or that he would no longer be the old Steve. She never would have considered motherhood without him. Imagined visions of such a baby's future taunted her. *Crazy Brie's kid.*

No. She squeezed her eyes shut; that wouldn't happen. She wouldn't let her child grow up fatherless, as she had. She wouldn't let her heritage chase Steve away.

The ringing of the phone startled her. She ran from the bathroom, dived onto the lamplit bed to grasp the receiver. *Don't be Mary, Sylvie, Cypress . . .*

"Hi." And at Steve's quiet, carefully steady voice, she almost started crying again. He was safe.

"Hi," she replied, and her voice shook. She had so much to tell him—and this wasn't the way she'd wanted to. *It could be false,* an annoying rationalism reminded her. *You could get his hopes up, then hurt him again.*

Assuming he'd think it was good news at this point. Assuming he didn't label the child a bastard. *Like hell.* She pressed a protective hand to her tummy, said nothing.

"I'm back at the *Sentinel.*" Steve took a deep breath. "I got your messages, and wanted to let you know I'm okay. I'm just . . . I'm going to stay here tonight. Do some typesetting, fillers. I need to think about some things."

She wanted to beg him to come home. She had news; she needed him. Surely he would come, if she said she needed him. Dutiful, dependable Steve.

And wouldn't that be as manipulative as if she summoned him by magic?

Instead, she said, "Nothing happened with me and Andy. He really was trying to contact ghosts." *And he said he'd felt whatever was there leave. He said he succeeded.*

After a long silence, Steve asked, "You believed him?"

It would take tact—not exactly her strong suit—to answer honestly without further threatening her vow. "It seemed worth a try. But you have to trust that—"

"No, I don't *have to*." But his voice remained steady, carefully neutral. "I don't have to do anything."

He could drive into the city, catch a plane, never come back. That would be out of character... but so was his temper, his diminishing appetite, his unfocused looks. So was her secrecy, her slapping him.

Their lives had stopped running by the rules she'd always counted on.

"I'm sorry," she whispered, cradling the phone against her cheek as if it were his hand. "I'm so sorry. I—"

"I know, Brie. It's..." But he wouldn't say it was okay, because he wouldn't lie to her. "Neither of us have been ourselves lately; things went too far on both sides. Let's just take a while and regroup, okay?"

*A while?* She hated the neediness that forced the next question from her, but she couldn't contain it. "When will you come home?" At least she hadn't asked *Are you coming home?* At least she hadn't begged. *Please come home to me. I'll do better....*

"Tomorrow," he said, and at the unspoken *of course* in his tone she released the breath she held. "Tomorrow night. We're going to talk about all this."

She bit her lip, foolishly nodded. *Thank you* sounded too clingy, even if she wanted to cling. *I love you* would prod him to return the sentiment. And *I'm pregnant*...

No. Not until she was sure. "Tomorrow night," she repeated. "Eat something, okay? Sleep well."

"You, too, Red." And even as the phone clicked in her ear, she closed her eyes, slumped against the headboard. He'd called her Red. There was still a chance.

Tomorrow night, if the second pregnancy test read positive, she'd tell him. She'd fix the perfect dinner, wear his favorite dress. She'd be everything he wanted.

She pulled the comforter securely around her, the witch and her all-powerful blankie, exhausted, though darkness had come only a few hours before. The sun set so early, lately. It seemed dark all the time.

Romeow hopped onto the bed, tested the covers over her legs and curled up atop them, like a vibrating heating pad. She'd left the overhead light on, and the hallway light. And she didn't want to get up again. Concentrating, she took a deep breath, then a deeper one, feeling the energy awake in her, directing it. One more, as the power peaked, and then: "Lights out." As the room plunged into darkness, she recognized the muffled thump of a blown fuse. Well, magic *did* work by natural means. Steve would call it coincidence, of course, but...

Steve would never accept *any* magic. If she remained a witch, he could never completely accept her. She held the responsibility for that deception, and only she could end it.

She couldn't break her sworn vow, but she could stop not just practicing, but *being*, a witch. Completely. With one last ritual, at full moon next Saturday, she could bid the Ancient Powers disown her and leave her to the mundane life of housewife and mother—the life she chose. It was a ritual, an amputation, that she should have performed years ago. Magic to sever her magic. Fighting fire with fire.

*But what do* you *want?* demanded her private demons. She hid her face in the linen muskiness of Steve's pillow, hugging herself—hugging her baby—for comfort. It had never been a question of what Steve would sacrifice, but of what she found most important. Her husband. Her family.

Without them, nothing else would matter.

It was getting late, but Steve knew he wouldn't sleep well on the vinyl couch. Besides, he thought, looking over the notes he'd taken, the books he'd bought, and his appointment book, all spread in the weak glow of his gooseneck desklamp. He had to make sense of all this.

He would far rather focus his attention on Brie and her eclectic circle of friends than on his own mood swings. His control was probably being strained by the secrets that Brie was keeping, he told himself, taking a sip of coffee. That was all. If he understood the secrets, he would regain his old self.

He told himself that he wasn't actually investigating either Brie or Sylvie. If he investigated them, he'd ask probing questions and take photos from bushes. No, he was just reexamining things he should already have noticed.

And he didn't like the pattern that he saw forming.

He'd first gotten suspicious on Halloween night. Though he didn't buy the idea of psychic hunches, his subconscious could have pieced together the information that his consciousness was only now noticing. He'd gotten home, and Brie had been wearing a black robe.

Halloween was some kind of Sabbath for witches.

She'd been out the night before that, too, he remembered—on the full moon. And, though his own appointment book, a yearly stocking-stuffer from Brie, didn't show any full moons, the puppy calendar beside Louise's desk did. On several of the dates, he couldn't place Brie's whereabouts, or his. But every full moon he could place her. Every full moon she'd gone out with her friends, including his weird sister and Mary Deveraux—whose other car was a broom.

Okay, so he had Brie on weirdness by association. Pushing his calendar aside, he flipped through the books he'd bought at the occult store in New Orleans. Weird? Its shelves had been cluttered with mason jars, hand-labeled Cat Bones, Chicken Blood and Graveyard Dirt. He'd found books about voodoo, satanism and black magic. One title, *Cult of the Occult*, had been "written by an ex-wizard, who only recently escaped the trap of occult forces." Another paperback, *Beginning Black Magic*, looked to be self-published, with a hand-drawn pentagram on the front, but sported a promising table of contents: spells to bind a lover, spells to defeat an enemy, spells to summon demons!

He almost hadn't bought them, but something mesmerizing about their sensational titles, the smoky bite of incense, the row upon row of perverted ingredients had held him.

In his deserted office, double-checking the dates of other witches' sabbaths from *Cult of the Occult* against his appointment book, he didn't think he'd forget that shop anytime soon. And not just because Brie had been out on Mabon. And Lammas Day. And Midsummer Night.

"Coincidence," he muttered unconvincingly to himself, skimming the book. She did go out on a lot of nights that *weren't* full moons or Sabbaths.

A passage about an orgy caught his reluctant attention. It told how witches and wizards performed sex magic with demons who longed for the fleshly pleasures of mortality. He shut the book and threw it across the room. Even discounting the bull about demons, this was sick.

And somehow familiar, as if he'd been imagining such things even before now.

He threw *Beginning Black Magic* across the room, too— four points, total—and opened the file of doomsday letters that Louise, after telling him off for calling her and Kent at 10:00 p.m., had admitted to keeping. All these letters to the "Editer," like the one he'd trashed the day after Halloween, warned of "whiches." And, he noted, deciphering the scrawl, "wearwooves," "demun worshipers," "vampirs," "the Honey Iland Swamp Monster." And, he noted with a grin, someone named "John."

All newspapers got wacko letters…and these put things into perspective. He'd lowered himself to this anonymous Chicken Little's level. Brie and the others would have to be a lot crazier than he'd give them credit, to consent to orgies or try raising demons. At the very worst, they were embarrassing themselves with New Age-y goddess-movement games. At best, he'd misread even that.

He would see Brie tomorrow. They would sit down together and *talk*. He'd lay everything on the table. If she wanted to save their marriage, she'd let the familiar out of the bag and she'd agree to joint counseling.

And if she didn't?

He refused to consider that. He turned off his desk lamp so that only the streetlight outside illuminated his office, and he made his way to the lumpy, patched couch. He kicked off his shoes, stretched out.

He tried not to think of orgies with demons.

* * *

They were going to *talk,* he reminded himself the next night, mounting the steps to the porch, unlocking the front door. They wouldn't fight, they'd *talk.*

The warmth and lights of the house enfolded him as he shut the door, the cat meowed in welcome, and he felt as if he'd been gone much longer than one night. The rich smell of roasting beef tickled his stomach, reviving the appetite he'd lost yesterday. A good sign, right? He laid his keys on the table inside the door, shed his trench coat and hung it on a peg, turned—

And saw Brie standing expectantly in the hallway.

God, she looked good. She wore her off-the-shoulder, short red dress, one he really liked, and she'd left her hair down, but that wasn't the true difference. She seemed to glow, from the inside out. Her smoky blue eyes sparkled with not-quite-restrained joy, even as she chewed her lower lip. He'd never seen her look so glad to see him, except maybe at their wedding, and it eased much of the pain he'd carried since yesterday. Things truly could work out, if she was this willing. Once they talked.

"I'm home," he announced, finally.

"I'm glad," she admitted. "I'm sorry you got hurt. Even though nothing happened—"

He raised a hand; he couldn't bear to hear it again. "I believe you. Leave it."

She came closer, smelling of roast beef, spicy perfume and Brigit. "It couldn't have been pleasant."

"No," he agreed. "It wasn't. I don't..." This was moving too fast—but what was he afraid of, lying? "I don't want to lose you. Us." It wasn't a lie.

She lifted a hand to his face, spread its warmth against his rain-cooled cheek. Her open expression hid nothing, though she did look excited. His own wooden posture relaxed. "Can we start over?" she whispered. "Brand-new? No more secrets?"

It was exactly what he wanted to hear, exactly what he needed. "No more secrets." And he drew her into his arms, just a hello hug... but instinctively he skimmed his hands down the tight silk of her skirt. It ended too quickly; lace teased his palms. Heat flared in him, familiar and sultry, painfully intense. It seared him when she raised up on tiptoe and leaned into him, her breasts arching forward from her raised arms, and flicked her tongue across his lower lip.

Yeah, they were supposed to talk. To hell with talking. This... this was practically a family tradition.

He bent and kissed her, deep, knowing. His Brie, who'd added mystery to his life, who'd filled his too-staid days with adventure and his nights with passion. She moaned into his mouth, burned him where she pressed against his need. She arched back from him, drew her nimble fingers down the collar of his shirt, parted the buttons as if by magic before pushing it from his shoulders. She stroked her hands down the bareness of his arms until linen caught at his wrists. Only then did he release her, let the shirt drift to the floor. As long as his hands were free, he yanked the red dress over her head and dropped it to the ground, as well.

She shook her loose, fiery hair free, while he stared.

Her lace panties were a bloodred color, almost purple, with a little black bow at each flared hip. Her skin still held a warm, golden glow from summer afternoons; he let his gaze lick down her gracefully curved legs, then back past the triangular scrap of the panties and up to where more bloodred lace held her breasts, high and round, with another tiny black bow tempting between them. The pendant her grandmother had given her gleamed there, and he followed the chain to the inward curve of her neck, her small chin, her heart-shaped face. Tendrils of red hair licked at her cheekbones. Those smoky eyes fairly sizzled at him from beneath her flared brows.

His heart raced, flooding him with hunger for her. His breath scorched into his lungs, caught in its hurry. When she unzipped his trousers, he let them slide to the floor, pulled off his socks with his feet as he stepped out of the wrinkled pants, caressing her with his eyes all the while. He loved her breasts, and the way that omnipresent pendant shone gold where it lay...

Huh. That was odd.

He must have looked at that medallion a million times— pushed it out of his way when making love to her, slid his fingers over it when sharing a shower, seen it at the breakfast table and beside him in the car, and yet the design suddenly looked...

Dizziness tripped him, and he caught himself with his hands on her bare shoulders, followed through on the motion by dipping his head again, taking her mouth with his. She responded willingly to the kiss, leaning back against the hallway wall to take his unbalanced weight until their lips parted. She was so beautiful, so seductive, standing before him like that in the golden light, and he wanted her....

*But what is she getting from it? She seduces you. She hides something...*

Fingers of anger mingled with his desire; he winced them away. Of course she wanted him. She was his wife.

As if from a distance, the cat yowled to get out.

"Steve?" Brie asked, her voice nudging away the dizziness. "You okay?"

Of course he was okay; this was about as okay as it got! Since he had her backed against the wall anyway, he trapped her more deliciously by leaning into her searing softness, again catching her lips with his own. Her nails scored lightly down his bare spine. He stretched under the delicious shiver of it, watching her beautiful, hungry face through his lowered lashes.

And that pendant, precariously balanced on the slope of her breast. *That pentagram.*

Her image blurred beneath him—same Brie, different circumstances. Lying on a forest floor at midnight, lit by the orange wash of a nearby bonfire. Witches' circles. Sexual rites. *She bewitched you, damned you.*

She stroked her hand around his ribs, across his taut nipple, down his stomach, branding him with her touch. He reached out, and when his fingers brushed the velvet curve of her breast she made a purring sound, not noticing that his true goal was the pendant. Her own scorching touch slid lower down his belly, skimmed the bulging front of his skivvies, flame to flame.

*What demon doth she take as her lover?*

She parted her lips, smoky eyes half closed, so sexy, so evil.... One of her legs skimmed up the side of his own, her thigh catching precariously against his hip. Her torturous, wondrous hand slid lower still, and his heart nearly stopped beating.... Oh, yes, she knew just what to do. She'd been practicing forever, hadn't she? She'd had such experienced partners....

*What oath hath she given him?*

His fingers closed around the pentagram, so tightly that its curved edge bit his palm, but he didn't notice. His mind was too full of the awful, erotic images of an orgiastic witches' Sabbath, glimpses of Brie tangled in the throes of ecstasy with...what? Evil. He could make out others, people half-recognizable in their bacchanal; the skinny blond arms of Moonbeam Beaudry; a wolfish man with a black ponytail, atop his sister...

But he didn't recognize her, any of them. Only the golden-skinned redhead, seductress, demon's whore....

*We art bewitched.*

And it felt good.

# CHAPTER TEN

*Be she a witch, or be I mad? I am not mad.*
— The Journals of Josiah Blakelee

The cat cried more persistently.

Steve took her mouth again, rougher this time, and Brie let him—his coming back to her made everything right. She'd packed away her magical tools—the sixteenth-century brass goblet, and the carved ashwood wand, the ebony-handled dagger and the hand-copied Book of Shadows that she'd had to keep hidden—and shipped them to her mother this morning, before she could change her mind. And she'd wanted to change her mind even as she turned away from the counter at the shipping office, but now she was glad.

Finally she could be the woman Steve wanted. Finally she could have the secure, happy family of her dreams. The second pregnancy test had been positive. She would tell him while they made love.

One of Steve's hands lay fisted against her breasts, but the other grazed down her ribs, and he pressed her head back against the wall with the force of his kiss. Only when he ground her lips into her teeth did she yelp a soft protest. "Ow...careful, hon."

"Don't you want it?" The length of his body trapped the length of hers while she caressed his hard thigh and hip with her leg. His roaming hand squeezed behind her to yank open the clasps of her bra.

"Oh, yes," she gasped, pressing harder against him.

His hand escaped from behind her, pushed her bra aside to catch a handful of her breast with unfamiliar roughness. "Be it on your head," he warned, before his mouth again captured hers. The heat of his breath seared her as he ravaged her mouth; she gagged on his thrusting tongue and twisted her head free. What the hell was *that* supposed to mean?

He kissed the length of her throat instead, nibbled too sharply on her shoulder. She lowered her leg to stand on both feet. Romeow's wails distracted her; something was wrong. "Wait."

"'Tis your will, this," he breathed, heavy against her, nipping again. "'Tis what you meant."

"No," she gasped, wincing away from his hot mouth, from his teeth. "I've changed my mind. Get off." She pushed at his shoulder. He didn't budge. Something burned against the back of her neck; her amulet chain. His fist clutched her pendant, pulling it tight like a noose. Her pentagram, she realized, her mind in turmoil. She'd forgotten to mail her pentagram. When she twisted against him to get free, he only moaned and held her harder. "Damn it, you're scaring me...."

He laughed, but it wasn't a familiar laugh. "You are the one damned. You tempt men to sin, tempt me to sin." His head moved downward, toward her breast, but she didn't want him touching her. She didn't even know him! She braced herself to knee him in the groin, but hesitated to actually hurt him. "Steve!"

Only then did he rear back from her, not enough to release her, but enough to look down at her, his face gaunt in the artificial light, his sharp brown eyes reflecting it in their empty depths. "Don't call me that," he commanded.

And he yanked her pendant, hard, so that the chain cut the back of her neck before snapping.

She cried out; he hardly noticed. *Don't call me—?* Lords above! The man against her—her husband?—didn't even blink as he clawed downward at her panties, eyes glazed.

She did try to knee him, then, but he blocked the blow with his thigh. The lust in his sharp eyes mixed with a fury that, in Steve's face, doubly frightened her. "Steve!"

He raised a hand to strike her; she caught it, clawed at his wrist. Fear became volatile power; she could feel it roiling within her, hot and pulsing.

But she'd given up being a witch.

Not until the next full moon! She aimed the energy at the bastard who had her trapped against the wall. Power burst from her. And scattered.

She was out of practice. Fear made for unstable energy. And he was shielded.

Stunned into momentary stillness, she stared up at his sneering face, in shock. She'd tried to blast him, and he was psychically shielded . . . and Steve, objective and empathic, had thinner natural shields than even average mundanes.

Against the quivering push of her grip, he lowered his own hand to her face. She felt warmth on her fingers, his blood, as he grasped a handful of her hair. "Bitch."

She tried to pull away from him, but only managed to crack her head against the wall behind her. She breathed hard, tried to raise more energy in the rhythm of her panting while she stalled. "Steve." It came out closer to a whimper than she would have liked. But where *was* Steve, her Steve? He couldn't do this, couldn't let this happen, how could he—

His mouth twitched in anger, and he clutched her hair harder, pulling at it. "No."

Deep, stabilizing breaths. She plumbed the recesses of her memory for childhood protections from when she had fully accepted her magic, grasped what power she could from the waxing moon, tapped her own life energy. If he was shielded, it was her will against his. "Steven, stop it. Now." This time it was a command, not a plea.

His awful, shadowed face lowered toward hers. With him holding her hair, she couldn't wrench away. But she could stop him, she *would* stop him. With each silent repetition, her power—arcane and otherwise—surged.

Her warning came out a low, forceful growl. "Steven Christopher Peabody—stop!"

He paused.

And she released his bloodied wrist and pushed him away with both hands and enough power to blast an un-shielded man across the room.

He made a strange, gasping noise as he collapsed back from her, hit the hallway wall immediately across from her, but she didn't stop to watch. Drained, light-headed, she stumbled for the front door. Steve might still catch her, but she made the doorway without being intercepted, and barely paused to grab his trench coat on the way out.

Romeow was scrabbling at the base of the door, as if trying to dig his way out; when she yanked it open, he streaked into the night. She pushed the door shut, prayed he didn't tear it open again. The wind moaned through the tall, dark trees as she shrugged into the coat, inside out. Where could she go? She swayed, barefoot in a thin puddle of rainwater; mist blurred the streetlight at the corner. Humidity pushed at her, thick in her heaving lungs, trying to suffocate her. No car keys, no license. Where could she go, when she had to flee her one true sanctuary—

She heard a scream inside, a masculine bellow of rage that, though muffled by the door, seemed to echo from every realm, from here to the netherworld.

She hurled herself at the other door, several feet from her, and gasped a wail of dismay when the knob wouldn't turn. "Open, damn you!" As good as a lock pick; it clicked around in her hand, and she fell through it, slammed it shut behind her, turned the lock again—and sank, empty, to the floor.

Even dark, Sylvie's living room had an airiness about it; light from the upstairs hallway spilled down the stairs, picking up yellow on the walls and golden wood on the floor. Safety. She could feel the welcoming wards as surely as if she'd pressed through a force field. Safety? From Steve?

Sagging back against the door, she began to tremble, and she barely noticed the voices above her.

"Wait, Syl, it could be—"

"It *is* Brigit," insisted her sister-in-law, and feet padded quickly down the steps. Then Sylvie was there, her hair mussed, wearing jeans and a misbuttoned, oversize shirt. She tried to lift Brie into her fragile embrace, raincoat and all. "What's happened? What is it? Come on, sit here on the mama-san. Is Steve all right?"

Brie could barely stand, couldn't stop shaking; she felt as if her very life force were flickering erratically, and not just because she'd overextended herself. Steve. She clenched her teeth against a hot surge of bile in her throat. Steve.

A strong male arm eased behind her. She spun with a gasp, luckily too weak to blast Rand Garner as she'd blasted Steve. "It's just me, ma'am," Sylvie's fiancé said soothingly. She noted vaguely that he was wearing jeans, fly unsnapped, and little else. His black hair hung long and loose, past his shoulders, nothing like Steve. She let him support her as she followed Sylvie's lead toward the pillowy mama-san couch.

"Where's Steve?" repeated Sylvie, her tone sharper now.

"He—" *Deep breath, Brigit. Ground yourself.* "He—"

Blanching, Sylvie whirled to go check herself.

"No!" Brie didn't want to scare her, but she couldn't let the kid walk into anything. Sylvie adored her older brother. "He's changed. He's...not himself. I don't think you should..." She looked at Sylvie's fiancé, who nodded and loped toward the door.

"I'll go check," he volunteered. "You stay here, Syl, and get her something to drink."

Steve's sister nodded reluctantly, pulling Brie closer into her protective energy, her own strength. "It'll be all right, Brie. It will. If anyone can fix it, we can."

But Brie continued to shake, because they couldn't make it okay.

Even Steve couldn't do that, now.

Hot, scalding needles. Eyes closed, forehead propped against hard tile, Steve realized that he was in the shower, half dressed, and he welcomed the punishment of the scorching water. He knew he'd dragged himself up here. Like the last time, when he'd come home to Moonbeam, he could remember everything—blurry, hesitant, nauseous. Everything.

Some of the water on his face wasn't from the shower.

He heard a door— Oh, God, not Brie! His stomach clenched at the thought of the one person he dreaded seeing; the one person he'd die to see again, safe and happy and with no memory at all of what—

His eyes opened, and he blinked at the billows of steam that writhed like ghosts around him. Of course she'd remember. Just like him.

A dark shape came at him through the searing fog—he hadn't drawn the shower curtain, the whole bathroom was soaked—but he didn't recoil from it. He'd welcome a murderer, a monster. Punishment. Instead, he got Rand Garner, twisting off the faucets, cursing the heat. "You crazy?"

"Get out," said Steve, but he had no heart left to put into his words. They stumbled from his mouth, pitiful things.

Distaste curled the lips of the man in front of him. Why not? Steve couldn't begin to imagine the scene from a stranger's point of view. The flooded room smelled like vomit. And here he stood in his skivvies, trembling, soaked.

"No." Garner grasped Steve's arm, yanking him forward so that he had to either step out of the tub or fall out of it. He stepped, but only from habit. "Man, you look like death. What the hell happened over here?"

The full force of the memory sent Steve diving for the toilet again, but he didn't have anything left to throw up. He was vaguely aware that Garner laid a damp bath sheet over his shoulders.

He'd tried to rape her.

It wasn't like he'd blacked out. It wasn't like he hadn't been there. He'd recognized the pentagram, and somehow all his rage at the way she'd been lying, all his suspicions about black magic, all his feral desire...somehow it had snarled up inside of him, gone wrong. Somehow—no matter how it happened—he'd lost control. He'd hurt her.

His stomach might be empty, but that didn't mean he wasn't sick. He was. Very, very sick.

He leaned his forehead against the toilet seat, so weak he could barely sit up. He was a kind of sick that made him dangerous.

He heard his uninvited visitor pace into the bedroom, shuffle through drawers and return. "Here," said Garner. "I've got some clothes laid out for you, okay? Let's get you dry, and you'll feel better. C'mon."

Because he didn't have the strength to resist, Steve rose and allowed himself to be led out of the foggy bathroom to the bed. His clothes. After staring at them for a minute, he began to put them on mechanically.

"Your wife's over at our place," said his helper. "Weirdest thing. Syl jumps up and says she's got to get dressed. Then the front door slams open. I coulda sworn I locked it, too, but it was Brie. She's pretty upset." Garner paused, while Steve finished buttoning and zipping by rote. "Not that you're up for the Zen award yourself."

Dry clothes did feel better. Well, maybe *better* was too strong a word. He felt more directed, though. More competent. He stepped to the closet, stared at the revolver case for a moment, then looked away to pull his suitcase from the upper shelf.

"Wait a minute," protested Garner. "What are you—?"

Steve didn't bother answering. He just opened the bag, opened his top dresser drawer, scooped out a handful of underwear. Then he snagged some shirts and trousers from the closet and draped them in, hangers and all. He threw a pair of shoes on top. It was his worst packing job ever.

"You oughta come over." Garner followed him into the bathroom again. Steve grabbed his toothbrush, deodorant, a bar of soap. He noticed something gleaming on the tile, in a puddle of tepid water. "Let your wife know you're okay."

Steve crouched, retrieved the medallion and stuffed it in his pocket. "I'm not okay," he pointed out, standing, and staring at the misted mirror. Narrow face, small, frantic eyes—who the hell was that? "Look!"

But even as Garner obeyed, the mist cooled away from the glass surface, revealing just the two of them. He really was crazy! Shaken, not bothering to explain his command, he carried his toiletries to the suitcase. He mashed his finger pushing some hangers out of the way while he closed it. Good. "I don't think I'll be okay for a long time."

He grasped the handle, dragged the case off the bed, headed down the stairs. Yeah, he was running away. And not just to protect Brie, as he'd nobly assumed yesterday. He was running away from the truth of what he was becoming.

His wallet lay in the heap of clothing, his and Brie's, that huddled on the floor, in the hallway leading to the kitchen. The only thing that made him get it was the thought of having to come back here. Unless he could conquer the dark anger deep within him, he couldn't trust himself ever to come back.

His car keys sat on the little table where Brie had kept the Halloween candy. Garner stopped him at the door, a hand on his shoulder. "Hey, bro, listen."

Steve waited. Sooner or later this longhair would get out of the way, and he could get the hell out.

"You need a place to stay. Go by my cottage. I can hang at Sylvie's until you've figured things out, okay? Lemme give you the key—"

"No." Steve pushed by him and out the door. The wetness of the grass squished between his toes as he crossed the shadowy lawn. Mist fell steadily around him. The scent of dying, rotting vegetation filled his lungs.

He could hear Garner at his heels, but he didn't look back. What if Brie was at Sylvie's window? He threw the suitcase into the Volvo, slid in and shut the door.

Rand Garner stood on the lawn, shifting uneasily from foot to foot. "Call me, if you need to talk," he called. "I mean, if you want to..."

Steve took a deep breath, started the engine, gripped the steering wheel too hard. He nodded. "Yeah," he said, and repeated it loud enough to be heard outside. "Yeah. Thanks."

Then he went onto the gas and got the hell out of there, only turning on his windshield wipers halfway down the block.

*The bellow of rage used every last shred of Josiah's strength. Peabody's abhorrence of their actions dislodged him from the dominion of physical existence, and Josiah immediately wasted away to little more than a presence, a thought form, a shade behind the Veil, on the other side of the portal.*

*She had distracted him again, as had the witch before her, and he had missed his chance to have vengeance. To have justice. The vixen had eluded him....*

*And now she baited him.*

*A door slammed open, scattering vibrations throughout the house, and the bright, angry glow of the witch appeared within her wards. If only he could reach out to her, if only he could snare her.... But he could not.*

*The frustration tore at him.*

"Who are you?" *He sensed that the witch screamed the words, though he mainly felt their spiritual echo as she moved through her home.* "What are you? What are you doing to Steve?!"

Saving him. *But Josiah had not even the strength to send that thought at her, as he had his questions.*

*'Twas like the bitch to taunt, to tease. She stood so close that her fury flared through the portal. He could almost taste it, but could do nothing but regather strength and hope his host body—one of his host bodies—returned.*

*There were things a physical being could do other than sin. He would not give in to temptation next time.*

*Next time, he would finish it.*


''Why Steve?'' shouted Brie, spinning full circle round in the middle of the workroom. When she got no response, she stalked back into the house, through the kitchen and living room, where she noticed that someone had picked up her clothes, and up the stairs. ''Why not me?'' she demanded of the ceiling, the walls, the floor—of whatever was ruining her life.

Sylvie hadn't wanted to let her return to her home, even after giving her a sweatshirt and a pair of too-long sweatpants to wear, even after Rand Garner came back with the news that Steve had gone. But as soon as the paralysis of shock began to wear off, as her strength began to return, she had known exactly where she had to go.

She had to go after whatever was manipulating Steve into not being Steve anymore. That was the only possibility, right? Possession or haunting or whatever, something other than Steve had tried to rape her.

She would not believe otherwise. Hadn't he said *Don't call me that* when she'd called him Steve? Steve wouldn't have hurt her. He wouldn't!

''Who are you?'' She knew Sylvie could probably hear her. Well, she had Rand for comfort. In the bedroom she turned completely around again, sure that whatever it was had to be lurking nearby, in the corners, in the vents. If it wanted a fight, she'd give it a fight it wouldn't forget, even if she had to expend every drop of life force in her. "Why?" Her voice echoed back at her, from the three-mirrored vanity, from her wedding photo. "It's me you want, isn't it? Then come after *me,* you sonofabitch! Come after *me!*"

She stumbled, dizzy from spinning, and fell to her knees. Nothing took her up on her dare. Nothing was here.

"Why don't you leave us alone?" she whispered to the emptiness around her.

It had left because Steve had left. Whatever it was, it existed through Steve. And she was its catalyst. As long as she stayed away from Steve, he remained himself. But when they got together...

They couldn't even be together.

She swallowed back a curse, a true curse, not spoken by anyone of her blood for generations. Even were she willing to suffer the karmic ramifications, she had no name toward which to direct her hatred.

And she had to remember the baby. Lords above, the baby! Here she sat, offering herself up to who-knew-what like a sacrificial lamb, albeit a poisoned one....

"I won't let it get you," she whispered at her lap. "I won't. Not you or your daddy. You've got—" The irony of her intended words struck her. Wasn't that where all the trouble started? "You've got my vow. May my powers desert me and my allies turn against me if I don't do everything in my power to protect you."

She couldn't just be rationalizing Steve's behavior, projecting his sins onto some phantom. She refused to believe that. It was something alien to him, surely.

Still on the wood floor, Brie let her face fall into her hands. She didn't know what she'd do, how she'd survive, if so hateful an entity was of Steve's own making.

* * *

Steve blinked sleepily at the rusty mirror in the *Sentinel*'s dingy bathroom. He hadn't been shaving, both because he'd left his razor and because he didn't care, and for the first time he noticed that he'd passed the "Miami Vice" look and now just appeared scruffy.

It had been the longest five days of his life.

Brie had tried to call, several times, but he wouldn't pick up. If he talked to her, he'd want to see her even more than he already did, and if he saw her, he might hurt her. Again.

He couldn't risk doing that to either of them.

Sylvie had shown up at his office the day after the incident, confused and hurting for them both. But if Brie hadn't told her what had happened, he sure as hell wouldn't. He could hardly admit it to himself, much less to his kid sister. He'd given her his credit cards to pass on to Brie, and asked her to have Brie change the locks.

"You've got to get help," Sylvie had said, like he hadn't figured that out, but he made her leave when she started talking New Age mumbo jumbo about strengthening his aura. What he *didn't* need was to excuse his behavior as something other than his own. He might be a sonofabitch, but he was a sonofabitch who took full responsibility for his actions.

Or he'd thought he did. But Sylvie wasn't the only member of the Friends of Brigit contingent he'd had to deal with. The day after Sylvie spewed that nonsense about shielding himself, Mary, who'd never tried to disguise her delusion, had shown. "If I could work a spell to help you, would you give permission?"

That had been Wednesday, two days before the paper went to press, when nothing could slow him down. This stopped him dead.

"Do I have a choice?" he'd asked, wary.

She'd nodded, little pentagrams bouncing from her ears. "Then *no.*"

She'd said his closed-mindedness wasn't helping his marriage. He'd noted that she wasn't even married. A low blow, and for which he'd apologized. She'd brightened immediately—"Make it up by letting me try the spell?"— and he'd thrown her out before thinking to ask her how much Brie was into this nonsense.

He'd remembered to ask Cy, who'd sensibly appeared the day *after* they went to press. She'd set a black rock on his desk. "This here is going to magnify any protective energies in the room," she stated. "You've got the choice, throw it out if it scares you. But it makes a fine paperweight. Have a nice day."

"Brie doesn't really think she's a witch?" He'd meant to ask more subtly, but Cypress was already leaving. She paused in the doorway, threw an embarrassed glance toward Louise's desk, and closed his door behind her when she stepped back in. "Son, you just keep pushing her about this, and you might as well buy her a plane ticket back to her mama—it'd save you both heaps of heartache. Now keep the rock." And she left, too.

He'd almost phoned Sylvie back, sure he could get her to talk, and then realized he was avoiding the real issue. Brie could think she was an avocado, and it wouldn't excuse his attacking her. That wasn't something he'd broken and could replace. God knew it wasn't something he could kiss and make better. No one made greeting cards with a sentiment that covered this kind of mess, and flowers would feel like a sleazy bribe.

Yet they couldn't stay in this limbo forever. At some point he'd have to talk to her. At some point they had to move on—he just didn't know where to. Time wasn't waiting for him to get his act together, so no more diverting himself with side issues. He missed her, like he'd miss an amputated limb. Last night he'd found himself driving by the house, hoping for a glimpse of her, like some stalker. He'd returned to the office with a fresh case of self-loathing.

Leaving the bathroom, he threw his towel over his shoulder, stuck his hands in his pockets and headed past empty tables and silent Sunday desks to his own office. Instinctively his fingers closed around Brie's pendant. He knew he should return it, but he savored the connection, some small piece of her that he could still touch. Besides, he admitted, flopping into his chair to look at the medallion, something about its Celtic knotwork fascinated him. Something he vaguely remembered noticing from *that night.*

Slipping the pendant beneath a sheet on his legal pad, he found a pencil and ran it lightly across the surface. The rubbing of the intricate design showed up as a negative, two-dimensional instead of three, and he stared at what he finally recognized, what his subconscious had seen for over a week.

He used the pencil to trace one single thread within the curving knot, and found himself drawing a perfect penta-gram.

That again. But he realized that, in the back of his mind, he'd assumed Brie had been drawn into this witch-idiocy by Mary or even Sylvie. She'd had this since the day he met her. Which meant that she'd not only kept secrets—distrusted him—from day one; she may have led his sister astray!

He sat back, pushed a hand through his hair incredulously, and only belatedly realized that he didn't feel any of that terrible, red fury. He felt disbelief, maybe disappointment, but he didn't have enough information to be angry. This still wasn't the main issue...but could it somehow be connected?

For the first time in a week, he felt in control.

He hoped that wouldn't make him careless.

He feared it would.

The mansion sat silent—silent as death, which fit, since someone had died there. Brie never felt uncomfortable at estate sales. All antiques outlived their owners. Besides, she'd been raised to see death as a natural part of life, a spoke on the ever-turning Wheel.

And yet, descending the thick-carpeted stairway, surrounded by paneled walls, high ceilings and a crystal chandelier, she felt not merely out of place, but ill at ease...as if there were unseen eyes upon her. She looked around, saw nobody but a white-haired lady picking over a table of knickknacks, and shook the feeling off.

She'd thought that, since her determined vigil at the house had revealed nothing, she ought to get out and make some acquisitions for Craft Queen...to add to the other renovations she hadn't finished. But estate sales were fairly well picked over by Sunday, and being away from the house made her feel guilty. The evil might choose today to show itself, and she wouldn't be there to see, and understand.

*Like that's going to happen.* If nothing else, this week had shown her that it wouldn't show up without Steve. It never had. Even when she'd felt it in the workroom, when she'd heard it in the bedroom, it might have just been Steve.

It could, she had to admit, *be* Steve.

She paused, her scuffed sneaker hovering over the last step. Was that a footstep? Stale floor-wax, furniture polish, and perfume laced empty air; she saw nobody. Even the knickknack shopper had moved on.

She felt them again, the unseen eyes.

She hurried through the ornate dining room and into the kitchen, where she'd last seen the estate solicitor. The big room, with its island in the center and its near-empty rack of tagged copper pots, sat equally silent.

A floorboard creaked. She spun to look around her, torn between anger and fear. Surely *it* couldn't have followed her here, independent of both house and husband after all!

In the deathly silence of the kitchen, she heard another creak. Then another.

They stopped.

Brie cut back through the dining room, through the front foyer, and escaped onto the porch, looking back. Nothing behind her—at least nothing visible. She paused, and shuddered off the chill of fear. This last lonely week had just made her paranoid.

But when she spun away from the looming structure to the crushed-shell drive, the path to her Blazer was blocked.

By a gray Volvo—and Steve Peabody.

# CHAPTER ELEVEN

*Why would man so lower himself, but that woman
hath evil power o'er him?*
                    —The Journals of Josiah Blakelee

Steve leaned against the side of his car, arms folded across
his chest, quiet as a hunter outwaiting his prey. Which
didn't mean he hadn't been inside the house only minutes
before. He was, after all, a runner.

Brie felt, as much as saw, his eyes upon her, and she
shivered inwardly. She gathered her nerves—and her scattered energies—more closely to her, and descended the
steps from the porch to confront him.

A long white drive, beneath a tunnel of sentinel oaks,
bisected the mansion's sprawling front lawn. Its oyster
shells crunched loudly beneath Brie's sneakers. Despite the
cooler weather, a blanket of humidity smothered the par-
ish, lending an air of unreality and expectation. Though
several sparrows fluttered about, and a rabbit sprinted
away, she and Steve seemed alone in the world.

She didn't give him time to speak. "How did you find
me here?"

"You sometimes do estate sales on the weekend," he
noted. "My paper ran the ad for this one. When I called
home and got our machine, I made an educated guess."

"Why?" She realized she'd spoken sharply, adrenaline
still burning through her, setting her nerve-endings ablaze.

He stiffened at her tone, then glanced away, just long enough to lose the defensive stance. He looked tired. Several days' growth of beard darkened his jaw with soft brown shadow. "Your messages said you wanted to talk . . . and I wanted to know that you're all right."

Despite the need to stay on guard, the concern she so badly needed lulled her. "You didn't have to lurk."

"Was I lurking?"

"In the house."

Steve glanced toward the mansion. "In there? I'm not *that* crazy." He sounded sincere. Then again, he'd sounded sincere before he'd . . . before he'd attacked her.

"I forgot that estate sales make you uncomfortable."

"Espe—" He broke off his comment, but not in time. *Especially this one? Especially here?*

"What?"

"Doesn't matter."

"What happened here?"

He still had his arms folded, like a child in a china store careful not to touch anything. "Right after we moved to Louisiana, remember? A woman's ex-husband killed her after he lost custody of their kids. Litigation held up the distribution of the estate."

Nausea closed her throat. "Killed . . ."

"More than half of all female murder victims are killed by—" He looked away, but she knew the rest: *their husbands or boyfriends.* "Never mind. Bad idea. We'll talk later."

"No." She put a hand on his arm; the tension that hardened it beneath his buff-colored sweatshirt surprised her. He didn't look back. "I do want to talk. I have—"

*I have wonderful news, darling. We're finally going to have a baby.* The perfect announcement to make in the shadow of a home where someone had died in a custody battle—and to a man who was leaning toward domestic violence himself. This raised bad timing to new heights.

When she didn't finish her sentence, he looked back at her. His eyes searched hers, curious.

"Not here," she decided finally, with a shiver that had nothing to do with the sixty-degree temperature.

"Not at the duplex," he said, with equal finality, and quickly added, "Someplace public."

Like meeting a stranger from the personal ads? "You're joking."

"I won't—I don't want to hurt you again."

She tightened her grip on his arm. Despite the pain and suspicion in his eyes, despite the tension that billowed off him, despite everything that had happened...this was *Steve*.

"I can take care of myself." *At least until full moon on Saturday*. If she went through with her ritual. She had to go through with it. "I'm not afraid of you."

He met her gaze with his own, so familiar and yet so unnaturally disturbed, intense. "You should be."

"I'm not. But I don't want to hurt you, either." *My lover. The father of my child.*

*My tormentor.*

Finally he unfolded his arms, only to grip her shoulders, almost too tightly, perhaps to prove his point? "If it comes to that, Brigit, you hurt me. It would be self-defense, and anything you do to me couldn't hurt so badly as what I might do to you. Promise." His voice fell hoarsely. "Hurt me."

She felt smothered, disoriented by his intensity. "I never had you pegged as the kinky sort," she teased, in a clumsy attempt to lighten up.

It didn't work. Steve let go of her, turned away from her, slammed a fist onto the roof of the car—the hollow thud frightened a flutter of sparrows from a nearby oak.

She knew she should remain wary, knew she could no longer trust him . . . and yet what she wanted to do, more than anything else, was to touch him. To hold him. To be held, in the futile hope that this *was* the Steve she'd married.

She gingerly extended a hand, touched the soft sweatshirt on his hard back. He flinched away, as if burned.

"The park," she suggested. Did she detect a slight tip of his head, a flicker of eyelashes to indicate interest, in his otherwise stony profile? "The weather's bearable. Let's have a Sunday-afternoon cookout."

Surely he remembered their earlier picnics on their apartment balcony. He *had* to remember.

When Steve finally turned his head to look at her, some of her fear melted before the spark of warmth in his eyes. Perhaps the fire wasn't dead, after all.

Perhaps it had only been banked.

They drove separate cars back to the duplex, but Steve stayed on the curb, making room in his trunk, while she ran inside for the food and charcoal. On a regular outing, she would have playfully challenged him for the right to drive. But he seemed to feel so out of control in other areas of his life, she wanted to give him this.

The drive out to the old park, on the other side of town, was silent until she flipped on the radio to quell her impatience. When a singer exulted about hearing the beating of an unborn heart, she had to look out the window to hide a tenuous smile. Bad timing or not, this news would be delivered—so to speak—properly. It merited celebration.

Stagwater might not have a twenty-four-hour supermarket or its own cinema, but it had a beautiful park surrounded by pines and oaks, with a children's playground and a large gazebo and several picnic areas with grills. Steve parked the Volvo near one of the empty sites, close enough to several families to keep him on good behavior—and, after killing the engine and setting the brake, looked hesitantly toward her.

Brie dropped her eyes when she saw the earnest longing of his gaze. It wasn't a sexual longing, but something much more intimate. He wanted *her*—her company, her approval. And, after almost a week away from him, she wanted his.

Suddenly, in the eye of the madness, this felt like the nervous first date they'd never had.

As if realizing that he'd been staring, Steve hurried out of the car and around to Brie's side, opened the passenger door for her. She fought an amused smile as she took his proffered hand and, for once, let him help her out. Even after they'd carried the cooler and the cookout supplies to the cedar-plank table, she couldn't shake the feeling that they were dancing around one another, so uncertain, so self-conscious, that they hardly dared say anything at all.

And yet something very important needed to be said.

She settled herself on the table so that her legs dangled, and dug into her purse. By the time Steve had set the burnbag in the grill, pushed up his sleeves and held out his hand, she'd found her lighter for him. She'd given up smoking after a week, years ago, but she'd carried a lighter ever since. He lit the bag, handed the lighter back, and she returned it to her purse. It was their own choreographed dance. He still hadn't cut his hair, she mused, watching how the autumn sunlight, breaking through a latticework of tree branches and pine needles, caught in its chocolaty waves. He'd lost more weight.

And yet, in the fresh air, serenaded by birds and insects while he threw someone's leftover hamburger bun to a squirrel and kicked pine cones out from underfoot, he looked as attractive as ever he'd been. *Lord of the Greenwood....*

The burnbag on the grill flared, and Steve turned back to her with a self-conscious grin of triumph, as different from the angry, accusing bastard who'd attacked her as any man could be. She found herself returning the smile, drawn into its sincerity and warmth, just as she had been on the day they met. *This* was the man she loved, the man she'd married, with whom she wanted to raise her family. Then, just as she drew breath to tell him about the baby, his smile faded to an expression of seriousness.

"I've been thinking about separation," he admitted. Her breath caught, hurtful, in her lungs. "Not in the abstract, I mean us. Separated, for...a while."

"We are." She drew her feet up onto the table with her, so that she could hug her jeaned knees against the jolt of his announcement. "We've been separated all week."

He found a stick, poked it at the burning charcoal. Trees shaded the picnic site, despite the sunny afternoon, and the flames cast orange highlights and shadows across his face in a way that didn't so much threaten as disturb her.

"It's not like we can pretend nothing is wrong," he cautioned. "I can't just come home. Not the way I've been recently."

"Recently. I've known you for three years, Steve. I can tell that the way you've been isn't you." *Literally, in fact.*

"It's sure as hell not who I want to be," he admitted, as much to the fire as to her. "Lately I've been...out of control." She could see his difficulty with that admission.

"And I won't put you at risk by coming home until I've figured out what's wrong. Right now there's still a chance, I hope there's still a chance, that if we work through some things we can save our marriage. But if I came home, if I turned on you again..."

"But I'd know it's not really you," she countered, distracted by her suspicions of possession—and how she could possibly release him. *Especially if I'm no longer a witch.* "You sound as though our marriage is in serious danger. But I know it's not you doing this."

His eyes cut over to her, strong, intense, burning. "But it *is* me. Who else, if not me? It's like the darkest part of me, unloosed, like all of my morality and my love for you are paralyzed by this anger. Like being drunk. And you know I don't consider being drunk an excuse for bad behavior, either."

Had the wind suddenly turned icy? "Except that you haven't been drinking."

"I must be doing *something* that's messing me up! If it's stress, I'm the one who's been working too hard. If it's an allergic reaction, or a chemical imbalance—I went in for tests, by the way—then I should have made a connection long before now."

She blinked at him for a stunned moment. He'd gone to the doctor for tests? She'd never even considered the possibility of a medical cause for his moodiness. Could her supernatural upbringing have biased her outlook more than she'd realized? The dichotomy between Steve being possessed or Steve being deep-down cruel expanded with this third, hopefully less extreme possibility; he might just be ill!

Trust her husband to arrive at so reasonable a conclusion. She belatedly noticed the flames dying to glowing coals, and opened the cooler. While she retrieved a plastic bag full of hot dogs, Steve said, "It usually happens around you." She turned to him, searched his face, but found no censure there. He had merely stated the obvious, and looked apologetic about even having done that. "Have you gotten a new perfume lately? New shampoo, new soap?"

She shook her head, handed him the hot dogs. "I'm using the same stuff as always. But if you're looking for a pattern, your... spells... usually happen at the duplex, too."

"We haven't done any major repairs. I checked for radon, lead paint, the whole nine yards, when we moved in. Have you noticed any new plants in the yard, or had an exterminator in?"

She shook her head. She hadn't, and no sick house syndrome would explain the voice in the bedroom, or the nightmares. "What if it's not a chemical, or a gas?" She let her legs dangle again. "What if you're picking up on some kind of... negativity?"

"Be serious," he chided, almost sharply, as he turned away to put the meat on the grill. "Even if you believe in that junk, don't push it on me, okay?"

*Even if you believe.* He hadn't questioned, but stated. She knew that her friends had approached him about allowing them to help him magically. Since ethically they could do nothing without his permission, she'd all but asked them to. Yet she felt a surge of annoyance at his expected condescension, and had to bite back a retort. She was giving up all arcane ties within the week, wasn't she? Why fight to defend what she couldn't admit to, and wouldn't keep?

"Whatever it is," she said, making herself change the subject, "if it's something medical, like allergies, if you're having some kind of attacks, then I can hardly hold you responsible.''

He sank onto one of the cedar-plank benches below her while the meat cooked. ''Logically, maybe. But, Red, how often do I have to come at you before emotionally you start to connect me with anger, or fear, or pain? And what if I did hurt you, really hurt you? Fault or not, you'd still be hurt, and I won't risk that.''

''It won't happen,'' she assured him, but sudden fear for what was at stake, for the baby, dammed her tone with uncertainty. ''And if it does, I can defend myself.'' But could she? Once she relinquished her abilities, could she really?

''I don't plan on giving you the chance. Even if you could handle it, I couldn't.'' He shook his head while she slid down onto the plank bench opposite him. ''I used to be so dammed cocky, never thought there was anything I couldn't handle. But this might be it. And, Brie, it's getting worse. Every time one of those . . . those moods hit, *I* get worse. So I'm not coming home. Not even for you. Not until I have this thing licked.''

It wasn't an easy decision for him. The pain in his brown eyes, before he glanced away to hide it, both wrung her heart and soothed her own fears of rejection; he wasn't staying away because he wanted to. ''We can date, can't we?'' she suggested, attempting a smile.

His own reluctant ease—his eyes falling closed for a moment, his lips pressing into the faintest of smiles—rewarded her. ''Yeah,'' he agreed, reaching across the table to take her smaller hands in his. ''In public. Or with chaperones. We'll do Thanksgiving next week with Sylvie, and—''

Then a look of concern struck his face and he lunged to his feet to turn the crisping hot dogs.

Despite the unpleasantness of the decision, the dubious security of having decided *something* raised their spirits. While the hot dogs finished cooking and the rolls toasted, Steve confessed that he'd been to not only a doctor but a therapist, as well, who was referring him to a psychiatrist in New Orleans. He hated living in his office, and if the moods continued, he admitted, he'd probably have to get an apartment.

"Can we afford all this?" She retrieved the potato salad and spoons while he slid the done dogs onto paper plates, but paused, hands in the cooler, when he said, "I can sell the Volvo."

"But—" But he loved that car. She knew that argument wouldn't pass his practicality test. "You could never get that good a car for that price again!"

"Doesn't matter. If we really get into financial problems, I'll..." He had to take a breath for this one. "I'll unload the *Sentinel* and send résumés out to city papers again. I'll do anything to get us through this, Brie. You've got to believe that."

He'd barter away every precious piece of his life to regain control of himself. But she didn't believe he'd agree to an exorcism. "Move?"

Handing her the mustard, Steve repeated, "Anything."

"The paper's been your dream since college. And Sylvie's here. There's the duplex—we were going to renovate it back into a single house, if we had a big enough family. And we wanted to raise children in the country."

Steve's grin was that of a near miss. "Thank God that isn't an issue yet. We'll shelve those plans until we've gotten past this, and—" His grin froze on his face, wavered against unblinking shock as he stared at her.

And she knew that she hadn't hidden her expression well enough, that she wouldn't get to make the celebratory announcement she'd always planned. "Guess what?" she said, her voice hoarse.

Oh. Oh, my. There were no words. Steve let his hot dog fall back onto his plate and stared at his wife. She was pregnant? They'd wanted children from the moment they were married, and even before then had only used birth control for the sake of pragmatism. After the wedding, they'd assumed she would conceive fairly quickly. Instead, they'd waited for over two years, with a few false alarms, but no success. By now, they'd started calling the front bedroom "the front bedroom" again, instead of the original "the baby's room." They hadn't bothered to hang the duckling wallpaper he'd found, and the antique cradle and dressing table Brie had restored remained under dust cloths. They'd stopped trying to think of names, and had already considered the possibility of infertility counseling.

And now that all hell had broken loose, she was pregnant. *They* were pregnant. Brie, who sat chewing her lip, looking pale and anxious, wasn't the only one responsible! It was the lousiest possible timing.

And, despite that, the best possible news. Steve began to fight his broad grin—he hated grinning like a goon—then let it have its way. This was a baby! He could look like a goon for once. "Are you sure?"

She nodded, wary relief lighting her blue eyes. "I've been to the obstetrician already, and she said we're both doing fine. I wanted to tell you—"

He nodded before she could explain why she hadn't told him. It was the same reason he was fighting back his physical reactions, so as not to scare her, so as not to risk harming her. He hadn't been there when she first suspected. He hadn't been there when she found out, or for the doctor's appointment. His moods, his damned insanity, had robbed him of a week he'd longed for, and he would never get it back.

*Whatever* it took, he would get past this. And in the meantime, he wasn't about to waste the time he had left! "Wha—I mean, when—?"

"Before Halloween."

"When are you due? Wait, nine months..." He started to count it out.

"July." Though still glowing, she sat fairly still. It wasn't until he'd asked his fourth question, "So when did you find out?" that he noticed this conversation had all the spontaneity of an interview.

"Just a few days ago," she assured him, her expression watchful, waiting... disappointed.

He hadn't wanted to scare her, but... He stood, came around the table, and extended his hands. When she took them, he helped her to her feet, looked her up and down. The same Brie, with her sultry curves, her slanted brows, her smoky eyes, her wildfire hair. She'd be even more beautiful, heavy with his child.

She lifted her chin against his examination, and he cleared his throat. "I've never asked this before, but...may I hug you?"

Confusion clouded her heart-shaped face. Then he could see understanding dawn, and she nodded. She was biting that lush, kissable lower lip of hers again.

*Down, boy. All hormones at full stop.* He was *not* going to lose control with her. Not again. So, when he drew her to him, his fingers caressing her palms, he did so very slowly. As she leaned into his chest, and he raised his arms to embrace her and protect her, he used smooth, careful motions. And then, the real test, he allowed himself to lean his cheek onto her hair and breathe in the spicy scent of her.

He'd missed her. He'd missed her so much, it hurt. "It's going to be okay," he murmured, feeling her arms encircling him, her hands splaying against his back. He tried to believe the words, for his own sake, as well as hers. "We'll make it okay."

She nodded. So far, so good.

"However," he warned, "there *is* one thing I've got to do." And he waited until she looked up at him, her expression somewhere between curiosity and suspicion, before he scooped her up and spun her around, squealing and laughing. "We're going to have a baby, Red!" As he set her feet carefully back onto the pine-needle carpet, she lifted her face to his, and he met the warm heaven of her lips instinctively—

Then backed away, cutting the kiss short. What if it happened again? What if he did something, and hurt not only her, but the baby, too? "Um...let's not push our luck, okay?"

Impatience clouded her eyes, but she nodded. "As long as you aren't using this mood-swing business to shirk your marital duties, Mr. Peabody."

That she'd joke about such a thing, after the way he'd abused her that night in the hall... Again Steve pulled her to him, and this time he buried his face in the curls at her shoulder. "I love you, Red," he murmured. "I really, really love you."

They settled onto the same bench, side by side, to eat their cold dinner, and spent the rest of their sunlit afternoon roasting marshmallows and planning, and tried to believe they'd be all right. But even when they walked hand in hand beneath the trees, or sat on a bench near the playground, they stayed in sight of the other families. And as those unknowing chaperones packed up to leave, as the sinking sun shot the sky through with autumnal red, he and Brigit packed up their supplies, as well. Their self-imposed curfew was a suffocating reminder of the problems they had yet to face.

When he pulled up to the curb in front of the duplex, Steve made sure Sylvie's Pinto and her fiancé's Volkswagen were both parked nearby before he cut the engine. Chaperones. "I'll carry the cooler, okay? You don't need to be lifting things."

"I carried it to the car this afternoon," Brie protested, opening her own door before he could get to her side of the car.

"Well, you shouldn't have," he scolded, helping her out. "The first three months are the most critical, aren't they?"

"But what about when you aren't here—" Her expression sobered as they both remembered that he wouldn't be staying.

To get through the moment, he lifted his palm to her cheek, drew his fingers across the fine hair at her temple. "Draft Garner to do anything I can't. He might as well get used to being treated as family, right? Abuse the man."

"Right." She ducked away to snatch the bag of cookout supplies—marshmallows, skewers, lighting fluid—from the trunk before he could stop her. Knowing it wasn't heavy, he contented himself with retrieving the sloshing cooler and following her up the walkway to the front door. Despite their problems, today had gone well. He hadn't felt his control slipping, even once. There shouldn't be any problem with him popping in just far enough to dump the cooler, popping back out, and maybe giving his wife a chaste goodbye kiss on the porch, in the fresh air.

It wasn't the kind of kiss he wanted to give her, he mused, watching her cute bottom sway in front of him as she climbed the steps to the porch and unlocked the door, but it was all he'd allow—

*She wants you. She wants your soul.* The thought struck out of nowhere, and, accompanying it, a red haze blurred his peripheral vision. He almost dropped the cooler; his hands clenched around it with a death grip as he fought the spell.

Where the hell did *that* come from?

Brie turned in the open doorway, cocked her head. "Steve? Are you okay?" Some of the haze faded at the purr of her voice.

But not all of it.

"Yeah. I'm fine." Hurrying now, feeling as if he were facing a deadline, he took the last few steps to the porch and deposited the cooler there, then backed away. It didn't make sense—he hadn't even gone into the house, he hadn't even been standing next to Brie. Delayed reaction to her company, perhaps? Or something else? Something psychological?

He backed away from the porch, wishing Brie didn't look so frightened, too concerned with getting away from her to put her at ease. Only once he'd reached the car and leaned against the Volvo's shiny gray flank, did he dare take a breath. And another. The red haze faded. He was okay.

For now.

Brie had followed him, frowning now. "Yeah, you look fine."

"I just..." He raised his eyes to hers, wishing she'd just let it go, just let *him* go. "I've got to get back to the office. Are *you* going to be okay? You haven't had any trouble here, have you—other than with me?"

"Steve, what's wrong?"

"I overdid it today, pushed too hard. I'll call you tomorrow, okay?"

Her nod of agreement came too slowly for his comfort; she was making connections that he wasn't getting.

Probably witchy stuff. He'd forgotten to ask her about that! Well, he wasn't about to start another discussion, not with the need to escape pounding through him. "Are you carrying your pistol?"

She shook her head.

He took a deep breath. "Carry it. For me."

And he hoped to God he didn't mean that literally. Against his better judgment, he began to extend his hand, but then he snatched it back before she could meet his reach. No. No touching. He was leaving her alone tonight.

She continued watching him as he escaped around to the driver's side, got into the car. When he raised a hand in farewell, she didn't return the gesture. Well, he couldn't blame her, he decided, pulling away from the curb. She probably thought he was as crazy as . . . as he did.

So be it. Whatever sick part of him threatened his control also wanted her. *It* wanted her. And he wouldn't let it have her.

Even if that meant he couldn't have her, either.

# CHAPTER TWELVE

*Confession brings salvation—why wilt she not be saved?*

—The Journals of Josiah Blakelee

On the curb, in the posttwilight darkness, Brie watched the Volvo's taillights shrink, then turn away. He'd left her again. But this time he hadn't left in anger. This time he'd been just plain scared . . . of the house? Or something that lurked within?

Allergies. Chemical imbalances. Stress. Like hell! She'd had a delicious refresher course in Steve Peabody this afternoon, and whatever—whoever—had demanded and accused and abused her these past few weeks could not have been him.

She'd bet her life on it. She'd bet her baby's life on it.

She returned to the duplex, her senses, all six-plus of them, alert for hostile presences. She felt nothing. The bastard was waiting for Steve.

*It's getting worse,* she remembered, hurrying upstairs to the bedroom. No arcane mysteries there. Whatever happened repeatedly would happen more easily. Practice makes perfect. And Steve's plummeting self-esteem didn't offer him much protection, either.

*She* knew it wasn't him. It was something in the house that connected with him, not him. But *he* still didn't know.

She grabbed an overnight case from the closet, and on second thought took the revolver, as well, charming it to be used by no hand but her own before she slipped it into her purse. Then she collected a change of clothes, assorted toiletries and, once back downstairs, a bottle of sparkling cider and two goblets.

Despite Steve's noble martyrdom, he needed her. Not as her husband, or her baby's father. He—*Steve*—was suffering.

And she meant to do something about it.

She'd had several backup plans in case he wasn't at the *Sentinel* offices—there were hotels in Slidell she could try—but when she pulled into the paper's front-yard parking lot, Steve's lonely sedan awaited her.

No lights were on in the refurbished house, neither before nor after she cut her engine. No lights came on when, descending from the Blazer with purse and overnight bag, she shut the truck's door.

It couldn't be much past seven o'clock. On a Sunday, on this side street, 7:00 p.m. had all the activity of a tomb. Pulling her jacket closer against the November night, she hurried to the front door and tried it.

Unlocked. Tsk, tsk, tsk. Frowning, she slipped inside. Only traces of light from a streetlamp provided any illumination, but her eyes quickly adjusted to the shadows, picked out the receptionist's desk, the layout tables. She moved, catlike, to the open doorway of Steve's office.

She recognized his silhouette first, leaning over the desk, hands propping him up, head hanging. He'd removed his sweatshirt, though he wore a white T-shirt against the chill, and shadows defined the planes of his muscled arms. Then she heard his ragged breathing.

"Steve?"

He spun so fast that some papers fluttered to the floor, and in the darkness he stared at her, eyes equally adjusted. "You shouldn't be here."

She dropped her bag beside the door, which she shut and locked behind her. "This isn't the duplex. We're safe."

"You can't know that." When she took a step forward, he took a hasty step back, tall and dark and oh, so handsome under the cloak of night.

"I know it," she assured him, shedding her jacket. "You know it, too."

She advanced.

He retreated, eyes narrowing. "Cut it out, Brie. And stay back. You're not the only one at risk here. Our baby's involved in this, too."

The baby they hadn't yet celebrated, created from a love she feared losing. But she *wouldn't* lose it. Not yet. And she wouldn't let Steve reject this bit of healing, either.

This wasn't magic. All rules were off.

She began to unbutton her blouse. Despite Steve's protests, she could see desire cloud his eyes, lightly part his lips. She'd been right. He wasn't just afraid for her. He was desperate for her.

"You wouldn't hurt the baby," she said soothingly, freeing the last button so that her blouse fell open, held in place only by her breasts. A momentary vision of the last time she'd undressed before him—of his harshness, his anger—choked off her breath. She swallowed away the fear, and stepped on the heel of first one sneaker, then the other, to pull them off. She did the same with her socks, to stand barefoot. She would *not* fear him.

Steve drew a deep, shuddering breath. "Don't do this. I can't risk it again, Brie. I can't let you..."

"See you lose control?" She unsnapped her jeans, unzipped them. "See deep down into the part of you that you

hide from everyone else? I've seen it, Steve, and I don't
mean recently. I saw it when you accepted a road trip from
a complete stranger. I saw it under the mistletoe, at your
parents' house. I saw it in the back seat of my car.'' She
tugged her jeans off her hips, taking her panties with them,
and stepped on the cuffs to climb out of them, as well.
"It's okay with me. It's part of what I love about you. Always have." She kicked the pile of clothes toward the door.
"Always will."

She could see his battle in the delineation of his muscles
beneath the smoothness of his skin, in the rise and fall of
his lean chest, in the sheen of sweat that caught the light.
She hoped by the Old Ones that he understood. The cru-
elty of such teasing would be unforgivable, if he didn't
come to understand.

"I—" The word emerged as a bare croak; Steve gulped
and tried again. "I don't want to..."

"To take advantage of me?" she finished softly, remembering similar words the first time they'd ever made
love. His eyes narrowed. He was remembering, too. "Give
me some credit," she recited. "I'm not that easy to take
advantage of."

And then Steve surged forward, caught her up and set
her on his surprisingly cluttered desk as he took her lips
with his own. While his mouth branded hers, she arched
back, trusting the support of his strong, bare arms to keep
her from falling, and spread her legs to feel the rub of his
jeans on her inner thighs, the hard heat of his arousal
against her own. Her lips felt swollen when his mouth left
hers, when his kisses seared down her neck, onto her
breasts. His new beard tickled her tender skin.

"Yes," she moaned, wriggling with delicious frustration. "Yes, Steve. It's okay. Risk it...."

The support of his arms seemed to lessen. She realized he was laying her gently on the desk, and she scooted backward, sending paperwork flying, to make room for him.

She smiled to see him pause long enough to toss a glass-framed photo and an empty coffee-cup safely onto the cushion of her overnight bag and jacket. Definitely Steve.

He stripped his shirt over his head, revealing the damp planes of his chest, the lines of his shoulders and arms. Then, as she lay back, waiting for him, he caught her foot.

She leaned up again, on one elbow. "Steve!" But then he kissed her instep, lingering there, and she felt herself melting back on the desk. "You tease!" came out a purr.

"Me?" He gasped the word somewhere between her ankle and her knee. Somewhere along her thigh he murmured something about glass houses, but he wasn't very coherent, and she didn't pay attention. Flickers of desire licked through her at every nip, every kiss.

Then he moved higher, and she nearly bolted off the desk. "Steve!" His strong, artistic hands caught her legs, held her still—not that she had any plans for escape. Hadn't *she* planned to seduce *him,* though? Hadn't she...

Mmm... His light whiskers brushed against her inner thighs, and yet more sensitive areas; the brand of his mouth seared through her physical body and into her astral being, into her soul. She moved helplessly, writhed against the pleasure of him. Her own gasps drowned the sound of his breath and became moans, mixing his name with a plea for...for...

Licks of heat became electric charges, increasing in voltage, higher, higher. Now Brie did break from his grip, convulsing off the desk with a cry of ecstasy. She didn't realize how loud she'd been till the sound echoed back at her, till she reluctantly grounded herself.

She moved one foot restlessly, accidentally kicking more papers to the floor, and tried to catch her breath. Slowly the stars faded and her eyes readjusted to the shadows.

Steve stood, propped against the edge of the desk, watching her in that intent, observant way of his. "I," he told her, with an almost-smirk, "am not the only one in this marriage who loses control."

She narrowed her eyes at him. His almost-smirk became the real thing, triumphant. Not because he'd mastered her, she realized. Because, in some small way, he'd mastered himself, and brought her pleasure instead of pain.

She reached for him, and he boosted himself up onto the desk, over her, and lightly into her arms. At some point, while she'd returned to earth, he'd shed his pants. *Good.*

"Let's lose control together, Mr. Peabody," she told him invitingly, lingering on the pleasure in his tired eyes—and the love.

He hesitated. "The baby..."

"The baby will be just fine, as long as its careful, thoughtful, wonderful father loves its mother."

"Wonderful mother," he murmured back. "Who can drive wonderful father wonderfully crazy."

And she did.

Much time and a half bottle of cider later, as they cuddled beneath a blanket on the patched couch, Steve still didn't understand Brie's certainty that he wouldn't attack her. True, he seemed to lose his temper exclusively at the house, but... "You couldn't be sure why. Something in the air, or power lines too close, or whatever, could have lingering effects, like alcohol in the bloodstream."

Brie stretched more comfortably atop him, her bare legs twining with his, and tucked her head onto his shoulder.

"You thought it might be psychological," she murmured sleepily. "Don't psychological problems have triggers? Like when someone sees a snake, and it reminds them of something they've repressed, and they freak? Maybe the house is your trigger."

"But it wasn't a trigger when we bought it?" he asked into his hair. He loved her so much it scared him.

"S'just a theory," she protested with a yawn.

"Good point." Tightening his hold on her, he re-adjusted his precarious perch on the couch. And he'd once thought doubling on a twin bed was difficult! "Couldn't hurt to mention it to the psychiatrist when I see him. That, and those Puritan nightmares."

Brie stiffened slightly atop him. "Those what?"

He stroked a hand down the indentation of her spine and let it rest on her bottom. "Nothing important, Red. I've just been dreaming about Pilgrims and such, that's all. Probably some twisted connection to Thanksgiving."

"Except..." She paused, as if measuring her words. "I've been dreaming about Puritans, too."

A strange chill shivered down his own spine, lifting the hair at the back of his neck. Then again, their camping out in his office did have a sort of sleep-over feel. "You're joking," he said, his tone challenging. "Tell me the one about the escaped psychopath with a hook for a hand."

She didn't say anything. Had she gone to sleep? "Red?"

"I've been dreaming about Puritans, too," she repeated, an edge to her voice. "So maybe we're picking up each other's thoughts. Or someone else's."

Or more likely Sylvie was playing a book-on-tape of *The Scarlet Letter*, or *The Crucible*, and they'd subconsciously heard bits of it through the wall. Still, since he'd already hurt her feelings once in the past minute or so, he kissed her head and let her have the point. "Maybe."

She relaxed again. "Would you consider hypnosis?"

Geez, humor her once, and she had him seeing some Malcolm the Magnificent! "No, I would not consider hypnosis."

She propped herself up slightly away from his chest; if he squinted, he could make out the heart shape of her face beneath a froth of curls, the shine of earnest eyes. "It's not like anyone's going to make you bark when you hear the word *zoo*, you know. Lots of psychiatrists use hypnosis."

"Mine won't."

"You don't have to do or say anything during hypnosis that you don't want to."

He didn't want to be annoyed; he wanted to savor this oasis of peace between them. But, sheesh! "Where'd you become such an expert?"

And he could have sworn she paled, before she laid her head back on his chest. "Never mind," she whispered.

Witches, he remembered. He should, after his visits from the Weird Sisters. Brie really thought she was a witch. It was almost a laughable concept, except that whatever it entailed for her had resulted in deception....

And he didn't want to be annoyed, damn it! He took a deep breath of her light, spicy scent, and released it slowly. By the third deep breath, he'd relaxed—well, relaxed as much as he could on this vinyl couch, with the nearest thing he could want to a sex kitten on top of him. When he confronted her with this witch thing, he would probably hurt her feelings, not that his weren't pretty bruised on the issue. He didn't want to face that tonight. At the rate things were disintegrating, it might be a while before they got together like this again.

"Don't have any nightmares about escaped Puritan psychopathic killers with hooks for hands," he whispered, to break the tense silence that had enveloped them.

She nudged him in the ribs. "Don't tease."

He gathered the blanket more closely over her shoulders and listened to her slow breathing. In her sleep, she nuzzled more intimately against him; he cuddled her to him and turned his head on their single pillow, trying to fall asleep himself. His mind had so much fodder, though. The baby. Brie following him here. Shared nightmares. And morning, when he would ask her about the witch business.

In the darkness, he blinked, frowned. Huh. Puritans. Witches. *The Crucible.* He saw the oddest pattern.

It took a long time for him to fall asleep, wondering what possible connection could exist between his life and the Salem witch trials.

Brie woke slowly, stretching under a thin blanket, and realized that she wasn't at home, but alone—*on a vinyl couch.*

She sat up, squinted at the room around her in the pre-dawn light, and then remembered. Steve's office. She'd come after Steve last night, and they'd made it through another twenty-four hours. If they kept this up, they'd survive this hellish month yet. She still didn't know what to do about the entity at the house. A full-scale exorcism was always a possibility, as was just cutting their losses and selling the place . . . to a really competent priest.

*Things that you run away from always catch up—three times as powerful.* Her mother had been telling her that for as long as she could remember. Brie stretched and swung her bare feet to the floor. "Not if you run fast enough, Mom."

It couldn't be much later than six, but Brie realized that Kent and Louise could come in early. Gathering the blanket around her like a toga, she found her overnight bag and changed into fresh clothes. Listening at the open door from Steve's office into the main foyer, she heard the sound of running water and knew that he was taking a shower. Though she wanted to, she realized that he'd probably disapprove of her joining him, this being his place of business. For all that she loved him, Steve could be a bit of a prude.

Then again, when you grew up with family friends who danced nude in the moonlight, prudishness had an awfully broad definition.

He'd be embarrassed as hell if Kent or Louise, or their high school intern, Timmy, guessed the kind of wild passion they'd shared here last night, she thought with a smirk, surveying the wreckage. An overturned pencil cup scattered pens and #2's across the floor, on top of an avalanche of mixed-up papers. At some point Steve had moved the phone to safety, and it sat smugly on the windowsill, but his clock radio hung off the desk by its cord, announcing the hour as . . . She had to tip her head to read it. Six forty-three. Smiling to herself, she began to restore some order before any observant reporter types showed up and assumed vandalism.

The papers, scattered willy-nilly, made the largest mess, and she hadn't a hope of organizing them, just stacking them neatly. For that reason, she almost missed the heading at the top of one of Steve's legal pads. She'd tossed a handful of invoices atop it before the words registered in her mind. With a knot forming in her stomach, she slid the yellow notebook from the stack.

"Full moons," he'd written, and then he'd listed the dates of every esbat for almost a year, following some of them with question marks and some with notations—about her. "Videos at Sylvie's," said one. "Cypress's house," said another.

Her soul became very, very still as she turned the page. The heading there read "Sabbaths." "Sabbats," she corrected in a broken whisper, staring at his list of Craft holidays. He'd written "Candlemas" for what her family called Imbolc, and "Lammas" for what she knew as Lughnassadh. But he got the dates right. And he knew she'd been out for them.

She hadn't been able to fool him, after all. A grudging respect for his intelligence—for his own innate abilities—warred with a deeper horror. He didn't just suspect, but *knew*. She'd gone so far without breaking her oath, and now, mere days from her becoming an ex-witch, he knew her secret.

She flipped past more pages of Steve's scrawled handwriting reducing her childhood traditions, her deep-seated beliefs, *her heritage,* to little more than a dispassionate collection of information bites. Her upset began to surface as temper; she bit it back. If she would be willing to reject those beliefs, what harm could his analysis cause?

Then she came across the rubbing from her pentagram.

Her hand raised instinctively to her neck, which had felt bare without Grammy's heirloom in the past week, as she stared at the familiar pattern and the darker pencil lines tracing the five-pointed star within it. He'd taken it. He'd taken Grammy's pentagram. And he'd let her worry, and apologize, and even plan to abdicate an integral part of her being, while he'd known that she was a witch!

He might not believe—but he knew.

She heard the door swing open behind her. "Geez, I *have* let this place go. You don't need to do that," Steve protested, tossing his towel over the back of his desk chair to crouch beside her. She tried to push the yellow pad back into a stack of papers. Too observant—why did he have to be so observant?—he looked sideways at her, tugged a corner of the legal pad back out to see what it said, then looked back at her.

He wore brown trousers and a slouchy khaki shirt, as yet without tie or shoes. His damp, uncombed hair, combined with the scraggly-soft fur of his whiskers, made him look older, woodsy and, with his high cheekbones and intelligent, velvety eyes, noble. *The Holly King,* she thought again. Samhain had passed almost a month ago, so why couldn't she forget the legend of the Lord of the Greenwood, the forest god, and his annual death for the sake of his people!

"Want to talk about it?" he asked quietly.

*May my powers desert me and my allies turn against me should I ever reveal my association with the Craft, or any of its secrets, to an unbeliever.* Had she been responsible for Steve's enlightenment? Had this last month been her retribution for carelessness? Maybe. Hopefully not. He remained a cynic, and she remained sworn. She shook her head.

Steve released an impatient breath; he took the papers and began to gather more. "*I* want to talk about it, Brie."

"I can't."

"Can't, or won't?" He stopped in his brusque cleanup to fix the intensity of his gaze on her; when she said nothing, the pressure of silence building in her chest, he went back to gathering papers. Sarcasm tinged his next words. "Can you maybe nod or shake your head if I ask questions? Stomp your foot to tell me how long this has been going on?"

*You stole my pentagram.* Even that was likely too damning an admission, now that he knew what it was. "Don't."

"You know I don't believe in this hocus-pocus. Is that why you never told me? What Steve doesn't know can't hurt him? Or was it maybe some kind of power trip, sneaking around behind—" He plopped a stack on the desk, then turned back to where she still knelt on the floor, took a deep breath. "Tell me. *Please.* I'll try to understand."

Her chest ached with the longing to tell him. But there must be a way, some way, to satisfy him and yet reveal nothing. "When I was young, I made a promise never to talk about certain things. Whatever I may or may not have been involved with, it's over!" Almost over, she reminded herself, belatedly standing. She had five days until full moon.

He shook his head, expression tightening, completely *un*satisfied. "No, I've got a problem with that argument, Red. If you haven't been straight with me since the day we met, how—" He paused, hand outstretched for emphasis, as if reconsidering his words. He went with them, spreading the hand. "How can I trust you to be straight with me now?"

*Because I'm carrying your baby. Because I want to be the woman you fell in love with. Because—* She wouldn't stoop to such tactics. Her Celtic pride wouldn't let her. "I *was* straight with you. I told you. When we got engaged, I told you there were secrets—"

He pushed off from the desk. "No! That's a cop-out. You *know* it's a cop-out! You said there were secrets, but I thought they were past. You never said you'd go on creating them." By the time he finished, he was pointing at her, scowling. They both noted his pointed finger at the same time.

He dropped the hand, then, his movements stilted, combed it through his hair. "Look," he said, more quietly. "Why don't you go home? We'll talk about this later."

Now there was something to look forward to! "I can't talk about it later, either, so you might as well get this off your chest."

He turned partially away from her, looked at the ceiling. "Brigit, *go home.*"

"Why?"

"Because I am really, really angry right now."

She could see the truth of that. His jaw was clenched, he seemed to be sucking on the inside of his cheek, his stare had turned belligerent. Instead of folding his arms, he'd shoved his hands in his pockets, but the posture was defensive all the same. It wasn't the kind of anger he'd been showing at the house—neither explosive nor violent.

This was one hundred percent Steve. Funny that it had taken her three years to see her husband at full boil. Maybe Mom had known what she was talking about. *Makes me wonder just how deeply he's buried his dark side...and what it's been doing while he wasn't looking.*

"So? Maybe it's healthy, every once in a while."

The look he cast her was one of pure disbelief—his mouth all but hung open. "Oh, yeah," he scoffed. "Right. C'mon, you of all people should know the consequences."

She folded her own arms. "Oh, no. *No.* You're talking about what's happened at the house, and that wasn't you."

"For crying out loud, we have *covered* this—"

"And you haven't convinced me yet that it's you, and not something influencing you!"

Steve paced to the window, spun, came back. Licking his lips, he surveyed the ceiling as he leaned back against the desk's edge, folded his arms in front of him. He was, Brie realized, seething. And she didn't feel threatened at all.

Not physically. But emotionally....

"The reason," he said finally, clipping his words, "that I have not convinced you, Brigit, is because you seem to have a hitherto-unobserved penchant for avoiding reality."

He was trying to intimidate her with words. She cocked her head to one side, holding her stance.

"Considering your fascination with ghosts, and hypnotism, and voices—"

"One voice."

"And *casting spells,* for chrissake," he finished. "You'll have to forgive me if I find your theories about my psyche just a little hard to swallow!"

She leaned toward him. "Don't condescend!"

"Give me a reason not to!" He'd leaned forward, too. Their faces were inches apart, eyes blazing, breath rough.

"One." She held up a finger before turning her back on him, collecting last night's scattered clothing from his floor and stuffing it into her bag. "You *used* to trust me."

"Maybe I didn't know you."

"Exactly. You didn't." Gathering her things, she stood and faced him again. "But you still trusted me, from the first moment you saw me. *Instinctively* you trusted me."

"Oh, geez." He hung his head, as if under the weight of her foolishness. She knew it wouldn't last long. It didn't.

When he looked back up at her, she said, "You take a while, Steve, and you figure out what your instincts are telling you about me. If you'd just *listen* to them, you'd know that I'd never hurt you, and that I'd never willingly lie to you, and that I know what I'm talking about with—" *With the ghosts, the hypnotism, the voices, and the spellcasting. With the hocus-pocus trash.* She didn't dare say something so close to a confession. "You'd know *me!*"

And she stalked out of the office, praying that he'd do just that. Surely his instincts could put him right. Except that she was beginning to doubt that Steve would—could—ever go purely on instinct.

Even to save their marriage.

# CHAPTER THIRTEEN

*That she would choose death with the devil o'er life
with her husband, rankles greatly.*
                    —The Journals of Josiah Blakelee

*Again he reached—again, he found naught.*

*Time had passed since his last failure, since the witch
seduced him into carelessness. He had regained strength to
extend himself again, to cross the tear in the Veil into the
physical realm. And for naught. But for one whiff of the
husband's presence, during the early dark-hours of the day
past, he'd found no vessel for his vengeance. He needed
eyes, hands, voice, to finish God's work, and his own.*

*Stymied, Josiah used the delay for thought. He knew all
too well the travesty of hangings, and the little good they
did. Was he not proof of that? The papists, for all their
heathenish ways, had it aright.*

*There was but one true end for a witch.*

Instincts! Steve shook his head, then turned and kicked
the desk. Then he cursed and fell against it, because he was
still barefoot. *Instincts!*

What about information? His *facts* told him that Brie
believed some supernatural idiocy of which he definitely
did not approve. Not that her life should run according to
his approval, but should his disapproval exclude him from
her life?

And that she'd dismiss his very real tempers as some kind of possession scared him. Had she based her trust on that, when she'd risked coming here last night? Did she think she could just snap her fingers or wiggle her nose, say "Bibbity-bobbity-boo" and make all their troubles go away?

Thank God he *hadn't* turned on her!

He rubbed a hand over his unshaven face and wondered how things had gotten so complicated. He wasn't who he used to be; it was *not* a change for the better, but at least, he hoped, temporary. On the other hand, Brie wasn't who he'd thought she was...and she never had been.

*You'd know me.* Weren't they supposed to have reached that stage a while back?

With a groan, he crouched and continued to straighten his office, wanting it in order before his co-workers arrived. Maybe he and Brigit would have done better to remain lovers, since that seemed to be the only relating they excelled at, lately. *You trusted me from the first moment you saw me,* she'd said...but maybe, just maybe, that hadn't been "trust," but something that rhymed, something that started with an *l* instead. How else could he have gone so long, never suspecting her weirder leanings?

His life had become a sixties sitcom.

And maybe now, with her pregnant, was not the time to be thinking like this. They'd meet somewhere safe, somewhere public, and talk some more. Hell, Thanksgiving was in three days. They'd meet with Sylvie, be a family, and...

And continue to live a lie? He hated to lie.

He'd thought Brie did, too.


"So the cat's out of the bag, eh?" Mary sat in the lotus position atop her massage table, surrounded by white

walls, blue counters and cabinets and posters with sea-
scape scenes and affirmations. The taped sound of waves
mingled with the gurgle of a fifty-gallon aquarium. Today the blonde wore clam-diggers and a white T-shirt that
read "Magic Happens." Brie loved that T-shirt. "Well...at
least you don't have to worry about *that* anymore."

"Wrong." After leaving the *Sentinel,* Brie had hesitated to return to the house. She hated to run to Sylvie,
who, as Steve's sister, already felt neatly trapped in the
middle of this whole situation. Then she'd found herself
heading for the Wellness Club, built in the renovated remains of an old, failed spa, where Mary Deveraux worked.

Though a newbie witch, Mary had her own special tal-
ents.

"This just makes it worse, don't you see?" Brie continued, shifting her weight in the massage chair she occu-
pied. Made to encourage its occupant to lean forward, the
structure included a padded chest support and a large,
doughnut-shaped pillow for one's face. She crossed her
arms against the chest support to stay upright. "My vow
didn't specify 'unless they find out anyway.' I still have to
stay silent, even if Steve knows—sort of—what he's talking about."

"Enough to be dangerous," Mary added.

"And all I can give him is 'No comment.'"

Mary winced. "Ow."

"Not the ideal situation to support a marriage." Now
she did lean her face into the terry doughnut. "Not the
kind of marriage I wanted, anyway. And it's my fault."

"Nuts," protested Mary, and Brie heard the light thud
of her friend's bare feet hitting the floor. "You've done
your best, eh?" Her hands found Brie's shoulders, not
massaging so much as sensing.

"I as good as sicced the circle on him." For a moment, she almost corrected herself—ex-circle—then gave up the pretense. They'd somehow always be her circle, whether she remained a witch or not. Just as Steve would always be her husband.

Even if he left her today.

"I might as well have hit him over the head with my wand, screaming 'I'm a witch, too! I'm a witch, too!' Neither you nor Cypress excels at subtlety."

She felt Mary sweep her hair away from her neck. "That's a fact. But remember *why* you sicced us on him." The massage therapist found and followed a line of tension down Brie's shoulder. "It was to help the old boy out."

*Old boy.* Despite relaxing under the gentle pressure of Mary's fingers, she made a face, then reared back from the massage chair. "Puritans! I'm not the only one having witch-trial dreams. Steve's been dreaming about Puritans."

Mary made the obvious connection. "*Salem* witch trials."

"Can you do a past-life reading, look for a connection?"

Instead of answering, the blonde leaned back against a counter. "Past-life reading?"

Turning, Brie nodded. When her friend looked down, as if uncertain, she added, "You know—preincarnation?"

"I know, I know. It's just..." Mary met her eyes, apologetic. "I already tried to see. Not past-life—I'm happier looking into the future than the past, 'cause the future can be changed, you know? I did some tarot readings that didn't turn up much, so I tried flying solo—without visual aids—a coupla times."

This didn't sound real positive. "And?"

"And I kept getting lost. Mixed up. Like a temporal knot. First I think I'm looking at the present situation, or a possible future, and then I'm slurped up, turned around, and I'm somewhere else, I think in the past." The younger woman shifted uncomfortably, as if torn between defending and understanding her confusion. "I know I should look around, try to get my bearings, but it freaks me so bad that I end up back in myself, sealing my aura and thankful to be home."

"It freaks you because you've lost control?" Brie asked, equally confused. *A temporal knot?*

Mary shook her head and folded her arms protectively so that her shirt just read "Magic." "No. 'Cause it has to do with death. I *know* death shouldn't bother me like this," she added quickly, as if Brie had protested. "I *know* it's all part of the cycle of things, birth to death to rebirth, chapters in a larger story. But I'm not like you, I wasn't raised with the idea of reincarnation, and quantum time. I'm not fearless and sure of myself...."

"Wait a minute." Brie dismounted the massage chair, staring at her friend. "Fearless and sure of myself? Me?"

Mary peeked up through her lashes and her blond bangs, her hazel eyes hesitant. "Uh-huh. You walk in and out of estate sales without a blink. You've been staying in that house, when you *know* something's not good in there. You make a decision, friend, and you go for it."

"Like the way I've gone back and forth about being a witch?" Or not being one. Or being one. Saturday would bring the full moon. If she still meant to quit officially, once and for all, she had five days left.

Mary hiked herself onto the white counter, like a kid on the side of a swimming pool, and swung her feet. "That's different—you *are* a witch, always have been. Only reason you're thinking to cut yourself off for good is 'cause of the baby."

"And for Steve." Brie stuffed her hands in her jeans pockets. "Though now that he knows, it's kind of like closing the barn door after the horses are—" Then she paused, and narrowed her eyes. "When did I tell you about the baby?"

Mary grinned, and pulled her tanned feet onto the counter, as well, to hug her knees. "I said the tarot didn't turn up *much,* not it didn't turn up *anything.* Congratulations."

The baby. If she wavered about quitting the Craft, hesitated to sacrifice so much for a man as closed-minded and stubborn as Steve, all she had to do was remember the baby. "Now you know why it's so important that Steve and I work through some of..." She spread out an arm, as if that could encompass the enormity of what they had to work through. It didn't even begin.

"Don't worry 'bout what I saw," Mary told her quickly, seeming to think she meant only the otherworldly problems. "Just 'cause I have a hang-up 'bout death doesn't mean nothing. I was looking at the past, eh? It's like you said about the antiques. Death and the past go together. Nothing eerie or upsetting there."

Brie watched a striped angelfish swim across the aquarium. "Depends on if it was your own death." The fish darted to the bottom, to examine the decorative wreckage of a tiny pirate ship. "And if someone killed you."

She wished she hadn't suddenly thought of a hanging tree—and Steve's dreamed voice. *Confess.* What if this wasn't the first life in which she'd sacrificed for him...or the largest sacrifice?

Mary lowered her legs again, eyes widening. "I know we supposedly reincarnate with the same groups of people, but you surely aren't thinking..."

"I don't know what to think. I'm probably just paranoid, what with everything else that's gone wrong." And yet she couldn't even conceive of having to face this latest possibility. If Steve *had* truly had her killed in a previous life, how would she handle such knowledge?

And how could she ever explain any resulting fallout to Steve?

He didn't believe in reincarnation any more than he believed in witchcraft.

Steve first noticed a nagging urge to go home around lunchtime. Kent had gotten them all po-boys, but in the middle of his roast beef on French bread, drafting a story about last Friday's Thanksgiving program at the elementary school, he started wondering what was in the fridge at the duplex. *Why not swing home and check it out?*

No way, and not because of Brie's fears about "some kind of negativity" lurking there. He lost his temper more at the duplex. And he wouldn't risk losing his temper.

But the urge didn't go away.

He could just imagine showing up at the house, telling Brie his instincts had brought him home, and falling into that red haze, attacking her again. Not just no—hell, no.

*Why not drive by, make sure she got home okay?*

Right. "She's casting a spell, to draw you into her clutches," he muttered to himself before taking another bite of French bread. Then he noticed Louise, who'd paused, coffeepot in hand, outside his office doorway.

He tried an unsuccessful grin, and Louise, looking more worried than ever, shook her head and moved on. Steve suspected Kent would be in at any moment, to subtly feel out his boss's sanity level.

As good a reason as any not to go home.

After leaving the Wellness Club, Brie went to the park, to watch mothers and their small children at the playground, and to think. Then she ate a late lunch at a fast-food chicken place. Finally, goading herself with Mary's words about her supposed fearlessness, she returned to the duplex.

This thing wasn't going to exile her from her own home, and besides, it was almost Thanksgiving. If she meant to make any money with her renovations before Christmas, she had to finish some of them. Steve hadn't let all this come between him and his work, after all.

She hated the part of herself that resented that.

A vast emptiness filled the house. The narrow staircase—its other half past the wall, on Sylvie's side of the duplex—looked miserly and ominous; the dark wood paneling chased away today's autumn sunlight. Her older furniture reminded her of Mary's "temporal knot"—and death.

"Not that it bothers you, O Fearless One," she told herself, hitching her purse's strap more firmly on her shoulder; the revolver added a good two pounds. "You've got antiques to renovate."

Colonial antiques. As in . . . Puritans.

Slowly she turned toward her workroom, and decided that, even fearless, she wasn't about to investigate in there.

An hour and a half later found her disgusted, in the sunny backyard, surrounded by a pair of pewter candlesticks, a chest, the Bible box, the spoiled still life, and everything she could detach and carry from the tallboy, including its drawers. First casting a protective circle, she'd gone over each Colonial piece as carefully as she knew how, and discovered nothing. She'd already worked most on the tallboy, stressing several new walnut panels to replace ruined ones, and she hadn't felt anything amiss, apparently for good cause. Neither did the Bible box prove her earlier senses wrong. She searched the chest for hidden compartments and, again, found nothing. The painting could have been an astral black hole, for all the vibes it put off, and the candlesticks held impressions only of age and of value...not so much material as emotional. Someone had once treasured them.

So much for her limited powers of telemetry. Frustrated, she used her hand to dispel the circle, since she'd sent away her arcane tools. She'd thought she had a lead. Instead, she just had a lawnful of antiques.

Maybe they *should* sell the house, she mused, carrying first the candlesticks and then the Bible box back inside. They'd planned to rent the second half of the duplex until they started their family, and until Sylvie found her own place to live, and then tear down the dividing wall and renovate the place for themselves. It seemed so long ago that they'd explored the big structure, thrilled that the depressed economy allowed them such a find.

Long ago, and far away. If Steve couldn't get near the place, that plan was moot. Their only chance to stay a family would be to find a safer place in which to be one.

She started to tote the disassembled tallboy inside, piece by piece, and wished their "only chance" didn't feel so slim. Even if they escaped *this* negativity, they'd still have problems. Big ones. How long would Steve's condescension haunt her? His cracks about witches didn't just insult her and her friends, but her mother, her grandmother, her long and proud lineage—whether she asked the Old Ones for release at full moon or not.

She might as well face the cold, hard truth, which was that Steve wasn't about to consider any reality outside his own realm. She either accepted his cynicism, endlessly aware of his scorn... or she no longer accepted him.

She might not even have *that* choice, as metaphysically outgunned as they were...unless she called in the big guns. Adjusting a drawer in the tallboy, Brie paused, considered, then went into the kitchen for the telephone.

"You know, dear," said Gwen Conway, "there's a good reason I've never come to visit you and your Eagle Scout."

Standing in the middle of the kitchen, Brie grew increasingly aware of the amount of open space at her back. "You and Steve don't get along, Mom. I know."

"Mother-in-law antagonism is practically a cliché." While her mother talked, Brie glanced, slowly, behind her.

Nothing but her dining room table and chairs. And yet... just to be on the safe side, she picked up the phone, eyed how much extra cord she had, and carried it and a wooden chair into the backyard, near the sprawling oak.

"The reasonable course of action is for us to stay out of one another's way. Your home is most definitely his territory," her mother continued.

Brie settled onto the chair, beside the easel and chest. "Not... lately. Steve hasn't been home, this last week."

"If you two are having trouble, I *definitely* shouldn't be there. Nonmanipulation doesn't just pertain to magic."

"Mom, he's staying away because something happens to him at the house. He changes. I think he's being influenced."

"Hence the possession question last month," her mother mused. Nearby, a squirrel paused halfway up the oak tree to listen in on the conversation.

She nodded, catching the phone cord with the toe of her high-top, then made herself stop fidgeting. "I can't figure it out, Mom, and I was hoping if you came here, you could."

"You and your circle are that much out of your depth? I'll admit, Brigit, I've never had total confidence in those new-recruit witches you've gathered around yourself, but at least you—"

"I'm quitting the Craft." Brie expected silence to meet her on the other end. She got it. "Permanently."

The squirrel chittered something at her, and disappeared into the foliage. Finally her mother said, "Oh."

"It's not just because of Steve."

"Oh?"

Realizing she'd started fidgeting again, Brie got up and went back to the workroom for her can of turpentine, bottle of alcohol, rag and cotton balls. She felt far too restless to sit quietly, and the still-life oak frame could still be saved "Mom, I'm pregnant." She uncapped the alcohol and dampened a cotton ball. Her hand shook; all the more reason to keep busy.

"Well," said Gwen Conway finally. "This is quite a phone call." Brie hadn't realized how much she'd counted on her mother's approval. Her heart sank, until Gwen added, "You couldn't have started with the good news?"

"You're glad?"

"How could I not be pleased? A granddaughter!"

"Or a grandson," Brie warned, starting to dab alcohol on the varnish and paint stains that smeared the frame. Luckily, her interruption the other week had damaged the painting more than the frame; half its ugly rendition of an apple had been eaten away, showing the paint beneath.

"Nonsense, our line always starts with daughters. But if you're pregnant, all the more reason to honor the Old

Ways! Don't you want your child to have a heritage, a past? To know the strength that runs through her veins?''

Put that way, of course, it sounded attractive. She'd never regretted the strength of her ancestry, just the complications. Still, she took a deep breath. "I'd rather she know her father."

"The two needn't be exclusive, dear. I'm sure even your Eagle Scout will accept a few eccentricities in his baby girl, until she's old enough to know discretion. You'd be surprised what fathers tolerate in their daughters."

"I wouldn't know, Mom. Was that your plan with my dad?"

"Was what my plan?"

"Discretion." Because it hadn't worked; he'd left anyway. She didn't know if he would have accepted her childish prattling about faeries and imaginary friends or not, because he'd left anyway, leaving no memories at all.

"With your father?" Gwen seemed to be having trouble following her daughter's line of thought, but Brie doubted she could clarify further without her voice breaking. It was so close, so damned close, to what was happening with her now. Another little witch baby, in danger of losing her father to twentieth-century rationalism. She swabbed at the painting with a turpentine rag, probably doing a horrible job, but could focus on only her mother's voice. "What should I have been discreet about?"

"The Craft, Mom! What about your vow of silence? How did you plan to get around it with *my* father?"

But her hand, her whole world, stilled at her mother's next words: "There was nothing to get around, Brigit. Your father was a witch, too. Surely you knew that."

* * *

"Mr. Peabody, I need to go," said Timmy, the student who interned with the *Sentinel*. "I just stopped by, ya know?"

Only then did Steve realize that he'd been holding the kid a conversational hostage, showing him more about layouts and headlines than a high school sophomore needed to learn.

"Yeah. Sure. Have fun," he said. His words came out halfhearted, at best. No insult taken, Timmy left even as he spoke. "Go."

*Home. Go home.*

He didn't conceive the thought as words, or images, but he understood it clearly, and no, he was not going to give in. Almost angrily, he stalked back into his office. Okay, so maybe he was a bit lonely this afternoon. Kent and Louise had left in a huff, after he refused to answer Kent's concerned, but personal, questions. Damned reporter types couldn't stand not to know every fact about an issue.

Staring belligerently at his again-neat desk, Steve noted the picture of Brie, her eyes smoky and mysterious, her hair wild. Damned if she didn't look like a witch—or at least the kind of woman labeled a witch to excuse some man's guilty fantasies about her. For a sane woman to consider *herself* a witch, though, just didn't make sense.

*You figure out what your instincts are telling you about me.* Oh, sure, he had names and dates, and her occult talisman, but he should ignore that. Trust his instincts.

*Because, Stevie-boy, she's not going to tell you squat.*

Looking around his dingy office, his hovel-away-from-home, with its patched couch and crowded shelves and out-of-date computer, he decided to face the cold, hard truth, which was that no one and nothing was going to make Brigit open up to him. Not the baby. Not the instability of their marriage. Not the idyll that marriage had once been.

The illusion of an idyll.

He also had a wedding picture, like the one beside their bed. Slowly sitting down, he lifted the silver frame and frowned at the happy couple matted behind glare-free glass. Geez, he looked confident. He'd known this was the right thing, Brie was the right woman, on so deep a level he could never have imagined cold feet. He'd known it instinctively.

And now he either went on with a marriage without trust and respect, or he went on without a marriage. Real good instincts there, Peabody.

*Go home.* This damned urge to check on her, he decided, was what he had a telephone for. Except that, when he dialed their number, the line was busy.

He slammed the phone down.

When Brie finally settled the telephone into its cradle, she was in shock.

"Well, of course Payne was a witch," her mother had said, honestly surprised that Brie had misread the situation for so many years. "Unlike my daughter, *I* kept my romantic involvements within the Craft."

"Then why'd he leave us?" Brie had asked, still stunned.

And her mother said, "I've *told* you. Because he was twenty years old, and he wasn't ready for the mundane responsibilities of fatherhood. It happens."

But, she realized, she'd never fully *believed* that until she learned he was a witch. He hadn't left because of the Craft at all. Mom's eccentricities hadn't chased him away. This faceless player in her mother's romantic past hadn't rejected them because they were witches.

He'd rejected them because he'd been an immature, unreliable boy who didn't want to grow up.

She wasn't sure how long she'd sat in the long shadows of the backyard, coming to terms with this latest news, before she finally focused on the painting at which she'd been staring all along. She'd been working on the frame, but something about the painting itself, something other than its sheer ugliness, drew her. The patch she'd overdosed in alcohol, that night when Steve scared her, hadn't eaten away to canvas, but to more paint, and what looked like a different painting.

Artists often painted over existing works, their own or those of others, what with the cost of canvases and the low pay of painters. A few treasures had been discovered in such a way. Dampening a cotton ball, swabbing away the rest of the apple and part of an ugly pear, she quickly treated the spot with turpentine as she looked more closely. The newly revealed paint looked like a floating hand, white fingers and white cuff stark against black background, and it reminded her of something from college, an old art history course.

This, she realized as her breath went shallow, was important. Even while she tried to place the reference, she began to swab away more of the still life—good riddance—to show the darkness beyond...and the image of a book, gripped awkwardly in equally white fingers. The perspective was all wrong, which somehow fit her half memory, and yet it was only when she wiped away paint— too carelessly; this had better not be a master—that she hit the white corner of a bib and finally placed the familiarity.

Early American portraiture. Usually second-rate, both in technique and in execution. A mixture of English provincial and Anglo-Dutch influences, and it dated from...

Colonial times. She'd had the frame's original painting, a portrait, in the house all this time.

"But why couldn't we sense you?" she demanded of the smear of paint, still propped on the easel before her, and tried to sense it even as she asked....

The world began to swim about her, blurring from the edges inward, and without physically moving she felt herself falling forward, through darkness, through some kind of tear in the dimensions.

She reared back with a gasp, knocking her chair over, but getting her feet beneath her so quickly she didn't fall. Backing away from the painting, raising a hand to her chest, she knew exactly what Mary had meant when she said she'd "freaked"—and Brie didn't blame her. The painting didn't exude a negative tingle, because, instead of radiating energy, as most items did, it seemed to be a void.

Which didn't make sense, but she wasn't about to hang around trying to figure it out. Digging into her purse, on the ground beside the fallen chair and the metal turpentine can, she pulled out her cigarette lighter—and paused.

The portrait waited on its easel, amid the quiet of the late-afternoon backyard. Somewhere on the street, a car cut its engine and another moved by. Toads croaked from the woods behind the yard, a heron swooped by, and a breeze rustled through the acorn-weighted oak leaves.

She hadn't uncovered the portrait's face.

*Destroy it!* But . . . she had to see his face.

Pocketing the lighter, she grabbed her bottle of alcohol and soaked a final handful of cotton, wrinkling her nose at its bitter scent. Trying to stay at arm's length—this had to be the answer, it had to—she swiped away the remains of the still life, and her shoulders sagged with relief.

The narrow face that seemed to float against the blackness of background and black-garbed torso was not

Steve's. The small, somehow frantic eyes of the painting were not Steve's. Logically she realized that reincarnates rarely carried over looks from one life to another...but she also knew, on a wholly instinctive level, that the clean-shaven, serious face that stared out at her belonged to a man bearing no relationship to her husband.

If they'd dreamed of another couple's lives, they'd merely picked up on someone else's memories, not their own. She would recognize Steve's soul—and his soul had never inhabited this form.

Not wanting to pause even to breathe relief, she dumped the remainder of the alcohol over the top of the portrait, letting the clear liquid run down the oily surface. As she pulled the lighter out of her pocket, she heard a twig snap behind her, began to turn—

And met a hard, male fist—and darkness.

*And Goodman Josiah Blakelee, now completely freed from the portrait and securely settled within a sufficient male shell, smiled down at the unconscious witch. She'd tried to destroy his portal, but his will had been stronger. He'd drawn salvation to him.*

*He again possessed hands, again eyes, again a form with which to do God's will. And his strength, now uncovered, pulsed through him.*

*His waiting had availed him. And this time, the sorceress would find no escape.*

# CHAPTER FOURTEEN

*E'en death hath not kept her from me.*
                    —The Journals of Josiah Blakelee

*Home. Go home.*

Steve stared through his office window at the still-light street, the occasional passing car, trying to distract himself from this growing dread. Hadn't he felt the same foreboding as he rushed home Halloween night? Nothing had been wrong. Hadn't he felt this way when he called to check on Brie, the day she thought they had ghosts? A lot had been wrong that afternoon, but she hadn't been in danger.

*That you know of.*

He blew out a sigh, paced back to his chair and sprawled in it. Then he grabbed the black rock o' protection that Cypress Bernard had given him and tossed it from hand to hand, eyeing the distance to the trash can. This need to go home was somehow connected to his psychosis, to whatever was driving him loony, and he'd be damned if he'd let illogical urges rule his actions any more! Especially not with so much to lose if he *did* go home.

Besides, he'd already called. Again. He'd gotten the answering machine, just as he'd gotten Sylvie's machine when he then called her. Probably his wife and sister were out together shopping, or at a movie, or a séance—God knew what.

*If Brie's not home, it's safe for you to go there.*

Right, so that he could completely lose his mind and end up hunkered beside the washing machine with an ax in his hands, waiting for her return. He'd once had to cover such a story, and had wondered how anybody could become so crazed as to sacrifice everything—loved ones and self—to so horrific an ecstasy of vengeance. Since he'd started getting these tempers, though, Steve had the sickening suspicion that he now understood, just a little more than a normal human should. Just enough for him to worry about his own sanity.

He would not—

*Go home.* A chill swept over him; the rock fell to the desk from his suddenly numb fingers. *Go home now. Something's wrong.*

He shook his head, but this time the sickening weight in his stomach didn't ease at his command. His skin tingled; he felt suddenly overaware of the late light blazing through the window, the roar of cars on the street. *Something's wrong!*

If he went home, this fear in his gut could prove a self-fulfilling prophecy. He could lose himself again, hurt Brie...hurt their child.

But what if—*what if*—the premonition was right...and he did nothing?

Oh, *hell.* Steve grabbed his keys from his pocket and hit the door of the *Sentinel* running. He hoped, prayed, that Brie had told the truth when she said she could defend herself.

Because he was going home.

The darkness faded slowly, from the edges inward, confused and disconcerting. With sight came further awareness—the feel of bark at her back, of rope on her wrists, and the sharp pain in her arms, pulled at an unnatural angle. She was, Brie realized, tied to the oak tree.

With that first clear thought, the rest of her comprehension flared back, clearing the last befuddled shadows from her mind. Someone had hit her. Her jaw and cheekbone still throbbed, sending bolts of pain through her skull and neck, and an elbow and hip ached where she must have fallen.... And she was tied to her oak tree!

She tugged frantically at the ropes, wincing as rough hemp burned the skin of her wrists, and for the second time that afternoon she found herself praying: lords above, not Steve. Let this be some mundane robbery. But she knew as she heard footsteps and the sloshing of liquid in a metal container, approaching from behind, that this was no robbery. This had to do with the portrait—the narrow-faced, frantic-eyed Puritan man in the portrait.

*Why hadn't her circle sensed him?* So clearly was the face from the easel now embedded in her mind that she stared, disbelieving, at the skinny young man who appeared in front of her, listing beneath the weight of a gasoline can.

Young Andrew Beaudry.

*There is no true power in fear.* How young had she been, when her mother taught her that? "Andy," she said now, trying to keep her voice steady. "What's going—"

"Wilt thou confess?" The anomalous voice, deep and stilted, that emerged from the blond youth's mouth struck at her. A too-proud posture hid Andy's natural gawkiness; his eyes had taken on a frantic edge. And his free hand, the one not holding the gas can, clenched and unclenched.

"If you untie me, right now, *maybe* I wilt not call the police," she answered. Fearless and sure of herself? If she were fearless, she'd be able to draw a decent breath. If she were sure of herself, she'd understand where this person, this *thing* had been when the circle investigated the portrait, and her frantic mind would conceive of some defense, like . . . names. Names had power. "Now, Andrew Beaudry, I know you're not—"

He hit her again; the blow knocked her head into the tree trunk, scraped her cheek against bark. She bit her tongue, and as the blast of dizziness faded, she tasted blood. "Silence, witch! If thou wilt not confess, be ye silent!"

Against her will, tears burned her eyes . . . and anger. She took a deep breath, then another, wishing she hadn't been denying her powers so vehemently. They now hovered outside her mental reach, coy and indistinct after such adamant suppression.

Surely she could dredge up enough power for one single psychic blast. She *was* still a witch. Witch enough to consider aiming at the portrait instead of Andy, who must be an innocent vessel of this Puritan bastard. Witch enough to recognize the dangers of destroying the portrait while that same Puritan bastard remained outside it, in her own realm.

Another deep, steadying breath, while Andy unscrewed the lid of the gas can.

Fear struck her as she recognized, belatedly, the significance of the gasoline; she had to start her deep breathing again. Deeper, grasping and collecting slim strands of power. *Sorry, Andy.* She would accept any karmic kickback she incurred by injuring the youth, if it saved her and the baby. Deeper—ignoring the sweet sharpness of gas fumes, directing everything into her spell. Deeper, and—

She struck out at Andy with everything she had; she could almost *see* the scarlet flare of her anger slam into the youth's chest and hurl him backward. She winced as he hit the ground, perhaps ten feet from her, and rolled once, twice, across the grass. Then she closed her eyes, near to passing out from weakness . . . and relief at her narrow escape.

Sylvie would come home soon. She could call the other witches. Together, somehow, they'd banish this bastard to his portrait, and then—

She heard a twig snap, and opened her eyes.

She stared.

Andy's hand moved, then moved again. Pawing at the grass, he managed to push himself up to his knees. He fell to one side, shook his head like a wet dog. And then he smiled.

The triumphant, satisfied smile, obscene on his puppy-ish face, chilled her soul. "The boy hath been taught protections," said the too-deep, wrong-accented voice. "Taught by thine own sisters in damnation."

"Then how could *you* get him?" she demanded, and regretted how her voice broke when Andy stood again, staggered back to her. She'd used all her strength.

She was completely alone.

"He opened himself to me." Andy's skinny hands lifted the red metal can, which hadn't even spilled over. "Questing for shades, delving outside of God's realm, he opened himself to me, and he invited me in. And now, thou shalt confess."

A splash of gasoline hit her chest.

Steve made it home in record time. Even the infamous traffic light, turning from yellow to red as he approached it, suddenly reverted to green. He skidded the Volvo to a stop too far from the curb, behind Brie's Blazer, and left his door hanging open as he escaped the car's interior and sprinted across the lawn, onto the porch.

"Damn it!" She'd locked the door. Though he'd wanted her to keep the place locked, he resented the seconds it took him to jam in his key, turn it, ram the door open with his shoulder. "Brigit!" *Serve you right if she shoots you, barging in like this.* But he was no longer listening to his rational side; this was his wife! *"Brie!"*

Nothing. No lit candles to say she was home; no smoky reminiscence of incense. He ducked down the hallway, automatically heading in the direction from which she'd emerged Halloween night, the last time he'd burst in with this pressure in his chest, this fear in his throat. She wasn't in the dining room, the workroom. He started to turn, to check upstairs—

When he saw the phone cord trailing out under the back door. *That* door wasn't locked. He pushed through, and in a single moment saw all. A litter of antiques spotted the ground beneath the tall shadow of the sprawling oak, and Brie herself sat against the tree's base. Her arms reached oddly behind her; she'd drawn her knees protectively up against her sodden chest. She was tilting her head upward at a severe angle, as a drowning person might strain for the surface.

Even as Steve took this in, smelled the gasoline, Moonbeam Beaudry emerged from behind the thick trunk of the oak to sling a final splash of fuel on her. She tried unsuccessfully to duck away from it; it splattered against her cheek, her hair. Moonbeam tossed aside the empty can, which rolled to a stop against the rest of the lawn's clutter.

And in the flash in which this happened, Steve knew fury. Not the red-hazed, self-involved, accusatory tempers with which he'd abused Brie, but murderous, single-minded rage. He stepped into the long, late-afternoon light, toward the bastard, the scrawny little bastard who'd dare—

But when Moonbeam held up a lighter, Steve stopped cold. Oh, God, not so close to Brie. The fumes! One spark...

"Confess," demanded a man's deep voice—Steve ducked back into the shadow of the porch. Was someone else there to stop his rescue of Brie? "How long hast thou been a witch?"

Brigit, staring at nothingness, said nothing.

"Thou can save thy soul through confession only!" There it was again, that deep, stilted voice. Steve tried to place its source visually. His senses had to be mistaken.

"Why didst thou become a witch?"

It *was* Andy Beaudry! But that wasn't the kid's voice. The eerie dread that had dogged him all day shuddered into his very bones, along with a nauseated sense of deeper, more horrifying recognition. Oh, God.

*It wasn't Moonbeam at all.* It was...him?

Suddenly, his terror for Brie met a second fear—fear for his own sanity. This was somehow *his* madness. He'd walked right into madness!

"What demon didst thou choose to be thy lover?"

Brie spat at the youth. He slapped her, open-handed, for the insult, made her cry out. "Confess!"

"No!" Maybe he *was* crazy, but no second man lurked to take him out from behind, and Steve stepped back into the light. Brie's eyes widened in a heart-wrenching mixture of hope and fear...and Andy's in slow satisfaction. Except that the expression fit Moonbeam no better than the voice. It, too, seemed illogically, horribly familiar.

"Leave her alone, you sonofabitch!" Steve strode forward, but stopped dead when Andy raised the lighter. He softened his tone, forcibly relaxed his posture. "You can't light that. It's the fumes that will explode, you know, not the gas. If you're close enough to light it, you're committing suicide.''

He managed one more slow, steady step before the deep voice challenged, calmly, "Again?"

*He didn't care?* So much for relaxed; the possibility that this thing in Andy could kill Andy as easily as it could Brie buffeted his comprehension.

"'Tis right, that thou shoudst see her end," continued Beaudry. Except that it wasn't Beaudry, of course, but someone in control of Beaudry, just as someone had been in control of *him,* before.

He tried not to be sick. No, that couldn't be true.

*How could it not be?*

"'Tis as it was, as it should be." And, holding Steve's gaze, this *being* extended the lighter nearer Brie. "Confess, witch, for thy husband, as well as thyself. *Confess!*"

Frantic possibilities jumbled through Steve's awareness. He could wrestle the lighter from Beaudry's hand, and, if either of them ignited a spark, they'd all die. He had hoses, fire extinguishers, his own jacket, to put out flames. But gasoline fumes would explode, not just burn— none of those measures would work. He couldn't save her.

*He couldn't save her!*

"Confess," insisted the unnatural, insane voice. "Bride of Satan, confess."

Steve caught his wife's agonized gaze with his own—and then she closed her eyes, shutting him out.

Well...why wouldn't she connect the two of them? The vile familiarity of the voice, of the questions, ate at his gut. This wasn't just *what* he'd been, but *who* he'd been ... or who had been *him.* Brie had known something weird was happening, and he hadn't believed her. Because he hadn't believed her, she'd die.

He extended a hand toward her, as if he could reach her across the lawn. But her eyes remained closed against him.

*I, Brigit Conway, willingly stake all that I am, was, and ever shall be on this vow. May my powers desert me and my allies turn against me should I ever reveal my association with the Craft, or any of its secrets, to an unbeliever. In this and all lifetimes—so mote it be.*

The stench of gasoline burned in her lungs, her sinuses, nauseated her and squeezed tears from her shut eyes. She'd *promised.* Other witches, her own blood, had gone to painful deaths for such a vow. They, she, believed in reincarnation, after all, in a greater scheme than a single life and death.

She knew of these witches, these Guineveres and Morgans and, yes, Brigits; she knew of them from bedtime stories and family reunions, and she believed in them. Alone, perhaps she'd find the strength to follow them. The baby couldn't yet feel pain, could she? The baby might not know....

But Brie had sworn to protect her. And, worse, Steve would have to witness whatever happened.

She opened her eyes, and through the blur of her tears, in the orange wash of the setting sun, she could see his anguish—for *her.* He'd come back here, for her. He hadn't had to face this, to face his own helplessness.

She noted the slightest movement of Andy's hand; it itched to strike the lighter. But his threat no longer held her complete attention. Only Steve's eyes, the horror and regret and deep, deep love in them, had that.

"Confess," urged the entity.

Steve might not fully believe in her, but she wouldn't withhold her love, barter for his belief. She did love him. Enough to sacrifice her powers, her allies, and all she was, would be, and ever had been. Enough to sacrifice her word.

She parted her lips; forced herself to form the syllables. "I...*am*..."

"Who the hell are *you?*" Steve shouted, interrupting her. Her head snapped up; she saw Andy's do the same.

Steve stuffed his hands in his pockets, physically non-threatening while his words did battle. The ruddy light threw the clean angles of his face into bright relief. "To whom is she supposed to be confessing, anyway?"

"To God!" snarled the voice, ill-suited to Andy's mouth.

Steve shook his head. "No dice. God knows everything already, right? This is a symbolic confession...so who are you, to take it? Some kind of priest?"

"A papist? Nay!"

Steve stepped forward, one step. It brought him one step nearer to her than he had been. And one step closer to danger. "Maybe you have some reason to hide your identity. Some secrets of your own?"

To her amazement, the entity answered. "I be Josiah. Goodman Josiah Blakelee." A name.

She had a name. And nothing left with which to use it.

"Josiah Blakelee of?" prodded Steve immediately. Lords above, he was interrogating the man! He was doing what he did best, being a reporter...and *stalling*.

She tugged at the ropes and tried to raise some energy, any energy, to help her escape them. She couldn't take a deep breath through the fumes, but the strength of Steve's support helped compensate.

"Of Andover Village," she heard the entity, Josiah, answer. "Massachusetts Bay Colony. In the absence of the general court, I demand full confession from—"

"Why us, Josiah?" Steve extended a hand. Brie almost smiled. He might as well be thrusting a microphone into Andy's face. "What gives you the right to target us for your witch-hunt?"

And then she felt a strength, bolstering her own meager energy: the protective power of the tree. Yes! By concentrating—concentrating harder than she should have to—she caught and eased her energy to the knots at her wrists. *Loosen. Loosen. As I will it...* Between that and her struggle, in a final twist, one hand came free.

And even as she held freedom at her fingertips, Andy, Josiah, turned on her again. "Treachery!" he cried, again thrusting the lighter at her. "Enough! Fire purifies even the darkest souls!"

She readied herself to slap the lighter, or the flames if she failed, away, one-handed.

And then she heard Steve cry, "Wait, Josiah! Use me!"

Close to her, too close, considering how fumes still engulfed her, the lighter hovered, still.

"I'm your first choice," insisted Steve. "I'm the husband. If you want to do this right, you have to use me."

*Don't invite him in!* She lunged for the lighter. Andy snatched it from her reach, threw it toward Steve as if this were a boyhood game of keep-away, and collapsed into a tie-dyed heap on the grass.

And Steve staggered backwards, his left hand clenching into a fist.

"Don't invite him in!" Brie screamed, straining at her remaining tie.

But she was too late.

For the first time since the "spells" had begun, Steve knew something possessed him. Through his own fear of losing control again, through his desperation to win this battle of wills, he studied the sensation. The now-familiar redness oozed into his consciousness, blurred his peripheral vision, but he recognized now that it wasn't his, and tried not just to fight it, but to shove it into a corner of his mind.

A corner neatly labelled "Josiah."

The anger nearly drowned him; some of it *was* his. He struggled futilely to differentiate between his own curbed angers—dark, so dark—and Josiah's rage at...at...

*His wife, Mercy. She sat by the hearth, mending, dressed in proper black attire, with her fine golden hair caught up in a cap...but she had stitched lace to the ruffle of the cap. Vanity! He had hoped she would leave such conceits in Boston, when he brought her to the village of his youth, yet he knew well she had not conquered the sin of pride.*

*And now he knew why.* "Thou hast been cried out against," *he told her.*

"'*Tis a lie,*" *she said, too brazen.* "*I be no witch.*"

"'*Tis no lie. I know so. 'Twould be best to confess thy sins, and so you will.*"

*And she had looked up at him, her eyes bright with defiance...*

No, pain. Betrayal. Raising a trembling hand to his already sweat-soaked face to ascertain his own physical presence, Steve realized what Josiah had not. The Puritan's accusations had hurt his wife, had hurt her even more than the accusations of the...

*The girls, and through them the general court. The trial's spectral evidence was undeniable; the girls writhed on the floor, begged Goody Blakelee to stop her magical torments. Why would she not confess? The costly imprisonment, Mercy wasting away in her shackles. Confess! But she didst not obey. She had held the power to win his hand, though she was not of his own village. She had held the*

*power to coax him into taking up the paintbrush, though
he had left his youthful vanity as a limner behind him, to
paint portraits of them both for her city-dwelling parents.
She had held the power to draw him into unholy, bestial
pleasures, past those condoned by God between husband
and wife—and so had she the strength, the strength of Satan, to resist.*

*He glared at her on the scaffold, betrayal as thick in his
throat as the rope around hers. He wished her obedience
and salvation, not her death. But he would have something. "Thou wilt not live, even for me?"*

But...was she blond, or redheaded? Double images
blurred, and Steve grasped at the flickering reality of a
backyard, cast in the otherworldly light of a flaming sunset. To his horror, he realized he held the lighter. No, he
was Steven Peabody! His wife was not named Mercy, but
Brigit, and she was—

*A witch! She hath betrayed us—*

"No!" Steve felt some of the sense of split personality
fade, momentarily, and realized that, though his left hand
held the lighter, his right remained in his pocket, clutched
around something smooth and disk-shaped. Brie's medallion. He was drawing strength from Brie's medallion.

Brie had somehow managed to untie herself; she scrab-
bled to her feet beside the tree, and he felt weak with relief.

And in that weakness lost himself again. *She could have
confessed, could have escaped damnation. Silent, she must
be punished. How could she not have respected her husband, her master? Could she not have trusted him, even so
much?*

Familiar thoughts—frighteningly, agonizingly familiar.
Through this Josiah had gotten him, through Steve's own
petty, mistrustful anger. He stepped toward Brie. She cir-

cled away from him, and before he realized he was moving, he'd darted to one side to cut off her escape.

Images of Mercy tortured his mind, her frail body dropping, then catching against the hangman's rope to dangle and kick, head off-angled. Images of Brie, when he would pin her to the ground and light the wildfire of her Judas hair...

She edged in the other direction; he cut her off again, caught her by the shoulder, threw her to the ground, and barely managed to fall back against the tree instead of tackling her. Along with the half-light of the coming dusk, scarlet anger again moved in from the edge of his vision. *Was it truly his...?* That wouldn't matter once it took him over completely.

Brie pushed herself up with her arms. "No," he gasped, his own voice rough with the effort to not be Josiah's. "Don't. I can outrun you...."

And grab her. Overpower her. Oh God, no.

The malignant anger spread through him; *Josiah* spread through him. How could his willpower combat that of a madman three hundred years old?

Brie, still on the grass, hesitated. He knew that, though he could barely move on his own, Josiah would be on her any moment now. And he knew what Josiah meant to do to her. And he couldn't stop him.

Plastering himself back against the tree, hoping to hold himself immobile long enough to allow Brie to escape, Steve moved the focus of his will from his actions and thoughts—*burn her, see her hair ignite, her clothes aflame, her skin crisp, hear her confession*—to his words.

She'd said she could protect herself. She'd promised. Damn it, she'd promised! Awkwardly he forced the breath from his lungs, closed his throat for the hardness of the first syllable, prayed for the rest to follow.

From the grass, Brie watched him, clearly unsure what to do.

And Steve said, "Kill me."

Brie stared at her husband, his back to the oak, his chin raised as he strained against—*it*. The it that wanted her. Steve's hair clung to his smooth forehead; a few strands had caught in the stubble beneath a cheekbone. The green shirt, plastered darkly against his sweated chest, completed his disheveled, wild appearance.

"No," she said, and his gaze cut down to her, intent, desperate.

"The only way... to destroy..."

Her heart caught in her throat as she pulled her legs beneath her. Lords above, was that truly the only way? Or—

"This could be one of his tricks. Spirits lie! He wants me to destroy you, because that would destroy me...."

A low moan strained from Steve's chest, through his throat, rising in volume toward a cry. His arms were starting to tremble from the effort to remain immobile.

"It's me!" Steve gasped. Even to turn his head, she saw, took supreme effort. If he relaxed for even a second, he would obviously be lost again.

They'd all be lost.

He drew another quick, sharp breath, almost a sob, as he met her eyes with his. Familiar. Brown. Loving. "For us, Red." His next breath was longer, nearly a death rattle. "Kill me."

At the teasing nickname, a sob stumbled from her own throat. Logical, always so damned logical! He wanted to trade himself for her and the baby. And maybe he'd even found the answer. Maybe, to destroy Josiah, she must destroy the vessel that held the Puritan's soul. But to barter his life for hers, even for the baby's...

"Shalt thou follow thy husband's bidding?" No, she didn't want to hear that voice, profane, from Steve's throat! "Or wilt thou see him destroyed?"

It would destroy him, to kill her. Then she realized the full significance of Josiah's words. He still held the lighter...and Steve stood against the gasoline-soaked tree. Could the fumes have dissipated by now? No; not yet.

Her purse lay nearby. Slowly she reached into it, found and withdrew the revolver. She stared at the weapon, heavy in her hand, and quickly looked back up. She couldn't use it. Not on Steve.

Now Steve's whole body shook; he couldn't hold out much longer. Pressed against the tree trunk like a prisoner awaiting execution, sweat dripping into his eyes and down his neck, he should have collapsed already. Could fighting possession kill a person? Andy hadn't fought it, and yet his prone form lay, still as death.

If she killed Steve, she'd almost certainly kill Josiah. But if Steve died from the strain of his battle of wills, where would the Puritan's spirit go? Could he take her over? Would such a misogynist try?

For a moment, the frantic madness faded from Steve's eyes, and they became as deep and soft as a buck deer's...they became *Steve's*. One last time.

He parted trembling lips. "Please."

She swallowed back her own sobs as she popped open the revolver's cylinder to check the bullets' placement, then closed it with a deadly click. She pulled back the hammer until it locked.

She raised the gun, her left hand cupping her right.

Each of Steve's breaths was labored now, shuddering and hoarse. She sighted the revolver on his soaked, heaving chest, then raised her eyes to his own. She couldn't do this, but she had to. If he could willingly sacrifice him-self...

So could she.

She shut her eyes tightly to squeeze the tears away, then resighted on his head, to ensure an instant and painless kill, and the complete destruction of Josiah Blakelee. She couldn't bear Steve's agonized breathing much longer.

"L..." She heard the sound in one of his gasps, but re-fused to lose her aim this time. "Love you," he gasped, his breathing labored.

She took a deep breath, tried not to whimper. "I love you, too, Steve." She tightened her finger on the trigger, felt its resistance. "Al-always have. Always will."

And she fired.

# CHAPTER FIFTEEN

*E'en death shall not keep her from me.*
                    —The Journals of Josiah Blakelee

Simultaneously with the solid "click," Brie had a brief image of Steve's—no, *Josiah's*—eyes widening, heard a snatch of his—its?—scream of defeated rage as she spun and shot again, this time on a loaded chamber. The double-action of the .38 kicked in her hands, hurt her shoulders; in the twilight she could see flame spout from the muzzle—prayed *she* wouldn't explode—as the roar momentarily deafened her.

And the gasoline can she'd aimed at, at the foot of her easel, exploded in an incredible billow of howling flames. Their orange appetite took everything within several yards: chest, chair, and the alcohol-treated portrait.

The portrait to which Josiah would—must—have fled.

"You believe in hell," she snarled, her voice an ugly thing. "Go there!" And she spun back to Steve.

He slowly slid to the acorn-strewn grass, not fainting, as Andy had, but using the faithful tree trunk to support his descent. Free? She leapt toward him, skidded to her knees before the sprawled form of her husband. He was swallowing breaths in great mouthfuls, gulping the air even as one of his weakened hands flopped toward her, across the

sweat-dampened front of his shirt. She grasped his sculp-
tured writer's fingers and squeezed them.

Steve, her Steve. The inhuman screams she sensed behind her, from the burning easel, told her that much.

"Are you all right?" She extended a concerned hand to
touch his tanned face . . . and froze. Momentarily, another
image transposed over his, the image from her dreams.
Not of a Puritan accuser, but of the Holly King, the forest
lord who made his yearly sacrifice for the people he loved.
Well, this man might as well be a god, the way she wor-
shiped him . . . and she, Brigit, was the person he loved.

He cut his gaze toward her, his intelligent eyes bright
with sarcasm. Despite the lengthening hair and the beard-
roughened cheeks, he was fully Steve again. *"Are you all
right?"* he mimicked, though weakly; a nervous laugh
bubbled from her. "I told you to kill me."

Now she did touch him. She laid her palm against his
flushed, beloved cheek, and for a moment cradled his face.
"Since when do I take orders from you?"

The unearthly wail behind her, she wondered if he could
hear it, faded, but continued. When Steve, wincing in that
direction, struggled to sit up she helped him, catching him
under the arms; he was as wet and weak as a newborn
fawn.

He'd put up one hell of a struggle.

Only once he'd sat up, propped against the oak, did she
also turn to watch the destruction of the portrait—the
*portal.* Of course! Her circle had sensed nothing evil from
the painting, because it had held nothing evil, nothing but
a gateway to . . . to someplace else, where Josiah Blakelee
had lurked. As long as the gate remained closed, it had
offered nothing to sense. And when it opened?

She shuddered, remembering this afternoon's sensation of being absorbed into that dark elsewhere.

The painting itself burned most quickly, Josiah's face blackening from the middle outward. The frame and easel took longer, embers falling free to be snuffed out in the grass. The turpentine can suddenly blew up in another sharp, smaller explosion; so much for chest and chair. And soon, not soon enough, the crackling of the flames drowned the last screams of otherworldly anguish. Josiah Blakelee was indeed gone.

"Fire purifies even the darkest souls," Brie murmured as Steve's embrace stole comfortingly around her. She laid her arms over the circle of his own, hugging them both, and the baby, leaning into his strength. The throbbing in her cheek and jaw intensified as she watched the brilliance of the flame against the newly fallen night; she felt sick. But only when she heard a groan from nearby, and saw Andy move his arm and groggily lift his head—very much alive, though apparently drained and disoriented from extended possession—did she have to swallow back relieved tears and turn her face into Steve's sweaty, familiar chest. *He'd come back for her...* whether he trusted her or not.

A door, a real door, shut; she recognized it not as her own, but her sister-in-law's, and peeked up to see Sylvie and Rand Garner staring at the chaos around them.

"Hospital," Steve managed to call at them. "Phone ahead to the emergency room. Let them know we're coming."

"You're hurt?" Sitting back, Brie ran her shaking hands over his sweated face, over the shoulders and chest that still trembled from fatigue. Had the nightmare not yet ended? "It hurt you? I hurt you?"

But he shook his head. The ghost of an exhausted smile played over his lips as he lifted a hand, traced the throbbing pain of her jaw, the stickiness of her split lip. "For *you*, Red," he clarified. "For you and the baby."

Rand Garner looked at Sylvie and said, "It's your turn to call the authorities, dear." But Brie was too busy melting in the concern of her husband's eyes to notice.

Under better conditions, Steve might have appreciated the irony. Upon arrival at the emergency room, the hospital staff immediately separated him from Brie, claiming "policy," though Sylvie was able to go back with her! After almost fifteen minutes harassing the poor nurse at the admissions desk, he finally understood when a uniformed police officer took him aside, on suspicion of spousal abuse.

This was *not* better conditions. Only Garner's supportive presence during the interrogation kept him from pushing past the cop and finding Brie himself. Garner's presence, and what Steve had discovered about himself this evening.

"What does my wife say?" Steve demanded, trying not to mention the word *harassment*. Brie didn't like lying, after all. And the truth, in this case, would be tricky.

"That you didn't do any of it," the lanky, white-haired officer assured him. "But she seemed a tad uncertain, won't say who did, so I'm askin' you. Neither of you boys helped with that job on her face, or the rope burns on her wrists?"

"No, sir," interjected Garner, before Steve could say something less appropriate.

"Officer, what don't you understand?" he demanded. "I arrived home, found an acquaintance mistreating my wife, and he and I...settled it." So far, he'd managed honesty, while avoiding the weird stuff. "If she refuses to press charges, I'll abide by her wishes."

"But you did not lay violent hands on her?"

He took a deep breath, and tried again to see past the man's shoulder, toward the hallway of curtained examination rooms. He didn't want to remember throwing her to the ground himself. She had to be okay—she *had* to!

"Now, son, if this was you, there's counseling..."

*For this?* Whether he'd really been possessed, or a victim of mass hysteria, or just projecting his worst traits onto an imaginary seventeenth-century villain, he knew how close he'd come to doing a hell of a lot more to Brie than pushing her. And he couldn't blame the anger that had churned within him on anyone but Steve Peabody. *"She's not pressing charges against me, either!"*

The policeman frowned. Steve ignored him to again try to see Brie's room, but only saw Mary Deveraux hurry in. Cypress Bernard had already arrived—their response time was incredible—so they were all there, now. Without him.

"...*your* wife...kinky stuff in the backyard...be upset?" His attention snapped back to where Rand was murmuring conspiratorially to the officer. What?

But the policeman nodded, and lowered his clipboard. "Well, now, I believe we can consider this interview over. Unless the lady changes her mind on filing charges 'gainst whomever, I can't do anything 'bout anything anyhow. You two boys keep your noses clean, though." He paused, gave them both the evil eye. "And I'd be careful to avoid speeding tickets in the near future, y'hear?"

"Yes, sir," responded Garner to the man's departing back, and went to sit next to the exhausted but ambulatory Andy.

Tossing his future brother-in-law an exasperated glance, Steve hurried back to the examining room but stopped himself outside the curtained entrance. Attitude check. Brie didn't need to see how scared he was.

Not yet.

"So if you've confessed," he heard Sylvie ask, "what happens now?"

"I didn't." The sheer relief in Brie's tone wrenched at his heart. "Steve stopped me."

Yeah. After trying himself, for how long, to force a similar confession, no matter how seriously she obviously took this "promise" she kept citing. It wasn't like he hadn't figured out the gist of her secret. She considered herself a witch, whatever that meant, and she wasn't supposed to tell non-witches. Did he really need to hear it from her?

Or had he just been trying to flex his husbandly muscles, like someone else with whom he'd had recent contact?

Not wanting to eavesdrop, he knocked on the wall beside the curtain, then swept the curtain out of his way to go to Brie's side. She still wore the fresh clothes she'd put on after hosing off, not a hospital gown, and she sat on the edge of the rolling bed, surrounded by her friends. She lit up when she saw him, as if he'd never tried to hurt her.

The women's conversation faltered at his appearance. Well, now he knew why. Into the uncomfortable silence, Mary asked, "How 'bout them Saints?"

"How 'bout we go check on Andy and give these two some privacy," Cypress said, and with some well-wishing, the three witches filed out.

Brie, bruises darkening her stubborn jaw, but smoky eyes as bright as ever, met Steve's gaze bravely. Did she suddenly realize he'd heard her comment about confessing? Did she expect him to demand answers . . . again? He didn't know how to reassure her without further threatening her privacy.

"It's okay," she assured him. It was a subject change if ever he'd heard one—a change to the subject he cared most about. "The doctor says the baby and I are both fine. She's going to prescribe some tranquilizers, and then we can go home."

But could they go home? Even if he had really been possessed, and that threat was gone, could they really go home?

"You need to know something, Red," he admitted finally, coming to sit beside her on the bed. "What happened in the backyard . . ."

Funny, he could feel the fear that flared into her eyes. She still didn't want to talk about it, didn't want to "confess."

"It was me, Red. So much of it was me—just amplified."

"No," she protested, shaking her head. Her hair was still damp. He raised a hand to touch it, and instead took her hand; their matching rings rubbed together.

"All that Josiah Blakelee stuff—let's say I buy it." Let's say that after seeming to share his mind, he knew more about the bastard than she, witch or no, probably did. He knew about the guilty self-righteousness that had haunted Blakelee after Mercy's execution. About how, in his increasing madness, he had burned the portrait of Mercy that he'd painted—half of a matched pair. About how, believing himself haunted by his wife's "shade," more likely by the repressed knowledge that he'd helped condemn an innocent woman, he'd hanged himself in front of his own portrait. If the story was a figment of Steve's imagination, it was the most intricate and least appealing fantasy he'd ever experienced.

"Even if I do, it doesn't change the fact that he... it... wasn't just taking me over. It was *amplifying* me, this awful darkness, this suspicion, this sense of betrayal that's been inside *me*, all along. *My* secret."

There, he'd said it. Now was her chance to pull back, to ask him to leave, and he wouldn't blame her if she did. She might have hidden that she considered herself a witch, but that was better than what he'd hidden.

"Maybe," she said slowly, finally, "there's a balance of light and darkness in everyone. Maybe as long as you recognize the darkness in yourself, you can control it... and appreciate the light more. The way I have always, always appreciated you."

It showed in her open face and her beseeching eyes and her hopeful posture. The little witch still loved him... all of him.

Much as he wanted to drag her into his arms again, to hold her and never, never let go, he knew there was one last thing he had to do to put aside the secrets and doubts that had lurked between them. Leaning away from her, he reached into his pocket.

Brie didn't understand what Steve was about until she felt metal pressed into her palm, and looked down at her pentagram. Her heart fell. She might have made it to full moon, undiscovered, if not for this. And yet, as her fingers closed around her grandmother's heirloom, she couldn't resent the necklace. She wished she could keep it. She didn't want to leave the Craft, to abdicate not just her powers, but much of herself, as well. Did that make her a bad wife, to so deeply regret doing something for her husband? She'd wanted to be so much better for him. "I'm sending this back to Mom."

"Keep it." When she lifted her face to Steve's, the depth of understanding in his brown eyes stunned her. "It's okay. I want—I love—all of you, not just the parts I understand. If I didn't trust your judgment, I would never have married you."

She continued to stare. Steve, seeker of knowledge, could do that? Just agree not to know?

He nodded. He could. For her.

She opened her mouth, couldn't make a sound, and decided simply to fall into his strong embrace, where she belonged. His arms closed firmly, protectively, around her. The woodsy muskiness from his shirt soothed the sterile hospital smell from her lungs, like the peace of a forest grove. Her lover, her Holly King...her husband.

She barely looked up at the rush of curtain rings that announced the doctor's return; barely paid attention as Steve accepted the prescription and the advice for her in his usual dependable, efficient way. He accepted her. Steve accepted *her*—magic and all.

"C'mon, Mrs. Peabody," he said, scooping her into his arms as if she couldn't walk by herself. Looping her arms behind his neck, she leaned her head onto his shoulder. She didn't mind at all. "Let's you, me and the baby go home."

"Sir?" As they left the curtained cubicle, a nurse came at them with a wheelchair. "Sir, for insurance reasons we'd really rather—"

"I've got her," Steve called back, not pausing. Catching the surprised looks of her friends in the waiting room, Brie laughed. Steve was in control again, and he loved her, and—

And a heavy blackness waited for them through the double glass doors. Night had descended full-force since their otherworldly battle.

"It's dark out."

She didn't know she'd whispered the words until Steve, after pausing to kiss her very thoroughly, said, "It's okay, Red. It won't last."

And, again resting her cheek against the solid security of his shoulder, she knew he was right. Together, with nothing else between them, they no longer had reason to fear the night.

Predawn light filled the baby's room as Brie tiptoed in, pulling her scarlet silk robe more closely to her against the December chill. Her footie slippers made no noise. The cat, lounging upon the baby's changing table, where he shouldn't be, sent her an expression of bored disdain, but didn't give her away.

She paused a moment, letting her eyes adjust to the gloom. She could make out the ducklings that waddled across the newly hung wallpaper, though she couldn't distinguish their pastel colors. Neither could she see which of the fat, unlit pillar candles, sitting on the shelves Steve had just installed, was red and which green—though of course she'd set them with the red one on the right and the green one on the left. That was how all representations of masculine-feminine deity were arranged, in her tradition. She could smell remnants of the candles' bayberry and cinnamon, mingling with the fresh aroma of the pine boughs she and Steve had hung over all the duplex's doorways last night—pine, holly, and some nice druidic mistletoe.

She smiled, hugging herself and thus the baby more closely. It had been a *very* nice night...particularly for the darkest night of the year.

"What are you doing up so early?"

She spun in surprise, not fear, to see Steve in the doorway, his jaw only faintly shadowed, his hair properly short again but deliciously mussed, his terry bathrobe looking particularly huggable. He leaned against the doorjamb, watching her...and yawned to unsuccessfully hide a grin. Oh, yes; last night had been enjoyable indeed. "My sister and I used to get up before dawn on Christmas, Red, but you're a few days ahead of the game."

He gave no indication that he knew this was the winter solstice. And with Steve's penchant for research, he must know that the winter solstice was a Wiccan holiday, Yule, after which the dark nights would finally decrease and the days' light would grow longer.

He *did* know she was meeting with Sylvie and the others this afternoon, so she didn't suspect him of trying to catch her in some clandestine ritual. True to his words in the hospital, he hadn't once prevailed upon her to break her somewhat obsolete oath. Even when they discussed what had happened with Josiah, he prefaced talk of their experience with qualifiers like "assuming this wasn't some temporary delusion...." He protected the mystery he loved in her, which in turn maintained the illusion of normalcy in their lives that she so valued.

Though the happiness they were discovering in one another, infinitely magnifying the love that had first drawn them together, was anything but average.

"Mom said not to put these up until this morning," she explained now, raising a fistful of crystal suncatchers. Their faceted shapes swung dully in the gray light.

"I'm glad your mom was able to visit," Steve admitted, moving to the cold paleness of the window, where he'd caught her on a stepladder, hanging cuphooks, several nights earlier. He extended a hand for the first crystal, not about to let her go climbing again. Besides, he didn't need the stepladder. "I think we resolved a lot of the distance between us. But, and I mean no offense by this, she is still one strange lady."

She grinned, passing him the snowflake-shaped crystal. Yeah, Mom was strange, and everyone had loved it. Though Mary had presided over Sylvie and Rand's handfasting, Mom had coached her, and Sylvie had felt honored to have a true, if undercover, Wiccan priestess overseeing the celebration. Mom had seconded Mary's and Sylvie's certainty that the baby, conceived before the spirit of Josiah Blakelee had awakened, had survived their recent ordeal unscathed.

And Mom had hugged Steve goodbye, before returning to Texas—with Andy Beaudry in tow for some *real* training.

"Well, Mom still thinks you're one strange man," she reminded him, handing him a suncatcher faceted in the shape of a raindrop, then a sun. Did he recognize the significance of their order, the seasons, the Year Wheel? Did it matter? "So that makes you even."

After hanging the final crystal, an autumn leaf, he turned and caught her against him, wrapped her in his warm embrace, lowered his mouth to hers. She stretched under the flame that sizzled up her spine at his kiss. He didn't taste like toothpaste yet; he tasted like her husband.

"What do *you* think?" he murmured against the corner of her mouth.

"I think," she whispered back, barely noticing the grayness fading around them, "that I always have and always will love you, Steve Peabody."

"Mmm..." He rested his cheek on her head. "Does that mean that if these things I just put up get too bright, you'll let me take them back down? I don't want my daughter blinded in the mornings."

"Daughter?" she asked challengingly, thrilled by his slip.

Instead of bristling at the implications, Steve kissed her on the top of her head. "I'm not saying your mother has some esoteric ability to tell these things...but if you've never had a relative conceive a boy first, well, that's practically scientific induction."

"Mmm-hmm..." she murmured, smiling. By the time their daughter was five, she suspected, there might not even be pretend secrets in the Peabody household. Then a flash at the corner of her vision caught her attention. "Look! The sun's come up!"

The first streaks of winter's dawn light had cleared the trees across the road, reached the window, and caught in the facets of the crystals. Tiny prisms of color, like a kaleidoscope of faerie lights, danced across the walls and the ceiling and the floor. She lifted her face to the splendor, and noticed with a sidelong glance that Steve had extended an open hand, as if he could catch a glint of brightness in his palm.

But he didn't try to close his fist around it.

He noticed her noticing him, and grinned down at her. "Okay, I give. The baby will love this."

She leaned happily into the support of his embrace and decided to take a tiny risk. "It could almost make you believe in magic, huh?"

And Steve, gazing into her eyes as he bent for another kiss, said, "Oh, yes."

When his lips touched hers again, she knew he already did believe. He believed in *their* magic.

And that was more than enough.

\*   \*   \*   \*   \*   \*

**And now Silhouette offers you
something completely different....**

**SPELLBOUND**
R O M A N C E

**In September, look for
SOMEWHERE IN TIME (IM #593)
by Merline Lovelace**

Commander Lucius Antonius was intrigued
by his newest prisoner. Although spirited
Aurora Durant didn't behave like any woman
he knew, he found her captivating. But why did
she wear such strange clothing, speak Rome's
language so haltingly and claim to fly in a silver
chariot? Lucius needed to uncover *all* Aurora's
secrets—including what "an air force pilot lost
in time" meant—before he succumbed to her
tempting lures and lost his head, as well as
his heart....

INTIMATE MOMENTS®
™ *Silhouette*®

Silhouette Books
is proud to present
our best authors, their best books...
and the best in your reading pleasure!

Throughout 1994, look for exciting books
by these top names in contemporary
romance:

**DIANA PALMER**
*Enamored* in August

**HEATHER GRAHAM POZZESSERE**
*The Game of Love* in August

**FERN MICHAELS**
*Beyond Tomorrow* in August

**NORA ROBERTS**
*The Last Honest Woman* in September

**LINDA LAEL MILLER**
*Snowflakes on the Sea* in September

*When it comes to passion,
we wrote the book.*

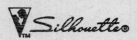

Fifty red-blooded, white-hot, true-blue hunks
from every State in the Union!

Look for MEN MADE IN AMERICA! Written by some of
our most popular authors, these stories feature fifty of
the strongest, sexiest men, each from a different state in
the union!

Two titles available every month at your favorite
retail outlet.

In September, look for:

WINTER LADY by Janet Joyce (Minnesota)
AFTER THE STORM by Rebecca Flanders (Mississippi)

In October, look·for:

CHOICES by Annette Broadrick (Missouri)
PART OF THE BARGAIN by Linda Lael Miller (Montana)

## You won't be able to resist MEN MADE IN AMERICA!

# JINGLE BELLS, WEDDING BELLS:
## Silhouette's Christmas Collection for 1994

---

### Christmas Wish List

*To beat the crowds at the malls and get the perfect present for *everyone,* even that snoopy Mrs. Smith next door!

*To get through the holiday parties without running my panty hose.

*To bake cookies, decorate the house and serve the perfect Christmas dinner—just like the women in all those magazines.

*To sit down, curl up and read my Silhouette Christmas stories!

---

Join *New York Times* bestselling author Nora Roberts, along with popular writers Barbara Boswell, Myrna Temte and Elizabeth August, as we celebrate the joys of Christmas—and the magic of marriage—with

## JINGLE BELLS, WEDDING BELLS

### Silhouette's Christmas Collection for 1994.

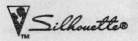

Dark secrets, dangerous desire...

Three spine-tingling tales from the dark side of love.

This October, enter the world of shadowy romance as Silhouette presents the third in their annual tradition of thrilling love stories and chilling story lines. Written by three of Silhouette's top names:

## LINDSAY McKENNA
## LEE KARR
## RACHEL LEE

Haunting a store near you this October.

**MIRA** ™

## The brightest star in women's fiction!

This October, reach for the stars and watch all your dreams come true with **MIRA BOOKS**.

### HEATHER GRAHAM POZZESSERE
*Slow Burn* in October
An enthralling tale of murder and passion set against the dark and glittering world of Miami.

### SANDRA BROWN
*The Devil's Own* in October
She made a deal with the devil...but she didn't bargain on losing her heart.

### BARBARA BRETTON
*Tomorrow & Always* in November
Unlikely lovers from very different worlds...they had to cross time to find one another.

### PENNY JORDAN
*For Better For Worse* in December
Three couples, three dreams—can they rekindle the love and passion that first brought them together?

The sky has no limit with **MIRA BOOKS**